D0542562

FAMILY PORTRAITS

LANCASHIRE COUNTY LIBRARY	
3011812689553 5	
Askews & Holts	24-Apr-2013
AF	£20.95

FAMILY PORTRAITS

Elizabeth Carden

WESTBOW
PRESS
A DIVISION OF THOMAS NELSON

Copyright © 2011 Elizabeth Carden.

All rights reserved. No part of this book may be used or reproduced by any means,
graphic, electronic, or mechanical, including photocopying, recording, taping or by any
information storage retrieval system without the written permission of the publisher
except in the case of brief quotations embodied in critical articles and reviews.

ISBN: 978-1-4497-2033-9 (e)
ISBN: 978-1-4497-2034-6 (sc)
ISBN: 978-1-4497-2035-3 (hc)

Library of Congress Control Number: 2011932553

WestBow Press books may be ordered through booksellers or by contacting:

WestBow Press
A Division of Thomas Nelson
1663 Liberty Drive
Bloomington, IN 47403
www.westbowpress.com
1-(866) 928-1240

Because of the dynamic nature of the Internet, any web addresses or links contained in
this book may have changed since publication and may no longer be valid. The views
expressed in this work are solely those of the author and do not necessarily reflect the views
of the publisher, and the publisher hereby disclaims any responsibility for them.

Any people depicted in stock imagery provided by Thinkstock are models,
and such images are being used for illustrative purposes only.

Certain stock imagery © Thinkstock.

Printed in the United States of America

WestBow Press rev. date: 7/21/2011

Acknowledgments

No book is ever published without the assistance of a group of talented people, and this is certainly true of *Family Portraits*. I would like to thank the entire team at Westbow Press for using their expertise to help make my dream of becoming a published author a reality. A special thanks goes to Amanda Parson, who guided me every step of the way and answered my numerous questions, no matter how trivial. Without the talented people at Westbow Press, this book would never have been published.

I would like to thank Mary Grace Paden, my creative writing instructor at John Tyler Community College several years ago, for reading the first short story I wrote featuring Cassie and her family. I doubt I would have written anything more had Ms. Paden not insisted, "You need to expand on this. This could become a great book."

Three wonderful ladies read the first draft of this book from beginning to end as it was being written. Thank you to Cass Harvey, Elizabeth Somerville, and Esther McNary—without the three of you, this book would not have been written. You all pushed me to continue writing when I wanted to quit, encouraged me through the long periods of writer's block, and gave me valuable feedback throughout the writing process. I can never thank you enough for your dedication to this book, and to me. I'm blessed to call you my friends.

To James Turney: thank you for the unbelievable photography for the cover of this book. You did a wonderful job and it turned out exactly the way I envisioned it.

To my "unofficial" editor, Michelle Wrage: thank you for taking so much of your time to painstakingly read every word of this book and determine where it could be strengthened. Your insights were priceless, and your friendship is even more so.

Lastly, to my family: you have believed in me when I didn't believe in myself. Thank you for always encouraging me to follow my dreams.

For my family.

And for the many young women who have told me their stories of abuse, scars, and redemption—without you, this book would never have been written. Your courage amazes me.

Cassie

"Cassie, you may come in now," Dr. Morton, our family therapist, calls into the waiting room. The rest of my family, except for my little sister Jade, is already in his office, here for the emergency counseling session that Dr. Morton has called. I think I know what it's about, but I'm praying that I'm wrong; it has to be something else.

I get up mechanically and shuffle over to the doorway of his office. I pause for a second, trying vainly to quell the butterflies in my stomach. *Help me*, I beg silently. *Please, please help me.*

Nothing could have prepared me for the sight that assaults my eyes when I open the door. My family is slumped on the various couches and chairs scattered throughout Dr. Morton's office, and … oh, the looks on their faces! *No. Oh, God, please, no.* I try for a smile, which probably looks more like a grimace, and I sink into a seat across from the rest of them. I sneak glances at each of them in turn as I attempt to breathe normally.

My older brother Levi's face is roughly the color of Cream of Wheat, and he is the only one who returns my gaze. His blue eyes, almost the same shade as mine, are anguished. "Cassie …" he mouths, then stops, shaking his head once and looking down.

Ben sits stone-faced, clenching and unclenching his fists. He looks like he's debating whether to reach for the paperweight on Dr. Morton's desk and hurl it at the wall. Or maybe at Dad's head. Ben, my little brother, was already having a lot of problems with our parents, especially Dad. What will *this* do to him? My throat closes, and I can't look at him.

Mom is the most outwardly composed. No surprise there. She's the queen when it comes to concealing emotions.

And then there's Dad. I just barely glance at him; not sure I want to look at him yet. His face is streaked with tears. *No, no, no. Please, please let this all be a dream.*

Dr. Morton clears his throat. I don't look at him either, keeping my eyes trained on the navy carpet. "So now that everyone knows the… ah, situation, I guess we need to talk about what happens next. But first, is there anything you'd like to say, Cassie?"

I shake my head vigorously before he's even finished asking the question.

"Okay, then. Peter, what about you? Is there anything you'd like to say now that your whole family is here?"

Dad clears his throat several times, obviously fighting for control. "Cassie, I just … I don't know what to say to you, other than I'm so, so sorry. I never should have … done those awful … awful things to you, and …." He stops speaking, weeping.

I force myself to look at him. Pure torment is reflected in his eyes, and I feel a sudden stab of compassion. I hate to see him suffering like this, especially over something that wasn't really his fault. "It's okay. I forgive you."

"You would," Ben snorts in obvious derision, and Mom drills him with a glare that could fry him. He glares right back, his chocolate-brown eyes shooting daggers at Dad.

Dad clears his throat again, seemingly oblivious to Ben's malicious stare. "Well, you say that now … but I really don't deserve your forgiveness."

"No kidding," Ben mumbles. Levi's jaw tightens, but he says nothing.

Dr. Morton launches into a description of the "next steps," and I zone out, staring at the carpet again. I hear bits and pieces: a mention of Social Services, a medical exam, Dad being out of the house for a while, weekly or even daily sessions with Dr. Morton for the next couple months. The words swirl around me, and I fight to keep them from truly sinking in. *This is all a dream*, I think. *You will wake up and laugh about this later.*

But something keeps circling in the back of my mind, a thought that won't stay quiet. After Dr. Morton finishes speaking, the rest of my family lurches to their feet, staring as if they've never seen each other before. I whisper tentatively, "Dr. Morton? Can I … can I … um, talk to you for a second in private?"

"Sure, sure," he says, hastily ushering the others out. Then he sits back down behind his desk and motions me to sit closer. "What's on your mind, Cassie?" The compassion in his hazel eyes is almost more than I can stand. I don't know him very well since Levi, Ben, and I have only had a few counseling sessions with him, but I trust him. That's why I told him everything in the first place.

"Um … well, I'm a little confused about … about what's happening. Or, I mean, what already happened." I fumble for the right words. "I … when I was telling you about, you know, my dad touching me and stuff, I thought I explained to you that I'm pretty sure, I'm actually positive, that I just dreamed the whole thing. Or maybe it was just an accident, you know? So I don't understand why the rest of my family had to find out. And I definitely don't think we need to see Social Services or anything. It just seems kind of … you know, extreme, considering this was all just an accident." My voice trails off, and I wrap a strand of my waist-length, coffee-colored hair— the same shade as Dad's—around my finger and twirl. I do that a lot when I'm nervous.

Dr. Morton won't look at me. And that's when I know. My stomach drops to the floor and for a moment, I forget how to breathe.

"Cassie," he says, still examining the stack of papers in front of him, "I'm sorry if I gave you the impression that the sexual abuse was unintentional or simply a product of your imagination. I'm so very sorry that I didn't explain the situation more fully. You see, what happened when I spoke to your father this morning during my session with him was …"

"Did you say 'sexual abuse'?" I interrupt, my voice unrecognizable to my own ears.

Dr. Morton sighs and finally looks directly at me, his eyes misty. "I'm sorry, Cassie. I'm so, so sorry. When your dad came in for his counseling session this morning, I confronted him with the things you had told me, and he confessed."

"He … confessed?" The room is spinning. "I … I don't understand. You mean, he … he *meant* to do those things to me? Like, he knew what he was doing the whole time? I didn't just have a nightmare and dream it all up?"

Now I think I really might throw up. I close my eyes tightly and try to remember how to breathe.

"Are you all right? Do you need some water?"

Water? Water? What I need is to wake up from this nightmare! "Did…" my voice is scarcely more than a whisper. "Did he say … for sure?"

"Yes, Cassie," Dr. Morton sighs again. He seems to have aged since I saw him two days ago and set this whole process in motion.

"Oh," I say faintly. "Okay. Well, thanks for clearing that up for me. I guess … I guess I'd better go. My family's probably waiting."

"Cassie, wait!" Dr. Morton calls as I stumble toward the door. "Are you sure you'll be all right, at least for the rest of the day today? Your mom's coming in for a session on Monday, and I'd be happy to see you as well. Or I can do a special session for you tomorrow, even though I don't normally see patients on Sundays."

"I … I think I'll be okay. Thanks, though."

It's a lie. I'm not okay. I'm not sure if I'll ever be okay again. The door slams behind me, and I hear the sound of my life, cleaving neatly into "Before" and "After."

Marianne

The full impact doesn't hit me until we're halfway home from our emergency meeting. Dr. Morton had offered to drive us home—the kids and me—and I had nearly laughed at him. Why on earth wouldn't I be able to drive myself? But now I understand what he meant. My hands are trembling so violently I think I may have to pull over.

Levi, sitting in the passenger seat, raises his eyebrows and says, "Mom, you want me to drive? You look really pale."

I manage a wobbly smile, take a deep breath, and force myself to hold the steering wheel straight. "No, honey, that's okay. I'm fine. We'll be home in just a few minutes, anyway."

My heart aches for him, my brave oldest. He has always been wise and mature beyond his years, the self-appointed protector of his brother and sisters. He and Peter were never as close as Ben and Peter—as Ben and Peter used to be, that is—but still, I know this is going to devastate him. What eighteen year old could handle knowing that his father …

No, don't think about this now, I order myself. I know I will lose it if I focus on this at all right now.

But, my mind refuses to cooperate, wandering down avenues better left unexplored. The thoughts beat through my skull, bringing with them a throbbing pain: *my husband is a child abuser. He sexually abused our daughter. He touched her the way he used to touch me. He went into her room and violated her. He fantasized about sleeping with her.*

"Mom?" Levi interrupts my mental self-flagellation. "You're completely pale, and you're, like, hyperventilating. I really think you should pull over. Or let me drive."

I veer over onto the side of the road, park the car, and tell myself: *Calm down, calm down, calm down.* I rest my forehead on the steering wheel and focus on breathing in and out, slowly.

"Mom?" Cassie's worried voice floats from the backseat. "Mom, are you okay?"

"Are any of us okay, Cassie?" Ben asks venomously. "Don't be so dense!"

"Shut up, Ben! Just shut your mouth! You say another *word* to Cassie and I will break your jaw!" Levi screams. My normally placid son appears to be coming unglued.

I hear Ben muttering, probably something I'd rather not hear, and Cassie whimpering. Levi turns back around in his seat and slouches down, his face contorted with fury. *God, what is happening to us? To my children!* I know I should say something to comfort them, to try to explain everything, but I'm suddenly so tired I don't think I can even lift my head. How can I explain something to them that I can't understand myself? What possible silver lining can I find in this dark cloud?

"At least Dad's moving out tonight," Ben mumbles.

There it is: the silver lining. We won't have to face Peter for a while, after this afternoon, which is probably just as well. With the frame of mind Ben is in, he might very well try to stab his father in his sleep. And so, I realize with a sickening jolt, would I. *God, where are You? I don't want to think these horrible thoughts. I love Peter! Help me remember that.*

But do I really love him? After this? I push the idea away; I can't think about that now. One step at a time.

I raise my head from the steering wheel. "Let's go home, guys."

"Home sweet home," Ben mutters darkly. "Whoop-dee-freaking-do."

I ignore him. All I want, right at this moment, is to go home, pull the covers up over my head, and sleep for about five years. Maybe I'd wake up and realize this was all a horrible mistake, or a dream. Because if this is going to be our reality now, I don't know how we'll survive it.

Peter

I've always known that this day was coming. Ever since the first time I touched Cassie, three years ago, I knew that one day I would confess. I had to; the guilt was overwhelming. All those years of carrying such a shameful, repulsive secret and now ... Admitting what I've done certainly hasn't made me feel better, but at least now I know I've been honest about everything.

The house is eerily silent as I trudge upstairs and head to the master bedroom to begin packing my things. Dr. Morton said to anticipate at least a two-week stay in a hotel while Social Services finishes its "investigation," but I doubt that my family will be ready to have me home anywhere near that quickly. If they ever do …

Not that I deserve their forgiveness. I don't deserve to come home again. I don't even realize I'm crying again until I notice the teardrops landing in the open suitcase laid out on the bed. Ever since my confession to Marianne and the boys in Dr. Morton's office, I seem to be unable to stop crying for long. I'm normally not an overly sensitive man, but then, I don't normally have to admit to my family that I sexually abused my daughter, either. Just the thought of Cassie and what she must be feeling right now makes my stomach clench, and I run to the master bathroom and throw up. Again.

How could I have done such a thing? How could I have been so stupid? So heartless?

Cassie has always been a Daddy's girl, with the possible exception of the year she was fourteen, when everything Marianne and I did, said, or wore was personally embarrassing and offensive to her. But she's sixteen now, and, despite the recent struggles Marianne and I have been having in our marriage, Cassie had gotten closer to both of us. She'd often sit at the kitchen table after supper and talk with us about her day; she even brings her boyfriend, Will, over occasionally. Unlike Ben, who rarely even introduces us to his girlfriends, much less invites them over to "hang out" with the family.

All that closeness between my oldest daughter and me is going to evaporate now. Not that I'll blame her for it at all; of course not. In fact, it's probably better for everyone. I don't think I could even look her in the eye right now, much less carry on a normal conversation. I just hope she realizes how sorry I am. How I would give anything—my house, my job, my entire life savings—to go back and change the decisions I made on those nights. *If wishes were horses …*

The suitcase on the bed is filled with clothes and toiletries I don't even remember picking up and packing. I zip the suitcase closed, grab my laptop, and walk slowly out of the bedroom and down the hall. I pause in front of the pictures on the wall—family portraits and the kids' school photos. Levi, whose blond hair and blue eyes give him an uncanny resemblance to Marianne. Cassie, with Marianne's eyes and my dark hair, a striking combination that, coupled with her lithe figure, turns heads almost everywhere she goes.

I sigh as I let my gaze rest on Ben's picture. Ben, who's so much like me, in both looks and temperament. He's growing into quite a handsome young man, with dark hair and eyes, and he'll soon be as tall as Levi and me. But in the past year, our precocious, sensitive fifteen-year-old has changed into someone I barely recognize.

And then there's Jade. Our "surprise child," she's the sunshine of the house with her curly golden hair and sparkling blue eyes. I worry how Jade will handle all of this; at only eight years old, there's no way she'll be able to understand, and Marianne probably won't try to explain much of it, either, at least not until Jade's a little older.

This is all such a mess … and it's only going to get worse. *What have I done?*

Cassie

Dad's nowhere to be seen when we get home. He's already packed his stuff and left, leaving a note for Mom on the bar with the number for the hotel where he's staying. There's another note, too, only two sentences long: *I love you. I'm so sorry.* Ben grabs it out of Mom's hands and rips it to shreds as soon as he reads it.

"I hate his guts!" he screams. "I hope he gets into a car accident and *dies*!" He takes off running toward his room, and Mom follows, screaming right back.

"Benjamin Michael! You get back here right now! You will *not* talk about your father that way, do you understand me?"

Levi and I stand there staring awkwardly at each other, listening to Mom and Ben yelling at each other from upstairs. "Cass, I just … I wanted to tell you that … you know, I'm really sorry about … well, everything."

"Thanks. It's no big deal, though. I'm just sorry that … well, it's going to cause so many problems, you know?"

"That's the last thing you need to worry about right now, Cassie. I mean, gosh, I can't even imagine what … what you must be going through right now. It's going to be hard enough for the rest of us, but for you …"

"Levi, it's okay. I'm fine. Really. I'm just—I'm worried about Ben. He's so angry, you know? And Mom … can you *imagine* how hard this is going to be for her? And Jade. How are we going to explain this to her? I mean, she goes over to spend the day at Sarah's house on Saturday morning and then she comes home at night and Dad's *gone*? And we have no idea when he'll be coming back? How is she supposed to be able to understand that?" Tears start streaming down my face, despite my efforts to hold them back.

"Hey, hey, don't cry," Levi whispers, putting an arm around my shoulder. "It's going to be okay. I'll keep an eye on Ben and Mom. Mom's an amazingly strong woman, Cassie. Yeah, this is going to be a living hell for her, but she'll get through it. And we'll all do our best to explain things to Jade. You just take care of you, sweetie. Promise me you won't keep all this inside? You're one of the strongest people I know, Cass, and I know you'll make it through this. We all will. But you have to be willing to let people in and help you. Okay?"

"Okay." I'm perilously close to losing it. "Thanks, Leev. I'm going to go change and … go over to Will's. Will you tell Mom for me?"

"You mean if the rebel without a cause upstairs stops screaming at her anytime soon?" Levi asks with a wry smile. "Sure, I'll tell her. And I'll try to talk to Ben later, too; get him to calm down a little."

I manage a wobbly smile for him and flee upstairs. My head is pounding violently, and my stomach is churning. I run to the bathroom and throw up until there's nothing left in my stomach. I rest my head on the cool tile of the bathroom floor until the room stops spinning around me. *Please make this stop.*

When I feel strong enough, I stand up shakily, brush my teeth and splash some water on my face, and stagger down the hall to my room. I lock the door—*why didn't I think to do that three years ago? Then none of this would've happened*—and change into my favorite jeans and warmest sweater. It hasn't snowed yet this year, but it's been unusually cold for mid-January. Besides, Will loves it when I wear dark blue; he says it makes my eyes stand out.

Will. Oh, God, what am I going to tell him? "Just tell him the truth," I order the girl in the mirror, scrutinizing my reflection. *But what if he hates me? What if he breaks up with me?*

Cassie, why would he break up with you over something that wasn't even your fault?

But he'll think I'm so … disgusting if I tell him. I mean, how am I supposed to tell him that the farthest I've ever gone has been with my dad? That's so...so...

I stop myself and try to think about something else. Anything else. I can't let myself believe that all this is really happening. There has to be some mistake.

I need to see Will. Now. I text him as I shove a change of clothes and a hairbrush into my backpack, and he texts back to say he's home alone all weekend. Perfect. I feel like I will literally fall apart if I have to speak to anyone other than Will right now.

I grab my stuff and practically run to the car, calling a good-bye over my shoulder to Levi, who's sitting at the kitchen table, brooding. I make it to Will's house in record time, and the second I walk into the living room and see him sprawled on the couch, I burst into tears.

He scrambles up and pulls me close. "Honey, what's wrong?"

"My dad …" I'm sobbing so hard I can't begin to form a coherent sentence.

"Shh, Cass. It's okay. Calm down. Just take a few deep breaths and tell me what's going on." He leads me over to the couch and holds me until I gain a modicum of control.

"Okay." I take a deep breath. "My dad moved out this afternoon. We're not sure when he's coming back."

Will's eyes, so dark blue they're nearly black, widen in shock. "Are you serious? Oh my God, Cass! What … I mean, why? What happened?"

I look into his eyes. *I can't do this. I can't tell him.* "I don't know. He and my mom have been having some problems, but I don't know why he all of a sudden decided to move out like that. Mom and I were at the mall and when we came home, he was gone. He left a note for her, and she said she doesn't know when he's coming back."

It's surprisingly easy to invent this story; I never thought I'd be able to lie so convincingly, at least not to Will. But he seems to believe me, tightening his arms around me and kissing my forehead. "I'm so sorry," he whispers.

"It's okay. I'm sure he'll come home soon. They'll work everything out. Thanks for letting me vent; I think I just needed to cry it all out, you know?"

"Anything you need," he promises. He's the most amazing guy; he really is. We've been together for a year, which is like three years when you're in high school. I try not to think about what's going to happen next year when he graduates, a year ahead of me, and goes on to college.

His parents aren't home, so it doesn't take long before we're making out. We have a pattern—we kiss until he tries to sneak his hand under my shirt, or he unzips my jeans—and then I push him away. I love Will, but I'm scared of going too far. I've always wanted to save sex for marriage; having been raised going to Sunday school and church, I figure it's the right thing to do. When I was twelve, my dad gave me a promise ring, and I've never taken it off. It's a commitment I've made—to God and to myself—but now …

Why should I keep my end of this bargain? God's sure not keeping His. What kind of God lets a father touch his daughter? *Couldn't He have protected me? Made him stop? Woken my mom up so she realized what was going on?*

I pull away from Will for a minute, inching the ring off my finger. "Is that the ring your dad gave you?"

"Yeah. It's a purity ring or whatever." *Purity. Right, like I'm so pure. My own father wanted to have sex with me! Pretty much cancels out the idea of purity, doesn't it, God?*

A wave of fury surges through me, so hot it sears the back of my throat. I toss the ring on the coffee table, enraged. *I can't believe You would let this happen to me! To my family! Forget it, God … all bets are off! You weren't there for me when I needed You, so why should I even listen to You anymore?*

And then I'm the one pushing against Will for more, and when he fumbles for the clasp on my bra, I don't push him away like I normally would. He hesitates a fraction of a second. "Are you sure?"

I hear my mother's voice in my head: if a guy has to ask you if you're sure, it's wrong. I push the thought away and kiss him back, unbuttoning his shirt. "Of course I'm sure. You know how much I love you, right?"

"Probably not half as much as I love you."

His fingers leave trails of fire on my skin. "You're so beautiful, Cassie."

Don't be afraid, sweetie. Daddy would never hurt you. You're such a beautiful girl, you know?

I tangle my fingers in Will's hair, pulling him closer, feel his hands fluttering against the valley of my spine. *Get out of my head*, I order the memory. *Just leave me alone. I don't want to think about this.*

And then most of our clothes are strewn on the floor and we're tangled together on the couch. "We can stop right now," Will gasps. "We don't have to go any further if you don't want to."

I smile playfully at him. "Do you *want* to stop?"

"I'd rather be thrown to a pack of hungry wolves," he grins back. "But I know this is a big step for you… for us … so if you're not ready, I understand."

Instead of answering, I pull him closer and kiss him as slowly and deeply as I can.

Shhh, Honey. This is a secret for just you and me, okay? Now lie still. This doesn't hurt, right? It feel good when I touch you like this, doesn't it?

Stop it! Nausea churns in my stomach as I realize that I've felt this way before; my body remembers how this feels. *He* touched me like this three years ago, and it felt so good … *I must really have been a slut, even back then,* I think. *How could I have thought it felt good for my* dad *to touch me like that? Oh my God.*

Will must have noticed me stiffen. "Honey, what's wrong?"

"Nothing," I grind out between clenched teeth, trying to force the memory away.

I turn my head and stare at the pattern of the couch so Will won't see me flinch and realize that he's hurt me. It doesn't hurt nearly as much as I thought it would, but then, I'm not paying too much attention to any of this. Because in front of my eyes, another scene is unfolding, three years away from Will's couch. In that scene, I'm younger and it's later at night. And I'm scared.

Not like now.

Except …Wait.

Which scene am I in? Is Daddy here? Is this Will? Or is it Daddy? Where am I?

Suddenly it's over, and I lie there, trembling and confused. Will reaches over to stroke my hair and I feel myself—I guess it's me, now? Not the girl from the bedroom scene? —jerk away. "Daddy, don't hurt me," I whimper.

Will yanks his hand away as if I've burned him. "What are you talking about?"

"Nothing. It's nothing."

"Cassie, what is going on? You just said …"

"Will, *please*! Just let it go. Please."

"Okay, okay," he soothes. "It's okay. I'm sorry if I hurt you, you know—before."

"No," I sigh. "*You* didn't."

He doesn't catch the emphasis in my words, and after a few minutes, he gets up to go take a shower. "You coming?" he asks.

"In a minute. I just want to stay here for a little while."

He bends over and caresses my cheek. "I love you so much, Cassie. You know that, right?"

I nod, unable to speak past the lump in my throat.

The scene is still playing—me, younger, lying in bed with my nightgown hiked up nearly to my shoulders, and ... *Make this stop.* It doesn't. I wonder if it ever will.

I roll over onto my stomach and cry. *I'm sorry.*

Ben

Cassie slept with Will tonight. I could tell right away when she walked in the door—not like I'm an expert or anything, but there were enough clues for someone way less observant than I am to pick up. She was about two hours past her curfew, for one thing, and that girl *never* stays out late. And she wouldn't have gotten away with it tonight, either, if it hadn't been for the fact that Mom was upstairs sleeping on a Valium-induced cloud. Gotta love Dr. Morton for prescribing happy pills; I hate to think what Mom would be like right now if she didn't have them. She's been pretty spaced out since this afternoon; she almost forgot to pick Jade up from Sarah's house this evening after dinner. Levi ended up going to pick up the little munchkin, since Mom was in no shape to be behind the wheel of a car.

And if you're like all the other poor suckers in this backwater town, you probably would think Jade's just the cutest, sweetest thing since, well, puppies or something. But if you're me, and you have to *live* with the little brat, you'd never look at her the way other people do. She's such a jerk sometimes—people think *I'm* spoiled? They ought to try living with Her Majesty for a week or two. Everyone else in this family waits on her hand and foot; not me. I was over that a long time ago.

But I digress; I have a habit of doing that. Back to Cassie and her little tryst with Sir William McLean.

So she comes home two hours late, right? And Levi noticed that, too, but Levi and Cassie are best buds, so there's no way he's going to call her on it, especially not after what else happened today. To hear Levi tell it, both our sisters are models of perfection, sweetness, and light. Riiiiight. And I'm the proud owner of a Lamborghini.

Anyway, when Cassie finally got home, Levi and I were both waiting up for her. *Someone* had to; I was honestly a little afraid she might have decided to slit her wrists or something. Not that I'd totally blame her—I mean, life probably looks a little hopeless to her right now. It does to me, at least.

So Levi and I were waiting up, and of course, Levi was all, "I'm so glad you made it home! We were worried!"

I, on the other hand, was scoping the situation out. She was wearing a different outfit than when she left, and her hair was damp, like she'd taken a shower not too long before. Cassie's hair is about a mile long and it takes for-freaking-ever to dry. And she seemed … different somehow. I know, I know. Lame. But trust me, if you'd seen my sister at Dr. Morton's this afternoon, and then saw her when she came home tonight—this morning, really, if you want to be technical about it, since it was like 1 a.m. —well, if you'd seen her those two times, you'd know that *something* had changed.

And I was willing to bet money it was more than just Will "talking her through everything," as she claimed. Talking her through everything, my tail! Does she really think that Levi and I are that stupid? Okay, maybe Levi is, but I'm not.

See, the thing about Levi is, he's not stupid. He's really book-smart—got a scholarship to the local university and all—but he's *way* too naive and *way* too nice. He's going to take Cassie at her word about what happened tonight because, well, that's Levi. He's also going to be the one who's going to try the hardest to "forgive" our scumbag of a father, and to try to help Mom and the girls get through this hell we seem to have found ourselves in. Levi is your classic knight-in-shining-armor. All the girls at church want to date him, and all their mothers wish he *would* date their daughters. But Saint Levi doesn't date; he wants to wait until he meets the "right" girl and then court her. Court her? *Court her?* Are we living in the eighteenth century?

Never mind, forget my perfect older brother. Moving on to my not-so-perfect-anymore older sister—the thing that convinced me she'd been doing more than *talking* to Will was that her promise ring was missing. That thing is like glued to her finger. I think she only takes it off when she's showering or swimming or something like that. She probably even *sleeps* with it on! She's really into "saving herself for marriage" and all that. Or she *was*. If that promise ring is missing. Yeah, I'm no dummy. "Where's your ring, Cass?" I ask, leaning casually against the bar, the picture of nonchalance.

I'll give my sister this much: she has a great poker face. She doesn't so much as blink. "I guess I lost it."

I nearly burst out laughing at her choice of words. *'Lost it'? Yeah, I just bet you did!*

"I couldn't find it earlier today; I about tore my room apart looking for it."

Levi is, of course, immediately concerned. "Want me to help you look for it in the morning?"

"Aw, thanks, but that's okay. I know I'll find it." Cassie smiles sweetly, satisfying Levi and making me want to puke.

Levi says good night to us, after some gag-inducing pep talk about "we're going to make it through this and I'm always here for you." Blah blah blah. I completely tune him out until he finally, blessedly, trudges off to his room. He has an apartment about ten minutes from here, but it's a safe bet that he won't stay there again until Dad comes home. Which will be never, if Mom knows what's good for her—or for us. Okay, I guess if they do get a divorce—we'll probably never get *that* lucky, since Mom's bought the to-death-do-us-part crap hook, line, and sinker—Levi will eventually move back into his apartment. But for now, he's 100 percent into his Savior of the Family role. Shoot me, please. Or at least knock me out. It would be nice to be unconscious for, oh, a couple months.

I snag Cassie's arm as she starts to follow Levi upstairs. "Hey, can I talk to you?"

"Sure." She barely suppresses a yawn, and I feel a tiny flicker of guilt. No matter how disgusted I am with my sister's hypocrisy right now, she has been through hell today. And maybe every day for the past three years—how the heck would I know? It's not like she ever really tells me anything, obviously. I had to find out from some idiot Doctor Freud that my dad was freaking *touching* my sister at night when she was thirteen—she couldn't even tell me! *So much for thinking we were close.*

That train of thought reminds me why I'm so angry at her—heck, at everyone, if you want to know the truth—and I feel my hands clenching involuntarily into fists. "So you lost it?" I try to keep the sarcasm out of my voice. I fail.

Cassie blanches. "What?"

"Your ring," I say as innocently as possible. "What did you think I meant?"

"Oh." Visible relief floods her face and I think I'm going to puke. She's such a hypocrite. Miss Save-Yourself-For-Marriage. *Ben, you really shouldn't make out with your girlfriends so much. You don't want to go too far too fast, you know? You're only fifteen! Don't worry about playing the field for now; you've got plenty of time to find the right girl. And I would hate to see you, you know, make a mistake you're going to really regret later.*

"Who would've thought?" I can't keep the acid out of my voice. "Little Miss Purity is the first one of the Wilson kids to shack up!"

All the color drains from her face. "How did you …"

"Oh, don't worry, Cass," I sneer, furious, even though my brain is screaming at me, *Don't say it! Don't say it!* I say it anyway. "Your secret's safe with me. And hey, I've heard it's way better the second time."

She backhands me across the face. She packs a pretty mean punch for such a tiny person, and it takes all of my self-control not to pop her right back. A broken jaw would suit her. I spit a curse word at her, which she more than returns with several choice words of her own. My, who knew Little Miss Perfect was capable of breaking so many rules?

But then her face goes from furious to—I can't even describe it. It's like she breaks right in front of me. Like watching glass shatter in slow motion. Her face crumples and she starts to cry—I mean, really, *really* cry. That makes me feel like the world's biggest jerk. I put my arms around her—awkwardly because, okay, maybe I'm a pervert, but I can't stop thinking about her and Will—and she leaves a trail of snot and mascara and some other eye-goop all over the front of my shirt.

"I'm sorry," I whisper into her hair, suddenly realizing that I'm a couple inches taller than she is. It seems like just yesterday I was a couple inches *shorter*. "I shouldn't have come at you like that."

She's trying to say something, probably apologizing, knowing Cassie, but I can't understand any of it because she's crying so hard. "Hey, hey, now. Calm down, Cass. It's okay. It's okay." Gosh, I sound just like Levi. Terrific.

Gradually she loosens her grip on me and calms down enough that I can make out some of what she's saying. "It was like I couldn't even *see* Will. All I could see, all I could hear, was Dad. From … you know, before. And I feel like such a slut! God, Ben, you don't even *know*! I'm so … I'm so … *dirty!*"

I try to keep my tone light, even though she's really starting to scare me. I'm in *way* over my head here. This is the kind of conversation she should have with Mom or, second-best, Levi. Not me. "Having sex with your boyfriend doesn't make you a slut, Cassie. I seriously doubt God will send you to hell for something like that."

"No!" she shrieks, her face contorting like she's about to lose it again. "No, it's not *about* Will! I mean, yeah, I feel a little bit guilty about that, but, well, actually, I don't, now that I think about it." She shrugs. *Shrugs!* This is a day for miracles, that's all I can say. Cassie's shrugging about giving it up to Will? Has the earth tilted on its axis?

"But … that's not why I feel like a slut. I mean, I love Will, and I know he loves me, and we were careful, so that's not it. I feel like a slut because I … I remember when Dad was … you know, doing that stuff to me and … and it felt *just the same* as tonight! Like, Dad was *violating* me and part of me … God, Ben, part of me *liked* it! And he was—he didn't, like, rape me but I know he wanted to, you know? I *know*. And that just makes me feel like … like …" Her face does that shattering thing again, and I hold on to her. Or maybe she's the one holding *me* up, because I think I could pass out right now. Or kill someone.

One specific someone.

I hate my dad.

I really, really hate him.

As soon as Cassie calms down a little bit, she starts apologizing all over herself. I barely hear her. I think I'm going to spontaneously combust if I have to stay calm around her much longer. Thank God, she finally kisses my cheek, apologizes one more time, and staggers upstairs to bed.

He didn't rape me, but I know he wanted to. I want to kill him all over again, just replaying the look in Cassie's eyes when she said that. I know—I *know*—my sister is never, ever going to be the same again. In one afternoon, one confession, our father has completely destroyed her life. I guess all of our lives, if you really think about it.

I walk into the dining room and stare at the portrait of Mom and Dad on their wedding day, just barely illuminated by the moonlight drifting through the window. "You better *never* come back here," I whisper fiercely. Like he can even hear me. Like he would listen to me if he could. Like *anyone* ever listens to me.

Then, with as much force as I can muster, I smash my fist through the picture and into the wall behind it. Glass rains down around me, and blood drips down my hand. I pummel the wall again. And again. And again. And it's still not enough.

Cassie

The past two weeks have been hell in every sense of the word. I have not seen my father since That Day. I'm not sure I want to. Haven't talked to him, either. He calls the house every day around the same time, talks to Mom and Jade and sometimes Levi. Not Ben, of course. And I always happen to be conveniently busy or out of the house when he calls. He sent me roses, too, about a week after he moved out. I threw them in the trash.

Part of me feels guilty for shutting him out like this, but I just … can't. I can't see him now, can't even talk to him. I'm so confused. It feels like everything I thought I knew—about my family, about my dad, about my relationship with God, about who I *am*—is a lie, and I don't know what to believe anymore.

As hard as I try to keep from thinking about Dad and how much everything has changed in just two weeks, the memories keep intruding. This seems to happen constantly, at the most inappropriate, random times. I'll be sitting in homeroom and suddenly my mind flashes to one of the many early-morning fishing trips we took together. The memory is so vivid I can feel the morning mist on my skin, hear the sound of the water gently lapping against the canoe, and smell the fragrance of pine needles hanging in the air. Or I'll sit down to help Jade with her homework and find myself thinking of all the nights Dad sat with me doing the exact same thing. He was always the one who helped us with our homework while Mom cleaned up the dinner dishes.

The pictures in photo albums and scattered throughout the house bear witness to the fact that family is everything in our household—*was* everything. Now the memories of those family vacations, t-ball and softball games, swim meets, and father-daughter dates shadow me everywhere I go, trailing me like a ghost. But just as haunting are the memories of all those nights that I now know *weren't* a dream; all I have to do is close my eyes and I see it all playing in front of me like a horror movie that I can't turn off.

I was so close to my dad before, but now … It's like I've split him into two people: the evil monster who did those things to me, and the dad I've adored since I was tiny. I can't make those two images reconcile, and there's no *way* I can sort through all this if he's here. Or even if I talk to him. I have to keep some distance—okay, a lot of distance—or I will lose my mind. I mean it; sometimes I think I'm literally going insane.

The medical exam, a few days after Dad moved out, was torture. First some lady from Social Services grilled me for an hour about the "incidents," while her *male* assistant sat there taking notes and occasionally asking questions. It was awful. Then the physical exam began. I'd never had a gynecological exam before, and I had no idea how painful and humiliating it was going to be. And, of course, it didn't even tell them anything. They were trying to rule out the possibility that Dad had raped me, but they couldn't.

It's been excruciating to watch the rest of my family go through this, too. Jade—poor baby, she just breaks my heart. Mom didn't tell her any of the details, of course, just that Dad had to go away for a while so they can work out some problems. Overnight, Jade went from a bubbly, outgoing little girl to a withdrawn, nearly silent shadow that glides around our house. She can't sleep at night, and every night around midnight, she tiptoes into my room and curls up next to me. "I miss Daddy," she whispers, her tears soaking the pillow.

Mom seems to be doing better in the daytime. I think staying busy helps distract her from everything—but almost every night, while I'm lying in bed trying futilely to fall asleep, I hear her sobbing. One night, I woke up around 3 a.m. and she was sitting on the edge of my bed, stroking my hair. "I'm so sorry, Honey," she was whispering. "I'm so sorry I didn't stop him. I'm so sorry I didn't know what was going on. This is all my fault, and I am so sorry. My baby … my baby …" I don't think she realized I was awake, but it made me sick to realize that she blames herself for this.

Levi is the most stoic, but I know he's hurting, too. Sometimes at night, when I can't sleep, I go downstairs and find him sitting in the darkened living room, staring at nothing. "How did we get here, Cassie?" He asked me one of those nights, his face twisted in anguish. "How could this have happened to us? We were … we were such a normal family. We were a *great* family! Is God punishing us for something? Why would He let this happen to us?" That was the first time I saw him cry since all of this started.

And Ben. Well, Ben has reacted exactly the way I knew he would. Since the first night when he put his fist through the wall, he hasn't physically destroyed anything, but not a day goes by that he doesn't get into some kind of screaming match with Mom or Levi, or sometimes even Jade. He leaves me alone, though. I think he's a little afraid that if he yells at me or starts anything, I'll snap like I did that first night. He's kept my secret, too, even though I know he thinks I'm a hypocrite for sleeping with Will. He's right.

Part of me—the part that's been going to Sunday School and church for sixteen years, the part that used to wholeheartedly believe in God and His plan for me and all that religious crap—feels guilty about Will and me. But then I flash back to that afternoon in Dr. Morton's office and all those nights I know now *weren't* a dream, and I don't feel anything except betrayal and rage. If God is truly loving and only wants the best for His children, like they say at church, then why would He have let something like this happen?

Yeah, I know, I know. *"We all have a free will and God's a gentleman. He's not going to barge in and change our mistakes for us or keep us from making them."* Right. That helps. I'll be sure to tell that to Jade the next time she's curled up in my bed sobbing because she thinks her daddy doesn't love her anymore. I'll mention it to Mom, too, when she's too upset to decide between Hamburger Helper and steak for dinner. I'll pass that lovely tidbit along to Ben when he's slamming around the house, screaming about how he hopes our dad will go to jail.

No, I just don't believe that God is who I've been taught He was. It's not that I don't believe in God anymore; I do. But if He would let something like this happen to my family, He can forget me wanting a relationship with Him. Kind of like my dad—part of me thinks I never want to see him again after what he's done. A tiny part of me even wants to kill him, but I try not to think about that too much.

See what I mean about thinking I might go insane? I can't think about this stuff for too long or I just feel like my head is going to explode. It doesn't make sense. And I can't *make* it make sense, no matter how hard I try. But I can't stop thinking about those nights, no matter how much I want to, because they invade my dreams at night. The most graphic nightmares start out with flashbacks to the actual abuse and usually end with Dad raping me and slitting my throat or putting a bullet through my skull. Yeah, lovely stuff. I dread falling asleep at night.

A couple days ago, I saw Dr. Morton, and he started the session by asking me if I'd been having any suicidal thoughts? Any thoughts about hurting myself?

"Should I?" I asked sarcastically. "Is this enough of a crisis that I should be thinking about killing myself?" *That* really flustered him.

I did tell him about the flashbacks and the nightmares. He nodded like it's totally normal to dream about your dad having sex with you and murdering you afterward. "I think I'm going to put you on an antidepressant, Cassie. And give you something to help you sleep better at night."

"I'm not depressed," I objected flatly.

He raised an eyebrow. "You're getting about three hours of sleep a night, and your mom says you've lost your appetite. She also says you quit the swim team and you haven't been spending time with any of your friends except for Will."

The acid crept back into my voice. "Yeah, well, finding out that your dad had a thing for you when you were thirteen kind of kills your appetite. And it doesn't do a whole lot for your social life, either, Doc."

I hate it when I get like this; I never used to be so cruel. Now, it's like I get angry at the drop of a hat, and I've become a completely different person. I look in the mirror and don't even recognize myself. Who *is* that girl, with dark shadows not only under her eyes but *in* them, with the deathly pale cheeks and the newly baggy jeans? It's the first time in my life I've lost weight without even trying. It's also the first time I've lost weight without caring that I've lost weight. I used to be so vain. Now, I'll go a couple days without showering and actually leave the house without makeup. Amazing what a little family tragedy will do for your perspective.

Dr. Morton took my verbal assault in stride, which made me feel even worse. "I'm sorry," I whispered. "I shouldn't have said that."

"You're supposed to tell me how you're feeling, Cassie. Don't apologize for expressing your feelings."

"But they're *not* my feelings!" I protested. "I mean, they are, but … I can't even explain it. It's like I don't even *know* how I feel anymore. It changes all the time and I just …" Tears started trickling down my cheeks. "I don't even know *what* to feel."

"Are you angry at your dad?" Dr. Morton asked gently.

"Yes. No. I don't know! That's what I'm saying: I don't *know* how I feel, or how I should feel, or anything! Sometimes I'm furious at him. Other times, I just …" The tears fell faster, my voice unraveling like a cheap scarf. "I just want to see him again. I want things to go back to the way they were two weeks ago. But I know they won't, so …"

I looked straight at Dr. Morton, hoping that he could recognize the torment in my expression. "What is *wrong* with me?"

Marianne

Something I've learned in the last two weeks: the rest of the world doesn't stop, no matter what kind of personal tragedy you may be going through. Even if your world has taken a blow that leaves you reeling, staggering around through the mess of your life trying to find some semblance of normalcy, the rest of the world continues on as before. Bills still have to be paid, lunches packed, kids dropped off and picked up from school and extracurricular activities, church functions attended. So, no matter how much I've wanted to crawl into bed and sleep for days, just to shut out the rest of the world, I haven't been able to. It's astonishing, really, how smoothly a person can maintain some sense of normalcy in the midst of chaos. It is so easy to paste on a plastic smile and reassure the people around you that you are doing "just fine," when in fact you are bleeding to death emotionally.

Peter calls every day, begging me to let him come home, now that the Social Services investigation is over, but I can't. The kids certainly aren't ready for that—except Jade, of course, since she has no idea of what's going on in the first place—and even if they were, I know I'm not. Not yet. The thought of having to see Peter every day, to talk with him, to try to resume our normal life—let alone share a bed with him—makes my stomach heave. I'm so confused about what I should do. Part of me wants a divorce as soon as possible, to never have to see him again except in a lawyer's office. But I've loved Peter Wilson ever since we started dating at seventeen, and twenty-two years of marriage isn't something I can walk away from so easily.

But when I look at Cassie and think of Peter going into her room those nights. When I look at the faces of my boys, especially Ben, and see their fury and the pain that their father's betrayal has caused. When I hear Jade sobbing in her room at night, begging for her daddy to come home. Well, it's enough to make me want to march over to the hotel where he's staying and set his room on fire. The violence of my anger shocks and frightens me.

Nights are the hardest. When all the kids are in bed and the house falls silent, I have no escape from the doubts and fears that assault my mind and my heart. *Should I divorce Peter? If I don't, when should he come home? How in the world can I even begin to forgive him for this? Should I force Ben to continue sessions with Dr. Morton or just let it go? Do I need to worry about how much time Cassie is spending with Will? When will Jade start sleeping through the night again?*

So many questions, so many complex issues.

God, where are You? Why have You left us stranded in this horrible dark place?

Nights are when I fall apart. And the next morning, the charade starts all over again.

Levi

I've known this talk was coming for a couple weeks, but I'm still not prepared for it when Mom corners me in the living room—just me; the other kids are who-knows-where—and says, "I think it's time for your father to move back home, and I wanted to talk to you guys each about it first. I talked to Cassie already—I thought I should talk to her first, since, well, considering everything, you know. She said she thinks she'll be fine around him. But I wanted to talk to you next, as the oldest. Even though you won't actually be living here, it's going to affect you, too. So I'd like to hear your thoughts, please."

From the moment she started speaking, I felt rage building in me—that once-unfamiliar emotion that I now experience almost daily. When she finishes her little speech, it all comes gushing out. And I don't even bother to stop it.

"Well, what did you *expect* Cassie to say, Mom? You know how she is; she'll do anything if she thinks it's what the rest of us want—whether it's what she wants or not. She knows how much you and Jade want him to come home, so she's giving in to you and saying what she knows you want to hear! But news flash, Mom! Cassie's *not* going to be fine around him! She's not fine *now*, after not seeing him or talking to him for two months. How the hell is she supposed to be fine once he's living here again, and she has to see him day in and day out and be reminded *all the time* of what he did to her?"

"Watch your language, young man! And don't talk about your father that way!"

"Then how *should* I talk about him, Mom? As a liar and a backstabbing, deceptive jerk? As a child molester? As an incestuous …"

Mom puts up her hand to stop me, bright spots of color in her cheeks. She's furious, but I can tell by the look in her eyes that I've also hurt her deeply. Not that I really care—all I feel right now is a toxic combination of disgust and anger.

"*Levi Aaron*!" Mom practically screams. "That is *enough!* I don't understand why you're acting like this! This is the kind of tirade I'd expect from Ben, not you. You were so supportive in the beginning, and you were so willing to forgive your father. What has happened to you?"

That's an excellent question, one that I've asked myself numerous times as I lie awake at night, simmering with anger and the tiniest bit of hatred toward my dad. "Oh, gee, Mom," I answer sarcastically—another change; I *never* used to be cruelly sarcastic, and especially not to my mom. "I don't know. Maybe I feel totally betrayed by my supposedly wonderful, loving father, whom I recently discovered is a total scumbag."

"Levi, your father is not …"

"How can you defend him?" I interrupt, my anger mounting. "How *can* you? How can you even try to justify having him back in this house? I don't understand why you didn't haul him to a divorce lawyer first thing that afternoon we found everything out. You're making it sound like *I'm* the one who's changed so much—what about you? What happened to the whole 'your dad is not coming back for a long time' and 'I don't think I can forgive him for this' speech you gave us when he first left? I've heard you crying yourself to sleep at night; why would you think that Dad moving back home is going to make any of that *better*? I don't understand why you'd change your mind about any of this!"

Her blue eyes are damp. "Sweetie, it's not that simple. When I … when everything first happened, you're right, I was angry, and I didn't want your father to come home. But it's been two months, and, over time, I guess I've just realized … well, that I shouldn't be so hasty to judge him or end our marriage. It's all so complicated, honey. Your dad …"

"He *sexually abused my sister*!" I yell. "Your own daughter! How is that complicated? It's like … it's like he was cheating on you, but it's a million times worse because he was doing it with his own daughter! And as if that weren't enough, he was also addicted to porn *and* fantasized about having sex with Cassie!"

Those two nauseating tidbits of information came out during one of Dad's "confession is good for the soul" phone calls, about a week after he moved out, in which he decided to tell me and Mom—Cassie and Ben wouldn't talk to him, of course—everything, in the spirit of full disclosure.

I could have lived the rest of my life without knowing those two things and been perfectly fine, I think. I mean, wanting to have sex with your own kid? Even *thinking* about that? *Who* thinks something like that, much less admits it?

Tears are streaming down Mom's face. "Levi, don't."

Now I'm furious with her, too. "Don't *what*? I'm not saying anything you don't already know. What I *am* saying is that I don't see what kind of person—what kind of mother—would allow a child abuser and supposedly "recovered" porn addict back into her home, especially one who has an eight-year-old daughter. I mean, setting aside the fact that having Dad living here is *not* going to be good for Cassie, no matter how you look at it, there's also Jade to consider. You remember Jade, right? Our little sister, the one who's still going to be living at home for about nine more years? Nine more years with *him*? Are you freaking insane, Mom? What if he decides to touch her, too? Do you really want to risk even the possibility that she might go through something like what Cassie went through?"

"Cassie told me she doesn't even remember much of …"

I bolt to my feet, using all my willpower to keep from punching my beautiful, tormented mother in the face. "Don't. You. Dare," I growl in an ominously low voice, my teeth gritted and fists clenched. "Don't you dare try to minimize what *your husband* did to Cassie. I don't care how much you think he's changed, or how sorry he is, or how much he swears things will be different. There is *nothing* that he can say or do that will ever erase the fact that he went into Cassie's room six different times and touched her the way no father should ever touch his daughter. Nothing is going to make up for that."

"I know," Mom sobs. "I know that, and your father knows it, too. But I *love* him, Levi! I love him, and I need him, and you kids need him, too, whether you want to admit it or not. I can't handle everything by myself. Do you have any idea how hard it is to be basically a single parent overnight? I don't know what to do about Cassie virtually living at Will's house, or Ben getting so angry I'm afraid he'll kill someone. I don't know how to make Jade sleep through the night. I *cannot* handle this by myself! And I know it'll be a tough transition at first, having your dad back in the house. But he has to come home, Levi. I just can't do this anymore without him! And I'm not going to divorce him, because it wouldn't be right to end twenty-two years of marriage over a … a mistake that your father made several years ago, that he's repented for, and that I believe he'll *never* do again! Levi, you're planning to become a minister! Surely you understand why I won't divorce your father!"

"Okay, Mom, if this were a case of you guys having some problems, needing to work through some stuff, whatever, then yeah, I would definitely say don't divorce him. But if you're going to throw the ministry in my face, I'll just remind you that the Bible says that marital infidelity is grounds for divorce. If your husband sexually abusing your daughter isn't marital infidelity of some sort, I don't know what is. At the very least, it's a huge betrayal, an enormous breach of the whole marriage covenant. Not to mention that it's probably going to scar Cassie for life!"

"It won't," Mom whispers, her face pale. "Cassie is a strong, resilient young lady. She'll move past this. She's seeing Dr. Morton, and I'm sure she's making great progress in therapy."

"Right," I snort derisively. "That's exactly what she's doing. That's why she's practically living with Will now—oh, I'd say she's making *great* progress on her way to becoming another teenage statistic!"

"Levi ..." Mom sighs, putting her hands to her forehead. She suddenly looks years older. "I trust Cassie. I don't believe she's physically involved with Will, and I do believe that she's going to move past this. As for me, I think I'm able to forgive your dad for what he did. It took me a long time—I had to think and pray really hard about it for weeks—but I think I'm ready to forgive him, or at least to try, and that's why I'm not willing to end our marriage over this."

"So, what—he's just going to move back home, you guys will share the same bedroom again, and we'll pick up right where we left off? Sounds great, Mom. I don't know why you're even asking us for our opinion. I mean, you've obviously made up your mind. But I'll just warn you: be prepared in case Ben decides to stab Dad in his sleep one night. I'm serious. And don't expect to see me around much if Dad's going to be here."

Mom starts tearing up again. "He's your father, Levi! Of all the kids, I thought you would be the most forgiving. You *need* to forgive him, honey."

I shrug. "I can't. Not yet. And maybe I'll never be able to. And frankly, it really scares me that *you* can forgive him so easily for something like this. It really makes me wonder how much you care about your kids."

With that, I head out the door, ignoring Mom's sobs behind me. I stalk to my car and peel out of the driveway. I'm halfway to my apartment before my emotions settle enough for me to really think through what I'm feeling. I don't like what I find. I hate the person I've become; it feels almost like

I'm living a double life. There's a clear division in—as Cassie, Ben, and I have all started referring to it—the *before* and the *after*.

Before, I was Saint Levi. That was my nickname all through high school, and I certainly deserved it back then (funny; high school graduation was only eight months ago, but it feels like a lifetime). Even compared with a lot of my churchgoing friends, I was Mr. Goody Two-shoes. I didn't drink, smoke, party, have sex, or even really date. I've been a Christian since I was five, and I take my faith very seriously. Since I was about twelve, I've felt that God was leading me to become a pastor. So that was what I was planning to do: take a year or two of classes at the local university and then transfer to Portland Bible College. I really *believed* that was what I was supposed to do.

But now it's *after* and I'm not sure what I believe anymore. Actually, that's not entirely true: I know what I believe—I'm definitely still a Christian, and I do still want to be a pastor. But I'm beginning to doubt whether I believe those things as much as I did, say, three months ago.

See, here's the thing: I want to be a pastor, but I also have fantasies, late at night when I can't sleep, about killing my dad. I want to do things that please God, to really live out my faith—but not a day goes by that I don't get nearly overwhelmed with rage and even hatred toward my dad. That's what I mean by living a double life: it's like there are two of me.

Saint Levi, the perfect son, brother, and friend, the popular one, the one who's everyone's friend, the one who's committed to emotional and physical purity, the one who would never hesitate to forgive my dad, even for this. And Sinner Levi, the one who's just as angry as Ben, if not more, even if that Levi doesn't punch holes in the wall to show it. The one who was able to say such cruel things to Mom without even blinking, who could look at her crying and feel no other emotion than disgust. The one who is so intensely furious—at everyone, all the time. The one who knows that Cassie is having sex with Will and, instead of feeling disappointed in her, is, sickeningly, jealous of her.

It's a constant battle in my mind: Saint Levi vs. Sinner Levi. I'm worried about all my siblings: Ben and his anger, Cassie and her relationship with Will, Jade and her personality transplant since Dad moved out. But I'm also sick of having to be the perfect big brother, the replacement dad. I feel horrible for my mom, knowing that I can't begin to imagine how hard this must be for her, but I also sort of hate her right now for even thinking about allowing Dad back into the house. It's like she's so worried about saving her marriage that she's forgotten about her children. "*I don't think*

Cassie's physically involved with Will." Is she *crazy?* Mom's obviously in denial about all of us.

And as for my feelings about my dad ... my fingers tighten on the steering wheel. I never knew, until two months ago, how thin the line is between love and hate, and how easy it is to cross it from day to day, sometimes even hour to hour. I love my dad—or at least a part of me does. I mean, he's my *dad;* he's the one who taught me to ride a bike, tie my shoelaces, hit a baseball, and change the oil in my car. We spent hours over the course of the last eighteen years playing basketball together, tossing the football around, going fishing or camping, or just hanging out on a Sunday afternoon watching the football game. When Ben and I were in Cub Scouts and Boy Scouts, my dad was one of our troop leaders. Before all this happened, I could talk to my dad about most things, and he always gave great advice. If someone had asked me a few months ago, I would've said we had a good relationship.

In some ways, that just makes it all so much worse. I thought our family was pretty great, all things considered, and my relationship with my dad was fairly close. But then I found out that he had done something so sick and perverted and awful and, on top of that, kept it a secret and basically lied about it for three years!

It was like he plunged a knife into my heart and twisted it around. *Take that! You were never really close to me! Take that! I never loved you the way I said I did! Take that! I've screwed your sister up forever! Take that! Our family will never be the same again!*

Two months ago, the bottom fell out of my world. And I still haven't been able to stop my free fall.

THREE YEARS LATER

Cassie

The darkness in the filthy warehouse is penetrated only by a few flickering overhead lights. The only sound is that of my footsteps, running furiously—and his, closing in with every step. He's going to catch me, of course; he always does, no matter how hard I run or how well I manage to hide. But even though I know he'll win in the end, I can't help fighting. Can't help running. I don't want him to think he's conquered me without a fight.

And, of course, despite the way I lash out at him with fingernails and teeth, it ends just as it always does. He rapes me, that hideous smile never vanishing from his face. "You're such a good girl, Princess," he whispers, the use of his favorite nickname for me a blasphemy under the circumstances. "You're Daddy's good little girl."

I jerk awake, soaked in sweat and gasping. My heart is beating so hard it feels as if it might come right through my chest. Half-asleep, Ian tightens his arms around me. "You all right?" he asks groggily.

"Just a bad dream," I assure him. "Go back to sleep."

The nightmare triggers an avalanche of flashbacks, as always. Shuddering with both fear and revulsion, I swing out of bed and walk down the hall to the bathroom. I turn the shower on and slip out of the T-shirt of Ian's that I sleep in, letting the water run until steam fills the tiny room. I step under the searing water, gasping as the heat steals my breath and flushes my skin. The disgusting reel keeps playing in front of me, though; the pain of the scalding water does nothing to distract me from it. I sink to my knees. *Please stop*, I whisper. *Please.*

It doesn't. And I've had enough flashbacks over the past three years to know it won't let up anytime soon. I clench my hands into fists and fight tears. *You are such a weakling! Why are you crying?* I berate myself. *You brought this all on yourself, and now you want to cry about it? Pathetic!*

His hands are everywhere, unmitigated lust in his eyes, his fingers easing inside of me, his voice, a soothing whisper: *it's all right, sweetie. I would never hurt you. You're just having a dream, okay?*

On the shower floor, I whimper and don't bother to stop the tears anymore, hating myself for giving in to them. *It's been three years! Three* years! *Why can't I just forget about this? Why can't I just let it go?* The torrent of scalding water pounds my back, and I have never felt so alone.

****

The following afternoon, an unusually warm Saturday in June, I'm back at Julia's and my apartment, getting ready for tonight. Julia and I became friends about a year and a half ago, near the beginning of our senior year in high school. *Just a couple months after Will and I broke up.* I shake the thought away and concentrate on the tangle of outfits that Julia has laid out on her bed, trying to find the *perfect* combination for each of us to wear tonight.

"This party is going to be awesome," she squeals, sounding more like a seventh grader than a nineteen-year-old college student. "Paul's parties are always the best! Have you *seen* his parents' house? Fully stocked bar, a pool …"

She chatters on, and I surreptitiously roll my eyes. Much as I usually enjoy hanging out with Julia, today she grates on my nerves. She stands in front of the mirror, tossing her mane of blonde curls and furrowing her brow at her reflection. "Should I straighten my hair for tonight?" she asks, suddenly diverted from the topic of Paul and his supposed "Greek-god hotness."

I shrug, listless.

"What's the matter with you?" Julia demands, turning away from the mirror and scrutinizing me, hands on her hips. "You've been acting so … *blah* all day!"

"I didn't sleep well last night," I sigh.

She smirks. "I'm sure. I wouldn't sleep well either if I was in Ian Davis's bed. In fact, I wouldn't sleep at all."

"That's not what I meant," I correct her, annoyed. "Never mind. Forget it."

"Is there trouble in paradise?" Julia cocks an eyebrow. Her green eyes are glowing with supposed concern, but I'm not fooled. Despite the fact that she's both my best friend and my roommate—when I'm not over at Ian's, that is—Julia is also a gossip. I merely shake my head at her, refusing to take her bait.

Now it's her turn to be annoyed. She purses her lips and pretends not to care. "Well, if there *is* something going on with you two," she shoots me a significant glance, "you'll have plenty to distract you tonight. Oliver's coming."

My throat closes. "I don't … we're not … I don't think we're, you know, still …"

Julia laughs at how flustered I am. "Oh, come on, Cassie! You know you still want him! And besides, it's not like it's any big deal. I'm sure Ian wouldn't care. He's not *that* uptight."

I wince at her veiled reference to Will. *Will.* It's been almost two years since we broke up, and I'm still not completely over him. "He wasn't uptight, Julia."

"Who wasn't?" She pretends innocence. "I thought we were talking about you and Oliver. I think you should go for it tonight. If he's interested, anyway."

That is a veiled reference to the fact that half the kids from our high school think I'm a slut.

My face flushes with anger. "If you have something to say to me, Julia, just say it. If you think I'm such a slut, maybe you should start looking for another roommate!"

Her green eyes glitter with mingled shock, irritation, and hurt—whether real or feigned, I can't quite tell. "I never said you were a slut! And I don't think you are. God, Cass, if you're a slut, so are half the girls from our high school! I mean …" She hesitates. "Okay, here's the thing: I know a lot of the kids from school thought you were … well, the whole thing with Will was pretty bad. People were way too hard on you, though. I mean, if it had been the other way around? Will would never have gotten all the flak you did. That's what we get for living in a man's world, you know? Sucks."

She takes a deep breath, turns back to the mirror, and starts to straighten her hair. "It's not like you were really cheating on him, you know? I don't think you were, anyway. It was just a random hookup, right? And since then—I mean, you've only really been with Ian. All the rest have been either friends with benefits or just hookups at a party or something, right?"

I swallow hard. "'All the rest'? You make it sound like I've slept with a hundred guys! Ian and Will are the only two that really … I mean, the only ones who really mattered. And even the others—I don't know, maybe four or five, total. So I've been with, like, six guys. Maybe seven. And only two of them were ones I cared about."

"So what's the big deal?" Julia scoffs. "A couple friends with benefits and one or two random hookups? *Everyone* does that! Gosh, people are such hypocrites! Seriously, I mean, if you were a guy, people would be spreading rumors about you if you *didn't* do stuff like that!" She smirks at me again. "You know, like they used to do about Levi. How's he handling your, um, romantic adventures?"

My stomach clenches. "He doesn't know. I don't think he's even heard the rumors. I mean, maybe he has, since he's home for the summer now, but I don't think so. He hasn't said anything, anyway."

"Oh, believe me, he would say something if he heard! I mean, come on, Cass, the dude is in freaking Bible college! He would have something to say about it! So would your parents, for that matter. Good thing you moved out once you graduated, huh? I'm surprised they didn't find out senior year. That whole drama with Will …"

I hate it when she fishes for information like this. "Well, obviously, they knew I broke up with him. I was a mess for weeks afterward, so it was kind of hard to hide that."

"You're still a mess," Julia states matter-of-factly. "Even Ian probably knows that you're not over Will yet."

My eyes sting. "Julia!"

"Oh, don't worry, Cassie. I don't think Ian really *cares* that you're not over Will. I mean, he's getting what he wants anyway, right?"

I try not to flinch, try not to let her know that the barb found its mark, but I can tell by her self-satisfied smile that she knows anyway. Sometimes I wonder why I'm friends with her at all. "I'm going to change," I announce, my back rigid with fury.

"Hey, wait a sec!" Julia stops straightening her hair and rummages in one of her many makeup bags. "Here." She tosses several tubes of lip gloss at me. I look at the garish colors—gold, silver, even a hideous shade of orange—and my heart sinks. "You'll need these tonight. A couple of the guys specifically asked if you'd be there."

I force a smile. "Great! Sounds like fun!" I walk to the adjoining bathroom, making myself keep my back straight and my pace normal. Once the door closes behind me, though, I sink down on the edge of the tub and close my eyes, willing the nausea and horrendous thoughts to disappear.

I don't often question the choices I've made over the past three years; I learned pretty quickly that moving forward, not looking back, was the only way to stay sane. But lately, I've gotten increasingly weary of the game: seducing boys at parties, or, even better, bars, complete with the fake ID Julia helped me get, isn't nearly as much fun as it used to be. Getting wasted over the weekend and spending all day Sunday trying to remember what happened the night before has lost its luster.

I know that Julia's mention of the guys who are hoping I'll be there tonight is her not-so-subtle way of mocking me, despite her little speech in my defense earlier. As if she doesn't do the same things. As if she's not the one who taught me nearly everything I know about how to seduce the poor fools who think they're in love with me. Julia can judge and insinuate all she wants—she's not as different from me as she'd probably like to believe.

But there are a lot of things that Julia doesn't know. She doesn't know about the nightmares that haunt me every night or the flashbacks that follow on their heels. She doesn't know that I see my father's face in all the guys I've been with, even Will and Ian; I can never escape Dad, no matter how hard I try.

Julia will never understand that all the things I've done—the wild parties, the guys I've slept with, the clubs and bars I've gone to with her and not remembered the next morning—have been a desperate attempt to forget, even for a night, even for a moment. To escape the demons that chase me. To erase the past.

Not that it ever works. Nothing's ever worked, not for long.

Even getting the chance to confront Dad about the abuse didn't help. He moved back home a little over two months after *That Day*. A few weeks later, Dr. Morton asked us all, except Jade, to come in for a family session to talk about how things were going.

When we got there, Dr. Morton looked at Levi, Ben, and me—all sitting together on one of the couches across from Mom and Dad, not looking at them—and said, "Okay. I want each of you to take some time right now to say whatever you might need or want to say to your father about the sexual abuse. This is a free and open place for you to express your feelings to him, and he is going to listen without comment and without judgment."

He raised an eyebrow at Dad. "Aren't you, Peter?"

Dad nodded, his eyes damp. "Absolutely."

"What about Mom?" Levi asked, looking at Dr. Morton for the first time. "Is she going to say anything?"

"No," Mom answered quietly. "I've already spoken to your father about my feelings. And maybe in our next family session, I'll share some of those thoughts and feelings with the rest of you. But today it's your turn."

Levi glowered at her, and Ben rolled his eyes. "Us versus them," he muttered. Meanwhile, I concentrated on not passing out. *This is not happening. This is* not *happening.*

"Okay, then," Levi began, a hard edge to his tone. "I can't believe you did something so disgusting to your own child. You make me *sick*. Do you understand me? Even if I ever forgive you for this—which I'm not sure that I ever will—it doesn't mean that I will ever, ever forget what you did." Levi slouched down and stared at the floor. I stared at him, shocked by the fury I had heard in his tone. Of all of us, Levi had always seemed to be the least angry over what had happened. Maybe I was wrong in assuming that.

"Okay," Dr. Morton continued gravely. "Ben, do you have anything to say to your father?"

Ben's face twisted into a grotesque mask of hatred and fury. He spit a succinct two words at Dad that made Mom flinch and Levi's mouth twitch in an effort to hold back a smile.

Dr. Morton's seemingly ever-present smile faded as he asked, "Anything else, Benjamin?" Ben leveled his fierce stare at him and crossed his arms over his chest.

"All right," Dr. Morton sighed. "Cassie, what about you? Is there anything you'd like to say to your dad?"

A hundred responses ran through my mind. Now was my chance to ask the questions that had been haunting me for almost three months, a chance to verbalize my deepest doubts and fears and insecurities. The biggest question rose in my mind: *How could you have hurt me like this when I was always Daddy's little girl? I trusted you and you* betrayed *me! How could you have done this to me?*

Those words were burning in my throat; they were on the tip of my tongue, but I could not speak them. I shook my head and looked down at the floor. "I don't have anything to say."

It infuriates me now to look back on that day and realize that I came so close to getting my questions answered and chickened out. But I just couldn't ask Dad those questions. I was too afraid of what his answers might be. What if he said it was all my fault, that I had done something or said something to entice him all those years ago? Or, worse, what if he said it *wasn't* my fault? What if it turned out that my father had never really loved me the way he said he did?

What if our entire relationship was a lie?

I couldn't ask him those questions. I just couldn't. But sometimes, I wish I had.

Ben

If Paul's party is any indication, this summer is going to be one of the best of my life. Two weeks ago, I *finally* graduated and ended the hell that was high school. Two more months and I'll be several states away at college, and after the past three years, there's nothing I want more than to get as far away from my family as possible. If it weren't for the fact that I have a sweet summer job as a lifeguard and the chance to go to at least a dozen more parties as awesome as this one, I'd already be gone. Between now and September, I plan to be at home as little as possible and to stay as drunk and high on the weekends as I can. Come to think of it, that's pretty much what I've been doing for the past two years or so.

Not much has really changed since Dad moved back home; I've probably only had three or four real conversations with him in three years. I'm still on the fence about whether I hate him or not—I go back and forth on that one a lot—but I've lost all respect for him, that's for sure.

Mom, too; I don't know if I'll ever forgive her for letting him move back home, especially if, one day, we find out that he's abused Jade, too. Mom acts like that would never happen, but Mom is clearly delusional; it took her about a year to figure out that Cassie's basically living with her boyfriend, and she still thinks that I spend most of my weekends playing video games over at Johnny's house. I haven't even *talked* to Johnny in probably a year or more.

But that's how it is with my parents: they see what they want to see. They both want to believe that Dad's changed, that he'll never "hurt" anyone again, that things are back to normal. *As if things could ever be normal again.* But hey, in some ways, I don't blame them. I mean, I think all of us have tried to pretend that it didn't happen and bury it and move on. Not that we've been very successful at it.

Why am I thinking about this now? I definitely need another beer—actually, I think I need something stronger. Much stronger. Something to keep me from thinking about all this. I scan the crowd as I head over to the bar: man, there are some *hot* girls here tonight! One of them, a tall brunette who looks like she just stepped off the cover of a fashion magazine, catches me staring and winks at me. That's all the encouragement I need …

I'm making my way over to her when I notice a crowd gathering near the bar and hear a mocking, insolent voice that stops me cold. All thoughts of the gorgeous brunette vanish as I shove my way through the crowd. I break into the circle that's gathered around three people, and my mouth goes dry when I realize what's going on.

"Oh, look," Will says sarcastically. "It's like a family reunion! How sweet!"

I hardly recognize Cassie in the outfit she's wearing. Mom would have a heart attack if she saw the barely-there tank top and obscenely short skirt, coupled with all the makeup. To be honest, Cassie looks a little too much like a hooker. No guy wants to see his sister being looked at like she's a piece of meat, which is definitely the way the idiot standing beside her is looking at her—along with most of the other guys in the crowd. I vaguely remember that guy—Oliver? Some loser she hung out with for a while before she started dating Ian. The fact that they're both standing there with guilty expressions makes me think that Will caught them doing *something*, but then, Will is such a jerk that he would probably accuse Cassie for no reason other than pure spite.

"What's going on here?" I demand, making no effort to disguise the hatred in my voice. I cannot stand Will McLean, and it's best that he's aware of that. Judging by the cold glint in his dark eyes, I suspect he feels the same way about me.

Cassie whirls around at the sound of my voice, her face pasty-white. "Ben …" she mouths. She's obviously more than a little tipsy and also clearly terrified. "What are you *doing* here? Go away, Ben. You don't want to hear this."

I completely ignore her, continuing to stare Will down. "I *said*, what is going on here?"

Will smirks at me, and I realize he's well on his way to being completely hammered. *Great.* "Well, what's going on here is that history is repeating itself. I caught your sister on her knees in front of Oliver a few minutes ago, and poor Ian here …" He jerks his chin toward Ian, who's standing on the opposite side of the circle from me, his jaw locked and his expression unreadable. "Well, of course, I had to tell him. Not that he doesn't already know that his girlfriend is a slut."

"Okay, that's enough!" Cassie's obnoxious friend and roommate, Julia, pushes her way into the circle before I can say anything. "In case you didn't notice, Cassie and Oliver were not the only people in that room. We were all playing a game, and there were probably five other couples besides them, including me and Paul." Her face flushes a little as she admits this, but she's just raised herself about ten points in my estimation. I never would've thought she'd defend Cassie; maybe she's not so obnoxious after all. "So you can take the 'Cassie is a slut' stuff and just screw yourself, Will McLean!"

Will just laughs at her. "Well, you know, Jules, it doesn't really matter to me how many of you were playing your little 'game.' Cassie's still a slut. She did the exact same thing when she and I were dating. Why else do you think I broke up with her?"

I take a step toward him, my fury rising. "Take that back. Right now. My sister is not a slut. *You're* the one who broke her heart!"

Will raises his eyebrows at me, then turns a critical glare on Cassie, his eyes going up and down the length of her body. "Am I?" he says coolly.

"Will, don't ..." Cassie whimpers. I can't see her face because she's turned to look at Will, but I think she's crying.

I feel a strange coldness begin to seep into me, like ice water running through my veins. "What are you talking about, McLean?"

Will's eyes don't move from Cassie's face as he answers, and pure scorn is inscribed on his face. "I'm talking about how Ian and I and half the guys in this town are sick of getting stuck with your dad's leftovers."

It takes a moment for the words to sink in, but when they do, all I can hear is a roaring in my ears. I lunge at Will, catching him off guard and knocking him to the floor. Because he's already pretty drunk and I'm not, I have a slight advantage. I pummel his face as hard as I can, but I only get in a few good punches before someone much stronger than I am pulls me off him from behind. I turn around, ready to take a swing at whoever is trying to stop me from leaving Will in a bloody pulp on the floor, and I narrowly miss slamming Levi in the jaw.

"Ben, *don't*," he says fiercely, before I've even fully registered that my brother is standing in front of me. "We have to get Cassie out of here. Right now."

That's when I notice the sound of my sister screaming. And she's not stopping. Julia has gone to her side and is trying to calm her down, but Cassie's not having any of it. The room vibrates with the sound of her screams—or maybe it just seems that way to me. I stand there, staring stupidly, while Levi grabs her arm and practically drags her away from the crowd of people who've all started to whisper and point. "Come *on*," he snaps over his shoulder at me.

Julia appears at my elbow, trailing after me as I try to follow Levi through the sea of bodies packed near the bar. "Ben! *Ben!*" Julia yanks my arm so hard that I skid to a stop and look at her. Her face is streaked with tears. "What Will said—is that ... is that true? Did your dad really do something ... to Cassie?"

I glare at her and keep walking, refusing to answer any of her questions. I head upstairs, figuring that's where Levi's taken Cassie, my head spinning. Everything is happening too fast. I feel so disoriented. And mad enough to kill someone.

By the time I find them in an upstairs bedroom where everyone's purses and stuff are tossed on the bed, Cassie has calmed down a little. She's still crying, but she's no longer screaming. She cries even harder when I step through the door, Julia on my heels. "Oh, Cassie!" Julia shrieks, hurling herself at my sister and clinging to her neck, sobbing. "I had no idea, sweetie! I'm so sorry, I've been such a horrible friend! I'm so sorry this happened to you! God, how awful!"

"Julia," Levi says through gritted teeth, "go away. Cassie just needs to go home. You two can talk about this later."

"Okay," Julia agrees, loosening her death grip on Cassie and wiping her eyes. "Do you want me to ride with you or come back to the apartment and stay with her or something?"

"She's not going back to the apartment," Levi answers curtly. "We're taking her to our parents' house for tonight. Maybe for a couple nights."

Julia and I both gape at him, but he drills Julia with a look that sends her scampering for the door, no questions asked. I'm not so easily intimidated, though.   "Are you *crazy*?" I hiss at him. "The last thing she needs right now is to be in the same house with ... *him*."

"That's exactly what she needs," Levi retorts, as if Cassie isn't standing right there beside him. Although I'm not sure she's *really* beside us, if you know what I mean—she's still crying, but her eyes are vacant. I wonder if she can even hear us. "We're going to settle this thing once and for all."

Something about the way he says it sends chills up my spine. "What are you talking about?"

"Drive her home for me, will you?" Levi continues as if he didn't hear a word I just said. "I'll meet you there, okay?" He turns to Cassie and kisses her forehead. "It's going to be okay, sweetie."

"Wait a minute!" I follow him to the door and grab his arm. "What are you going to do? You're not going to, like, try to *kill* Dad or something are you?" Depending on how you look at it, it's hysterically funny that *I* am the one asking *Levi* this question. But I don't feel much like laughing.

"He needs to understand what he's done to her," Levi says simply, as if that explains everything. "To all of us, really."

I stare at him, suddenly realizing that I don't know him. At all. "Mom?" I stammer. "Jade?"

"Jade's at summer camp for a month and a half, which you'd know if you weren't stoned out of your mind every chance you get. And Mom needs to hear what we have to say, too."

"So we're just going to … *talk*?"

Levi shrugs. "If he listens. If not …" He gives me an enigmatic smile. "See ya' at home, little brother. Be careful with her, okay? She's pretty shaken up." Then he walks away, leaving me standing there with a mixture of fear and anticipation churning through my insides.

"He hates me, doesn't he? You both do." I nearly jump out of my skin at the sound of Cassie's voice behind me. I had almost forgotten that she was standing there.

"What? No, of course we don't hate you! Are you nuts? Why would we hate you?"

"Because Will's right. I'm a slut. Come on, don't pretend you haven't heard the rumors. Maybe Levi hasn't, but I know you have." Her voice is totally flat, no emotion at all, but when I turn around to look at her, I see that tears are still pouring from her eyes. It's downright creepy.

"You are *not* a slut," I say firmly, holding her shoulders and forcing her to look me in the eyes. "You're not. And I could never hate you."

She shrugs, that same lifeless look in her eyes. "You hate Dad, don't you?"

I hesitate, sighing. "That's different. And it's way more complicated than hating him or not hating him." Cassie shakes her head but doesn't say anything else. "Come on. We've got to get home before Levi blows Dad's head off or something."

Her face gets even paler, if that's possible. "You don't really think he'll *hurt* him, do you? Levi wouldn't do that. I know he wouldn't."

I chuckle mirthlessly. "I think no one in our family really knows each other at all."

Levi

No matter how fast I drive, no matter how hard I grip the steering wheel or how loud I blast the music, I still can't forget the look in Cassie's eyes at the party. I can't block out the sound of her screaming, the way she seemed to shatter, right there in front of me. Ben didn't see it because he was too busy beating the crap out of Will, but I did. Only for a split second, but it was long enough to imprint itself on my memory forever. If I live to be one hundred, I will never forget this night. And if I have anything to say about it, neither will my father.

This is crazy, I think, drumming my fingers on the steering wheel as I speed down the darkened streets toward my parents' house. And I probably am crazy—except that this feels like the best thing I've done in a long time. How many nights have I tossed and turned, fantasizing about having a confrontation with Dad, a real, no-holds-barred showdown? How many times in the past three years have I been on the verge of lashing out at him—but I held back, out of fear or just plain cowardice? Well, no more. Maybe I *am* crazy, maybe I will regret this one day, but I don't think so. Hearing what Will said to Cassie tonight and watching her all but crumble in response forced me to realize that our father has never really had to answer for what he did. I'm going to change that.

I could tell that Ben was shocked when I told him we were taking Cassie home to confront Dad. Ben thinks he knows me so well; he thinks he has the market cornered on anger, on rage, on hating our father. The truth is, he doesn't have a clue. None of them do, not even Cassie.

But then again, after what I saw at the party tonight, it's obvious that I don't know the first thing about the person my sister really is. I mean, I already knew that Ben was in trouble—he's been drinking and doing drugs for the past couple years, not that my parents seem to notice or care. But until tonight, I had no idea about how much Cassie had changed. I didn't even recognize her when I saw her at the party, and even though I didn't immediately step into the fray like Ben did, I heard everything that Will said. The thought of her giving that loser Oliver a blow job makes my stomach heave—not to mention the implication that she's been sleeping around. Clearly, the days of the two of us telling each other everything are long gone.

And it's all *his* fault. None of this would have happened if my dad hadn't done those sick things to Cassie. Okay, maybe Ben would've ended up spending most of his weekends stoned, because he was already turning into Mr. Rebel Without a Cause before everything happened with Dad, but Cassie definitely wouldn't have done the things that she has. Mom wouldn't have turned into some space cadet who obviously has no idea what her kids are really up to, and Jade wouldn't have morphed into a quiet, cautious, overly-sensitive preteen.

I would probably be at Bible college and *not* feeling the need—the obsessive, driving need—to come home every summer and take care of my family, to make sure everyone's all right, and my siblings aren't spinning too far out of control. I would still be able to talk to my dad, really talk to him—instead of suffering through a few minutes of polite, stiff conversation here and there. I probably wouldn't have questioned my faith the way I have the past three years, wouldn't have vacillated on the bitter knife's edge of unforgiveness and hatred. Will wouldn't have broken Cassie's heart all over again tonight, and Ben wouldn't have tried to beat Will to a pulp. And I wouldn't be pulling up to my parents' house at eleven o'clock at night with a metal baseball bat in the trunk.

If my dad hadn't done this, our lives wouldn't be ruined. But he did, and they are, and someone has to answer for that.

Cassie

What started out as an awesome party—all right, a semi-okay party—has turned into my worst nightmare. Absolute worst nightmare. Now nearly all my friends, if "friends" is even the right term for them, know that my dad "did something" to me. They don't know the details, of course, but that makes it even worse. I know those kids, know how their minds work: they'll dredge up some story that's far, far worse than what actually happened, and I'll never be able to show my face around them again. Most of them already thought I was a slut; now they'll think I'm a slut who had some sort of incestuous relationship with her father. *Great.*

I knew things weren't going to end well when Will caught me with Oliver, but I never imagined that he would stoop that low and blurt out my secret in front of everyone. And the look in his eyes when he said: pure hatred. I literally could not breathe for a moment, realizing, for the first time, just how much he hated me. *Your dad's leftovers. Is that really what he thinks about me? Is that what he's thought ever since I told him?* A wave of nausea sweeps over me. *Oh, God.* I lean back against the seat and close my eyes, ignoring Ben, who's asking if I'm all right, focusing on the memory of that night, about eight months after *That Day*, when I finally caved and told Will everything.

I was spending the night at his place, since his parents were out of town that weekend. Will had known for months that something was very wrong, but he had been pretty good about giving me space and letting me know that he was here if I ever wanted to tell him what was really bothering me. I think that maybe, deep down, he knew what had happened—or at least suspected it—but he never let on.

That night, I was lying in his arms and I just felt safe. There is no other way to describe it. I knew he loved me, and I believed that he would never hurt me. He was the closest person in the world to me by then, and I was suddenly overwhelmed with the need to tell him everything. And I did. Will held me while I cried, and he even got choked up himself.

"I'm so, so sorry that happened to you, baby," he whispered into my hair. "It doesn't change the way I feel about you, not at all."

I think he meant it when he said it. But he was wrong. It did change the way he felt about me, the way he looked at me. It didn't happen overnight, but it didn't take long for me to notice the subtle changes—the way he suddenly couldn't spend nearly as much time with me; the way he stiffened, ever so slightly, when I touched him; the way he stopped calling every night. All of it confirmed my suspicions that what my father had done to me had left me as damaged goods, a girl no one would want for anything other than sex, maybe not even that. Will certainly wasn't as interested as he used to be. When I realized that it was driving him away from me, I hated myself for telling him. We were technically still "together," but in so many ways, we couldn't have been farther apart. I felt numb and empty and bereft without him.

And then one night, about three months after I told him about the abuse, Will caught me exactly the way he had caught me tonight—on my knees in front of some guy who didn't mean anything to me. And I couldn't make him understand that I wasn't cheating on him, that the guy meant absolutely nothing to me—putting aside the fact that we weren't actually having sex, anyway—that I was just trying to *feel* something. To make myself believe, even for a few minutes, that someone still wanted me—even if it was only for sex, even if Will didn't.

Of course, Will didn't see it that way at all; he broke up with me and proceeded to act as if what we'd had for the past two and a half years didn't mean anything to him. Which may have been true for him, but it definitely wasn't for me. Even when I started dating Ian, about a year ago, I still thought about Will and what I'd had with him before.

"Cass?" Ben says tentatively, as if he's a little afraid of me. "You okay?"

"Do I *look* okay?" I snap, not opening my eyes or turning my head to look at him. "Sorry. That was rude. I'm … I mean, how could I be okay, Ben? Half the town just found out that our dad …" I stop before I let the tears fall.

"Hey, hey," Ben soothes. "It's okay. Um … you're not, like, really wasted, are you?"

I try for a smile, which probably looks more like a grimace to Ben. "As if. Seeing you beat the crap out of Will sobered me up pretty fast."

He clenches his hands tighter on the steering wheel. "I should have finished the job. If Levi hadn't gotten in the way, I would've made sure Will left that party in an ambulance."

"Ben …"

"I'm serious. I don't care what he was to you three years ago; he's a complete jerk now. I mean, what kind of person says something like that in front of a crowd of people?"

"He was right, though," I say softly.

Ben slams on the brakes so hard I nearly hit the dashboard. Luckily there's no one behind us. "Don't ever say something like that!" His voice is nearly as fierce as it was when he was talking to Will earlier. "You hear me? I'm sick of hearing you say things like that: oh, I'm such a slut; oh, Will was right; oh, I'm not worth anything because of what Dad did to me."

He swears at me. "You know that's total crap, right? You can't say stuff like that about yourself, Cass! Dad is the one who's not worth anything— *not you.*" He starts driving again, still glancing over at me. "You got that?"

I nod, and Ben lapses into silence. That's not the first time he—or Mom or Levi or Dr. Morton or, before everything went wrong, Will—has said something like that to me. *Don't talk about yourself that way, Cassie. Don't think like that. Don't blame yourself. Don't, don't, don't.*

They can say those things all they want. It doesn't change the fact that I don't believe them. It doesn't change the fact that every time someone says something like that to me, I want to scream, *But that's how I feel! Why can't I say it? Why can't you just listen to me?*

Of course I don't say that, because nobody wants to hear it. Nobody wants hear how much I hate myself and blame myself for what my father did to me. Why should they? I don't even like admitting it to myself.

When we get to the house, Levi's car is already parked in the driveway. "Great," Ben mutters as he pulls in behind Levi, "he's probably in there beating the crap out of Dad."

Something tightens in my chest. "You don't really think he'll do anything crazy, do you? I mean, I know you said earlier that you think none of us really knows each other but … come on, Ben, it's Levi! If there's anyone in this family I would expect to beat Dad senseless, it would be you, not him! Maybe you don't know Levi very well, but I do."

The corners of Ben's mouth tip in a sardonic smile. "You sure about that? I bet, right now, Levi's thinking he doesn't know you very well, either."

My face flushes, and I can't look at him.

"Come on," Ben sighs, unbuckling his seat belt. "Let's get this over with."

"I … I don't know if I can." I am so exhausted that I feel like I could sleep for days; my limbs are so heavy they might as well have turned to stone, and I'm not sure I can even get out of the car. "What am I supposed to say to him? I don't … I just … I'm so tired, Ben."

"Yeah," he says softly. "I think we all are. That's why you have to do this, Cass. You have to tell him how you feel. You just have to, okay?"

For some reason the gentleness in his voice makes me want to cry. Again. "Why? Why do I have to? Why does it always have to be up to me to fix everything in this twisted family?"

Ben gapes at me for a minute. He starts to speak, then apparently thinks better of whatever he was about to say. "Because," he says after a moment of awkward silence, "you're the one he hurt the most. So you're the one who can hurt him the most now."

Marianne

I know something's wrong the minute Levi walks through the door—his face is tense, his eyes darting around like he's afraid someone is hiding in the corner. Peter must see the baseball bat behind Levi's back before I do, because his jaw tightens. When I notice it, I scream. "Levi, what are you doing?"

"Hey, Mom, Dad," he says bitterly, practically spitting the words. "What's going on?"

"Shouldn't we be asking you the same question?" Peter asks, the picture of calm and composure.

"Me?" Levi leans back against the wall across from Peter. "Oh, nothing much, Pop. Just waiting for Cass and Ben to get here. And then we're going to have a little talk, okay? Actually, don't answer that: I don't really care if it's okay with you or not. We're going to talk, and you're going to listen. And if you don't, if you say one word before I tell you it's okay, I'm going to bash your skull in. Are we clear?"

I feel all the blood draining from my face. This cannot be happening. Is Levi actually threatening to kill Peter? *Levi?* I could almost imagine Ben doing something like this—in my worst nightmare, of course, but I *could* imagine it. But Levi? Never. "Levi." My voice does not sound like my own, but rather the raspy voice of some old woman, some stranger.

He doesn't even spare me a glance but keeps his eyes trained on his father. "Be quiet, Mom. Nothing you can say right now is going to change this situation, and it might actually make things worse. So please, just be quiet."

My mind is racing. Should I try to sneak into the kitchen and call the police? Call the police on my *son?* Should I just do as he asks and keep quiet, hoping this will all blow over?

As if he can read my mind, Peter looks over at me and smiles, that placid calm never disappearing from his expression. "It's all right, honey. Let's just wait for Ben and Cassie to get here, and we'll all talk."

"No, no," Levi interrupts, glowering at Peter. "There's no 'we' here, Peter. Cassie, Ben, and I are going to talk. You are not going to say anything. Neither is Mom. Unless we ask you to."

"Okay, okay, son," Peter holds up both hands in a gesture of surrender. "I understand."

The minutes drag on, and I begin to wonder if Ben and Cassie will ever get here. I'm praying under my breath, a desperate jumble of pleadings and promises. *Please, God, please ... Save my husband and I'll do anything. Keep my children safe.* But I don't feel the usual sense of peace, the whisper in my soul that is God's response. God is clearly not talking to me tonight.

After what seems an eternity, I hear a car pull into the driveway. "Oh, thank God!" I blurt out before I can stop myself. Levi shoots me a withering look but remains silent.

It takes all my control not to exclaim again when Ben and Cassie come through the door, though. I have never seen my daughter this way. The clothes she's wearing—hooker clothes, my mother would've called them—are absolutely appalling.

I raised you better than this ... The words are on the tip of my tongue, but before I can speak them, Cassie raises her head and looks straight at me. The words die in my throat. *Oh, Cassie ...*

My daughter looks haunted. Even that word is too paltry to describe the anguish filling her eyes and twisting her expression; it's all I can do to restrain myself from running to her and taking her in my arms. *My baby ...*

"Okay." Levi looks at his brother and sister. "Let's get this party started, huh? Who wants to go first?"

Ben nudges Cassie, and I really look at him for the first time. He doesn't look much better than she does, and if I didn't know better I would think he was drunk. *But of course not—Ben would never ...*

"I don't ... I don't ... know what to say," Cassie stammers.

"Just tell me how you feel, sweetie," Peter encourages. Levi glares at him but Peter pretends not to see.

"I ... that's the problem. I don't know how I feel. I think ... I just feel really ... really angry at you about ... you know, what you did to me."

My face floods with heat. "Is *that* what this is about? Honestly, Cassie! After all this time? Why are you bringing this up now? I thought we talked about this with Dr. Morton—you said you were doing fine. I thought you were moving on. We really don't need to discuss ..."

All the uncertainty vanishes from Cassie's face as she whirls around to face me. "Would you just *shut up*? You are the last person I want to talk to right now! You never, ever just listen to me, Mom! You're always trying to tell me how I should feel and what I should think and what I should say, and I'm sick of it! And you don't have a freaking *clue* about any of it! You want to pretend everything's fine, and we're still the perfect family, and everything's so normal but it's ..." She begins to sob, animal-like sounds ripping from the center of her like I've never heard.

"Cassie ..." I begin, but Levi cuts me off.

"For God's sake, Mom, look at her! Shut your mouth for once in your life, and just *look at your daughter*! Does she look fine to you? Does she look like she's 'moved on' from everything? Are you really that delusional? I told you three years ago that Dad moving back home was a mistake, but would you listen to me? No! You never listened to any of us—you just made up your mind and did what you wanted to do. You never cared about any of us as much as you cared about him!"

"That's ... that's not true," I gasp, the force of my children's words hitting me like physical blows. "I put you kids first—you were always first."

"Stop saying that!" Cassie screams. "We were *never* first! You were never there for me the way you should've been! As soon as Dad moved back home, you just ... you abandoned me, Mom! You chose your marriage over your kids; what kind of mother does that?"

I'm dimly aware that I'm crying. "That's not how it was at all! I told you all the time that I was here if you wanted to talk, that I would always be here to listen to you."

"But when I told you stuff, you totally blew me off! You just—you didn't want to hear anything that was sad or difficult or messy. All you wanted to hear about was how 'well' we were doing. And you completely ignored *everything* I ever said to you about it! Everything!"

"I was trying to protect you! All of you, but especially you, Cass. I didn't want to see you get hurt again."

"Protect me from *what*? What could possibly have happened to me that would be worse than what Dad did? News flash, Mom: I would rather have been raped by a stranger than sexually abused by my own father! Do you have any idea how disgusting I feel, knowing that he did those things to me, that he thought about doing worse than that?"

"Sweetie ..."

"No, you don't know! Because you never listened! I tried to talk to you about it once, and you completely missed the point!"

My stomach twists. I remember the day she's talking about: it was in the middle of her senior year, shortly after she broke up with Will—*that* was a shame; he was such a nice young man. Cassie brought me her iPod and asked me to listen to a song. I don't remember the title now, but it was about a girl trying to recover from sexual abuse. I listened to half of it and then removed the headphones and gave the iPod back to her.

"You didn't even listen to the whole thing," she'd said, disappointment etching itself into her expression.

"Honey, that's a very disturbing song," I'd responded. "Are you sure you should be listening to music like that? Doesn't it just make you focus on all the wrong things? You need to be more focused on the relationship you and your dad have now, not dwelling in the past."

Walls had gone up in her eyes as I spoke, and she'd jammed the headphones into her ears. "Fine," she'd said flatly and stalked off. As she walked away I'd heard her mutter, "See if I ever tell you anything again."

At the time, I thought I had done the right thing in encouraging her to move forward.

Cassie's beautiful blue eyes are swimming with tears. "You remember, don't you? I was trying to show you how I felt through that song, because I was too scared to actually tell you in words. But you wouldn't even listen to the whole thing! And then you basically told me I shouldn't feel that way. But here's the thing, Mom: that's how I feel! And maybe it is wrong, or bad, or inappropriate or whatever. But that doesn't change the fact that the lyrics to 'Damaged' describe exactly how I feel! And you just blew me off—you didn't even try to understand it!"

"I'm sorry, sweetie," I plead, my own face wet with tears. "I'm so, so sorry. I should've listened to you."

The walls that I saw in her eyes two years ago are back. "Yeah. Well, it's a little late for that now, isn't it?"

She turns her back on me, leaning into Ben's chest and letting him comfort her. My stomach turns to stone. *I am losing my daughter. Right here, right this minute, I am losing her. I wasn't there for her when she needed me the most; how could I have been so blind?*

Another memory springs to life, this one from just a scant few days after Peter moved out. So much of those early days is now a blur to me, but this I remember clearly: it was the day Cassie had the exam at the hospital—the exam that the social worker had told me would be an external exam that I didn't need to be present for. When Cassie came out of that exam room shaken and white-faced, staggering, I knew immediately that it hadn't been just an external exam, and I was livid. I confronted the social worker and gave her a piece of my mind—probably a bit more intense than she deserved, but at the time, it felt like just one more betrayal from someone we were supposed to be able to trust.

When I had finished my tirade, Cassie had slipped her hand in mine and whispered, "Can we please go home, Mama? I want to go home."

She was sixteen. She hadn't called me "Mama" in nearly seven years—or held my hand in public for at least as long. But she refused to let go of my hand until we got to the car, and, once we got home, she curled up on the couch with a blanket. "Sit with me, Mama? Please? Just hold me."

So I sat there and held her until she fell asleep in my arms, the way she used to do when she was a tiny girl. "I'm so glad you're here," she had whispered right before she fell asleep. I remember sitting there, watching her sleep, and weeping, thinking of all that my precious girl had lost and all that she still had to go through.

How did I ever lose sight of that? How did I ever make my sweet daughter believe that I had chosen her father and our marriage over her and her feelings and her needs?

Or did she believe that because that's exactly what I had done?

Ben

About the time that Cassie falls into my arms and starts sobbing against my shoulder, I make a decision: if Levi doesn't use that baseball bat to beat Dad senseless, I'll grab it from him and do it myself. Remember how I said before that I go back and forth on whether or not I hate my dad? Well, that's over: I officially hate him, after hearing my sister fall apart. She said more in her tirade at Mom than she has in, well, since all of this started. I had no clue she felt that way, and clearly Mom and Dad didn't either.

Dad's standing there slack-jawed, like he's suddenly gone mute, and tears are streaming down his face. He looks so pathetic that I almost feel sorry for him. Almost … until I remember what he did, and then all I can feel is rage.

"Cassie, I …" he starts to say.

"Shut *up*!" Levi screeches.

He seems to have had a complete personality transplant sometime in the last two hours; the Levi I know would never yell at someone, much less our dad. I'm starting to believe that he really will use that baseball bat. If he does, I'll stand here and cheer—or maybe help him out with my fists. Just the thought of punching Dad in the face calms me down a little.

Levi's pacing back and forth in front of Dad, muttering something I can't hear, even though I'm only a few feet away from him. He's probably having a nervous breakdown. *Great. How perfect.*

So is Cass, for that matter. Her screaming match with Mom has sapped whatever strength she had left; I'm basically holding her upright while she leaves a trail of snot and mascara all over the front of my shirt, just like she did that night that I smashed a hole in the wall.

"Hey, maybe you should go upstairs and lie down?" I whisper. She shakes her head fiercely. "I'm not leaving you two here with him. Levi'll kill him."

She's probably right, so I just shrug. "At least sit down or something. Please, Cass. Come on. You're shaking like a leaf." She lets me lead her over to the sofa, where she sits like she's made of wood. I clench my hands into fists and turn to face Dad.

"Are you happy now? Look what you've done to her!" I'm shaking almost as badly as Cassie, trying to restrain myself from flying across the space between us and grabbing him by the throat.

My father apparently is too overcome to speak—which only makes me feel more disgusted. "Say something, for God's sake! You coward! You owe us some kind of explanation!"

"I ... I ... Ben, I don't have one."

If I weren't so angry right now, I'd be tempted to feel at least some pity for the man; he's obviously tormented. I've never seen him so emotional. His eyes are anguished, and his face is wet with tears. But the words he just said obliterated any spark of compassion I might've felt.

Fury surges through me, even hotter than a few minutes ago. "You have no explanation? Nothing? You ruin all of our lives, and you have nothing to say for yourself? What a load of ..."

"You have to have some kind of reason." The whispery, paper-thin voice that interrupts me doesn't sound anything like Cassie's voice; she's scaring me. She clears her throat and continues, her voice a little steadier.

"You can't ... you can't ... do something so ... sick to me and then try to say you don't know why you did it. You can't just—you can't completely ruin our relationship and destroy our family and stand there and say you don't have *any* idea why you did it. There has to be a reason. There has to have been something about me—something I did wrong or ..."

Dad's shaking his head before the words are even out of her mouth. "No, no, sweetie. It was not your fault! It had nothing to do with you, honey! I promise you that. I just ..."

"I wasn't finished," Cassie stops him. *Wow, Miss Passive-Aggressive is finally asserting herself.* She's still crying—I don't think she's stopped crying for the past fifteen minutes—but otherwise, she's very calm and composed. Levi and Mom look as astonished as I probably do.

"What I was going to say," Cassie continues, "is that, for the past three years, I've felt so dirty and disgusting and ... just ... evil ... because I knew that you wouldn't have done those things to me if I hadn't done something to make you want to. I just knew that! I felt like, well, I was so close to you before, when I was younger, and it didn't make sense that you would ... I mean, of all the people you could have sexually abused, why did you choose me?"

Um, isn't a better question: why did he choose to sexually abuse anyone? I keep this thought to myself, though, because Cass is on a roll now. She's definitely not as composed as she was a minute ago, either, and it's killing me to watch her suffer through these questions. I hope Dad's feeling about a thousand times worse. Judging by the look on his face, I'd say it's a safe bet that he is.

"I didn't ... I didn't *choose* you, Cass," he croaks. "It's not something that I planned out or ... or thought about a lot ahead of time. It just ... it just happened. I ... I made a mistake. A terrible, horrible mistake. But it had nothing to do with you, or anything that you did or didn't do. I just—I screwed up, sweetie. I would give anything to go back and change that moment. I would, I promise. But I can't and so now—I have to live with this for the rest of my life, Cassie."

She stares at him, unmoved in the face of his emotional meltdown. "So do I. So where does that leave us, Dad? You tell me what we're supposed to do from here, please, because I really don't know. Honestly, there's a part of me that doesn't care if I never even see you again. But then there's the other part of me that ..."

Cassie stops, struggling for control. "I still remember what a great dad you were when I was a kid, and how special our relationship was and, God, Dad, part of me wants that back! But—we're never going to get it back, no matter how much I want it.

"That's what hurts me the most, you know: the way you betrayed me. I was—I was Daddy's little girl, and you just...you just ruined it! All of it! It was like you took a sledgehammer to our relationship and smashed it. And then you want to try to put the pieces back together but we just ... we can't. Why do you think I moved out as soon as I could? Do you have any idea how hard it was to sit across the table from you at breakfast and talk about school or whatever, when I'd just spent the whole night having flashbacks and nightmares of you raping me? Do you have any clue what that's like? It felt like you had actually raped me, even though I know you didn't. Not that you didn't want to," Cassie adds, glaring at him.

"So is that all you can say? That you 'made a mistake'? Thanks, Dad. I'll try to remember that the next time I can't sleep because of the nightmares—which will probably be tonight, actually. So, thanks for the consolation. I'm so glad to know there's a legitimate reason for the *hell* we're all living through!"

Dad starts to speak, but Cassie cuts him off with a shake of her head. She stands up shakily and starts to walk out of the room, but then she turns back when she's halfway to the stairs. My jaw almost hits the floor at what she does next: Cassie walks right up to Dad and slaps him in the face, hard. Then she crumples into tears again and takes off running upstairs, probably heading for her room.

Everything is so still after she leaves; it's like someone dropped a bomb in the middle of the room. Levi looks both triumphant and angry, and Mom is dissolved into tears in the armchair across the room, behind Dad. As for me, well, I'm shocked and proud that Cassie actually slapped Dad—*Cassie, of all people!*—but hearing all the things she said gutted me. I think I'm angrier at Dad now than I was before Cassie said anything, if that's even possible.

I need to get out of this room, before I hurt him. "Just so you know," I begin without looking at Dad, "pretty much everything she just said applies to me, too. I think you're a sick coward. And I think it's pathetic for you to say that you 'have to live with this for the rest of your life,' because Cass is right: all of us have to live with it for the rest of our lives. You make me sick. And you didn't just betray Cassie, by the way. You betrayed all of us."

I start to walk toward the stairs, but I pause, remembering. "Oh, yeah, and Mom? Cassie's right about you, too. You chose him over us. I hate you for that. I really do. I mean, I don't hate *you*, but I hate what you did. I hate what you're *doing*. And I think you're a pretty lousy mother to choose your husband over your kids, especially after something like this. Both of you suck."

"That pretty much sums it up for me, too," Levi shrugs. "Now, if you'll excuse us, we're going to go check on Cass."

We both turn and walk out of the room, the sound of both our parents' sobs rising like a tidal wave behind us. Neither one of us look back.

Cassie

I can't stop shaking. As I try to remove the layers of makeup from my face, my hands are trembling so badly that it takes me twice as long as usual. I hear Ben and Levi tromping up the stairs and the muted chorus of our parents' tears rising through the tiled floor beneath my feet. I know my brothers are looking for me, wanting to make sure I'm all right, but I cannot face them now. Not yet. I lock the bathroom door, flip on the fan, and turn on the faucet in the bathtub. I pour in nearly half a bottle of Jade's lavender-scented bubble bath and run the water as hot as I can stand it.

Levi taps on the door. "You okay, Cassie?"

I close my eyes tight, willing my voice to remain slightly steady. "I'm fine. I just … I'll be out after I take a bath."

When he walks away, I lower myself to the floor, my back against the cool hardness of the wall, watching the tub fill with bubbles and the mirror disappear in a cloud of steam. Once the tub is full, I shut off the faucet and remove my clothes. The water flushes my skin an angry crimson as I gingerly step into the bathtub, and I gasp at the intensity of the heat. I lower myself into the water by degrees, trying to let my body get accustomed to the heat. I stretch out along the length of the tub, my hair fanning out around me, wondering if I will ever feel clean again.

My head throbs, and I close my eyes, trying desperately not to think of what happened here tonight. *What's still happening.* I can hear the faintest sounds of my parents talking downstairs. Their conversation is frequently pierced by shrill, harsh sobs from my mother and, though I can't hear it, I know that my father is crying, too. I imagine that he hasn't stopped crying since I slapped him. The sounds of their grief, however hushed through the floorboards and insulation that separate us, seem to invade the bathroom like a suffocating cloud. Their grief, my brothers' anger, my own confusion and hurt, and, yes, even anger, combine into a noxious mixture that makes it difficult to breathe.

I didn't realize how angry I was until tonight. I'd always known that there was a part of me that was angry with him—I did a good job of burying it and ignoring it, but I always knew it was there. Just as I always knew that I hated myself for what my father did to me. What I didn't know, until the moment my palm connected with his face, was that there was small part of me that hated him.

It was that realization, more than anything, that left me shaking and hardly able to walk up the stairs. I never wanted to hate him—before Dad moved back home, whenever Ben would fly into one of his tirades about how much he hated Dad, I would always cringe and try to jump to Dad's defense. I never even considered that I could feel the same way.

How can you love someone so much and yet despise him at the same time?

I cover my mouth with both hands to stifle the sound of my weeping. *God, where are You?* I silently beg the God I am not even sure I believe in anymore. I used to believe—believing used to be as natural to me as breathing. But God seems a million miles away from this house, tonight. *Why did You let this happen to us? Why is my family falling apart like this? I don't want to hate my dad…I love him! Why do I feel this way? Why am I even asking You, anyway? It's not like You care …*

Silence. God's not answering. Not that I'm surprised. I mean, if He's there at all, surely He wouldn't want to wade into the middle of the mess our once-picture-perfect family has become. No one else does; I don't expect that God would be much of an exception.

Even Dr. Morton, our "dedicated" family therapist, quit seeing us after a year, when Levi moved to Portland, and Ben flatly refused to come for sessions anymore. He didn't question my assurances that I was fine and that I didn't mind ending our sessions together; I secretly hoped that he would see through the façade. But if there's one thing I've learned in the past three years, it's that people see what they want to see.

I guess You're pretty much the same way, aren't You, God? Tears are streaming down my face, and I remember the Bible verses I memorized as a child, the ones about God always watching over His people. The memory infuriates me. *Are You seeing this? Can You see what's happening here tonight? Why didn't You stop it? Why, why, why is this happening?*

Nothing.

I attempt, in vain, to stop the tears. I don't even know why I'm crying, or for whom. Out of pity for myself? For my brothers, after everything they witnessed tonight? For my parents? All of us? Wave after wave of emotion crashes and recedes, leaving me even more distraught. Memories of how things used to be collide with scenes from tonight, how things are now, producing such a profound sense of loss and grief that I want to scream. *Daddy, Daddy, why did you do this to me? Why did you hurt me like this? Why did you do this to us?*

The water is nearly cold by the time I compose myself. Weariness has seeped into every bone in my body, as if my heart were pumping exhaustion and numbness instead of blood.

I run my hands over the length of my body, pressing down until I can feel my collarbone, ribs, hipbones, knees, and ankles. Suddenly I think of Ian, remembering the way I betrayed him tonight and the look on his face when Will was gloating about having caught me with Oliver. *Oh, Ian …* I didn't know how much I loved him until I saw his face tonight. I'd always thought, somewhere in the back of my mind, that he was just a replacement for Will, that I would never love someone the way I had loved Will. And now that I've realized how wrong I was, it's too late. I've lost him, too.

That thought sends me perilously close to sobbing again, but I grit my teeth and force the emotion down. *Not now.* I can fall apart later. Maybe much later, when all of this is over. *If it ever is.*

I'm shaking again as I rise from the tub and dry off slowly. I pull on my oldest pair of pajamas—I didn't even realize I had any pajamas left in this house, since I thought I'd packed everything when I moved in with Julia—and their softness enfolds me like a familiar friend. All I want right now is sleep. But I brush my hair and plaster a smile on my face, ready to brave my brothers' questions and concern. After what happened at the party tonight, I owe them at least that much.

Levi

When we were kids, my grandma used to say that certain people looked like "death warmed over." I never understood that expression—I thought it was the most morbid thing I'd ever heard. But the way Cassie looks when she finally staggers into her bedroom where Ben and I are waiting for her reminds me of that expression.

"God, Cassie …" Ben breathes. "You look awful."

She smiles weakly. "Thanks a lot. That's what happens when a girl takes off her makeup, you know."

My heart twists at the way she's trying to be normal, trying to joke around with us like it's a typical night. "Cassie …" I realize with horror that I can't speak past the thickness in my throat and my eyes are filling with tears. I haven't cried in front of anyone in years—not since those first few weeks after Dad moved out. I clamp my mouth shut and try to get ahold of myself.

Ben, perched on the edge of Cassie's bed, looks away, and Cassie kindly pretends not to notice me fighting for control. She shoves Ben over and flops down on the bed beside him. "I am so tired, you guys. And it's only, like, what? Midnight? I'm turning into an old woman, I guess." She tries to laugh but it comes out strangled. Next thing I know, she's curled into a ball, sobbing.

Ben shoots me a desperate glance, but I know if I try to comfort my sister right now I'll end up sobbing myself. *And why would that be such a horrible thing, you spineless weakling?* I chastise myself. *She needs you!* But my legs are concrete, rooted to the floor.

For someone who's practically allergic to a girl's tears, Ben does a fantastic job of consoling Cass. "It's okay. It's okay," he whispers. "Just cry it all out. It's good to get all of this out of you, you know." On and on, he keeps up a steady stream of encouragement as she cries. All I can manage is a steady supply of tissues, but I guess that's something. This is definitely a night for role reversals, that's for sure.

It seems like an eternity until Cassie starts to calm down, but it's probably only ten minutes. "I'm sorry," she apologizes as soon as she's able to speak coherently. "I didn't ... I really didn't want to fall apart like that. I feel like all I've done tonight is cry."

"Hey, that's not a bad thing." My voice is still too hoarse, but at least I'm not blubbering all over the place. "You probably needed a good cry. And come on, after what happened at the party tonight, who wouldn't be crying?"

"Not to mention," Ben clears his throat and glares at me, "*someone's* brilliant idea of an impromptu family therapy session!" I didn't even know words like "impromptu" were in my stoner brother's vocabulary. Apparently he's actually pretty smart when he's sober.

"Hey, Ben, it's okay," Cassie reassures him. "I think Leev did the right thing, bringing us here tonight. I think we ... I mean, I think we needed to say those things to Mom and Dad, you know? We probably should've said some of that a long time ago. I know I should've."

Her face starts to crumple again, and my stomach heaves. I hate to see her so tormented like this. "It's just hard, you know? I haven't even—before tonight, I'd never even said some of those things to myself out loud, not to mention to him. Or Mom. I didn't even really realize how mad I was at her until she said something, and then it was like ..." Her voice trails off. Her blue eyes are vacant; I don't know if she realizes she's crying again.

I sit down on the other side of her, so that she's sandwiched between me and Ben. "I think it's the same for me and Ben, too. Not that we know exactly how you feel—just that I didn't really know until tonight how mad I was at both of them. I've known for a long time that I was mad at Dad." I shrug, the casual gesture belying the intensity of my feelings. "I didn't know I was so mad at Mom."

"Me either," Ben adds quietly.

"I just ... part of me feels so guilty for being mad at them, though! Especially Mom. I know she was just doing the best she could—I remember how hard it was for her when he first left. Don't you guys remember? She was just ... a total wreck. And having to deal with all of us and try to keep the whole thing a secret from everyone, the neighbors and everyone at church—I know it was so hard for her. And when I remember that, I feel so awful that I'm angry at her. I mean, she didn't *do* anything!"

"That's the whole point, Cass," I remind her gently. "That's why I'm mad at her, anyway: she never did anything to help us, especially you. She just shipped us all off to therapy and tried to pretend things were fine once he moved back home. She never wanted to deal with any of it. Or maybe she wanted to, but she didn't know how; I don't know. All I know is, I warned her that she shouldn't let him move back home, and she didn't listen to me. And now I know that I was right."

Cassie shrugs her thin shoulders. That's another thing I hadn't really noticed until tonight: how fragile she's become. The pallor of her skin accentuates the shadows under eyes, and her always-svelte figure seems thinner than it was when I saw her at Christmas break. It's like she's changed into another person over the past year or so, and I didn't even know it. The days when we were best friends and told each other everything seem like a distant memory; I'm vividly aware that I hardly know her any longer.

"So are you mad at him?" Ben asks.

"Yeah …" Cassie sighs, as if it's difficult for her to admit to this. "It's complicated, though. Like I told him, sometimes when I think about what he did, I never even want to see him again. But most of the time, I think about what he did, and then I think about how close we were before that, and I start remembering all the good times and …" She presses a hand to her mouth, her lips trembling. A minute passes before she can speak again.

"And I know he's sorry for what he did. I know he is! And … and I love him—so I don't understand why I get so angry. I don't understand why I … why I said those things to him tonight. And I slapped him! Why did I do that when I … I love him and I know he's sorry for what he did?"

"Maybe that's not enough," Ben suggests. "I mean, I love him, too, deep down. He's our dad, and it's not like he was a horrible father before all this happened. But that's not enough to make me want to have a real relationship with him anymore. Sometimes it's not even enough to keep me from hating him, to be honest. And the whole thing about him being sorry … he should be sorry! That doesn't mean a whole lot to me, Cass. It really doesn't. It makes me feel a little better about Jade still living here with him, but other than that …" He shrugs.

Cass stares at him for a moment, as if she's absorbing the full weight of his words, and then she starts crying again. I can tell she's fighting the tears, trying to force herself to remain composed, but it's clearly a losing battle. "Why can't that be enough?" she whispers. "Why does this have to be so complicated?"

This time I hold her as she cries. "Shhh. Shhh. It's okay." Even though I know it's not okay. That it might not ever be okay again, not really. Things are never going to go back to the way they were before. All the good times Cassie likes to remember—they were real. But they're gone forever now, and there's no manual for navigating our way through this new reality. "It's okay, Cass."

"The one thing I don't understand," she says when she isn't crying as hard, "is, well, I don't understand why Dad came and apologized to me after the first time. I don't know why he would do that if he thought I was sleeping when he was … you know … touching me and stuff."

Ben shoots me a glance, his jaw tightening. "What are you talking about?"

Cassie looks between us, hesitating. "Don't get mad at him," she pleads, her gaze resting on me the longest. "What I mean is, the first time he … you know …"

"Sexually abused you," Ben interrupts.

"Shut up, Ben!" I snap.

"Well, the morning after that happened the first time, Dad … called me into his office and said he needed to apologize to me because he had … you know, touched me the night before while I was sleeping. And I pretended that I didn't have a clue what he was talking about, and that was the end of it. But then, a couple nights later, he was in my room again. I don't understand why he would apologize and then just turn around and do it again. It doesn't make any sense."

The roaring in my ears that was there earlier, during our confrontation with Dad, comes back. "Let me get this straight." I jump up and start pacing around the room. "You're saying that Dad came into your room and touched you and then *apologized* the next morning? Did he tell you not to say anything to anyone about it? He told you not to tell Mom, didn't he?" She doesn't answer and she won't look at me, which is all the answer I need. "*Didn't he?*"

"Levi, stop," Cass begs. "It's not a big deal. Don't …"

I'm already heading for the door, spewing a string of obscenities that would make my mother faint. I grab the baseball bat from the doorway where I'd left it. I'm vaguely aware of Cass screaming something and Ben chasing after me, but mostly all I hear is that roaring in my ears.

I tear down the stairs as if the house is on fire. *You are going to pay for this.* The thought drums through my brain like a mantra. Dad is standing in the living room, talking to Mom, his back to me. I tackle him from behind and drop the bat, using only my fists. And suddenly, all the tears I thought I'd held back earlier are pouring from my eyes as I pound his face as hard as I can. "I hate you!" I scream, my voice ragged with sobs. "I hate you! You're a liar and a hypocrite and I hate you!"

I'm dimly aware of both Mom and Cass screaming at me to stop, of Ben pulling on me from behind. "Levi, Levi, stop it!" He manages to pull me off of Dad, but not before I've gotten several fierce blows in. I stagger away from him and sink to the floor, sobbing like a little boy.

Dad just stares at me, blood streaming from his mouth and nose. "I'm sorry," I whisper, horrified at what I've done. "I didn't … I didn't mean … I didn't mean for that to happen."

Dad manages what might pass for a sad, crooked smile, a smile drenched in blood. "Now you know how I felt," he whispers.

Cassie

It's 3 a.m. before I'm able to collapse into bed. Things went crazy after Levi attacked Dad—Mom kept begging Dad to let her take him to the hospital, which he refused to do; Ben went up to his room and didn't come out for an hour and a half; and Levi sat on the floor and cried for almost twenty minutes. As for me, I sank into a chair in the living room and let the chaos swirl around me, pretending that I was somewhere else. Anywhere else.

I never would've believed that Levi would try to beat Dad up the way he did. Judging by his emotional meltdown afterward, I don't think even Levi believed it at first. I also thought that Ben would jump right in there with him and start punching away, but he didn't. Nothing about this night has turned out the way I thought it would.

Except for one thing—he invades my dreams when I finally drift into a fitful sleep. I knew, from the moment Levi said we'd be spending the night here, that the nightmares would follow me. I knew they would creep into my room, pin me to the bed, and leave me trembling and terror-stricken. I was right.

I wake up to sunlight streaming through my window; it's the fourth time I've been awakened since my first attempt to sleep. My head throbs, and I know there's no chance that I'll fall back to sleep. I slip on a pair of old jeans and a sweatshirt that I find in my dresser—Mom hasn't changed anything about this room since I moved out over a year ago. My old collection of stuffed animals still lines the top of my bookshelf; pictures from as far back as middle school almost cover the mirror on my door. Posters of bands I haven't listened to in at least three years plaster the walls. It's an eerie sensation, as if I've stepped into a time warp. I shiver involuntarily and hurry out of the room, closing the door firmly behind me.

Levi is in the kitchen, making a pot of coffee, when I stumble through the doorway, no doubt looking as horrible as I feel. "How you doing, little sister?" he asks, the corners of his mouth tipping in what might constitute a smile.

I grimace. "Is it possible to have an emotional hangover? I think that's what I have … That and lack of sleep. I think I got maybe three solid hours last night."

"You and me both," Levi chuckles mirthlessly. "And I bet we're not the only ones. That was one heck of a night, huh?"

I raise an eyebrow at him. "Especially after you decided to beat the crap out of Dad … What was up with that, anyway? I mean, you didn't say a word when I was telling him how I felt about everything, and then I mention one stupid detail after everyone's calmed down and you decide to beat him up? That's just so … I mean, it's so unlike you, Leev."

He shrugs, tracing the pattern of the Formica countertop with his finger and refusing to look at me. "I just … it was hard enough to see you so upset last night, and to hear what you said to him. But when you said he told you not to tell Mom—I don't know, I guess I just lost it. I've been so angry at him for all this time, but I've tried to ignore it and just pretend it doesn't matter. But last night, I couldn't do it anymore. I just couldn't. I couldn't stand there and let him get away with it."

I choose my words carefully. "You saw how he looked last night when I was telling him how I felt. I don't think he's gotten away with anything, Levi."

"I know," he sighs. "I know, but I didn't really realize that until after I hit him. I didn't mean to hurt him, Cass, and once I did, I realized that he wasn't the one who deserved to get beaten up. The person who deserved it was me."

I'm sure my mouth is hanging open, and before I can fumble for the right words, he continues. "I owe you an apology, Cass. I'm sorry. I'm so, so sorry that I didn't protect you from him. I'm sorry that I didn't realize what he was doing to you."

"Are you crazy?" I sputter. "Levi …"

"No, no, just listen to me …" He finally looks up at me, and I'm startled by the tears swimming in his cobalt-blue eyes. "I'm sorry I didn't stand up for you when Mom decided he should move back home. I'm sorry for everything Will put you through; I'm sorry I wasn't there for you all this time. I'm sorry I didn't realize how hard things have been for you. I'm just … sorry that I wasn't the brother I should've been."

"Levi …" I'm fighting my own tears now. "There was nothing you could've done to stop him, or any of the rest of it. It just … it just happened, and it's something we all have to deal with, you know? But you absolutely don't deserve to get beaten up! Geez, Levi, are you completely nuts?"

"Probably," he laughs shakily.

"Listen to me." I thought I didn't have any tears left after last night, but Levi's face blurs as my eyes fill. "Listen to me, Levi. You were always there for me when I needed you. Always. I never for one second thought that you wouldn't be there if I needed you—not for one second, do you understand me? And I know things have changed a lot the past couple years, and we're not as close as we were before, but, Leev, that's my fault, not yours. I just … I knew I should talk to you about everything with Will and Ian and … all that stuff but I …" I shrug feebly, staring at the countertop.

Levi puts a hand on my arm. "Did you think I'd be mad at you if I knew?"

"I don't know. I guess. I didn't know what you'd do. I mean, come on, Levi—you're going to a freaking Bible college! How on earth was I supposed to tell you about …" I blush in spite of myself. "Well, you know, everything with Will and … all that stuff." I can't look at him.

"Well, I'm definitely not going to judge you; you're my sister and I love you. I may not really agree with what you're doing, but it doesn't change how I feel about you. Besides," Levi snorts, "I don't think I'm really in much of a position to become a pastor after everything I did last night. I wanted to kill my own father! How can I possibly be a pastor when I have those kinds of thoughts? I can't be telling other people how God wants them to live their lives when I'm clearly screwing up my own."

"I … don't think that's how it works," I offer tentatively. "I don't really know what I believe about God anymore, so I'm probably not the best person to say this but … Well, you're exactly the kind of person who should become a pastor, because you know what it's like to fall short. You know how easy it is for even Christian families to keep secrets and lie to each other, and you would be able to help other people who are dealing with things like what we've been through. I mean, to be honest, that's one of the main reasons I don't go to church anymore: there was no one at church who I could talk to about what was happening to our family. Nobody would've understood. They would've just given me some trite sermon about it all being 'God's will' and that's not what I needed. And then after I started sleeping with Will …" I shrug, trying to make light of the embarrassment I feel at admitting this to Levi. "I guess I felt like too much of a hypocrite to be going to church. I *was* a hypocrite."

Levi doesn't say anything for a few moments; he just sits there, clearly mulling over everything I said. I shift my weight uncomfortably, then decide to leave him to his thoughts. As I'm walking away, his voice stops me. "Hey, Cassie?"

"Hmmm?" I turn around to face him, leaning against the door.

"Thanks for saying that. And what you said about not believing in God anymore, or that you're not sure you believe?"

"Yeah?"

"He still believes in you. Trust me."

If anyone other than Levi had said it, I would've rolled my eyes. But something about the conviction in his eyes makes me pause. "Maybe so. Thanks, Leev. I'm going to go see if I can make myself look a little more decent. I probably look like I haven't slept in days."

Levi's words echo in my mind as I walk up the stairs and down the hall to the bathroom next to my room. *He still believes in you.*

"You've got a funny way of showing it, God," I mutter as I rummage through the cabinet above the sink for any makeup I might've left when I moved out. No such luck. I should head back over to the apartment. Julia's probably worried sick.

I don't want to leave until I can talk to my parents and Ben, though, just to make sure everyone's okay, or whatever passes for okay in this family these days. And I don't think I can handle Julia's inevitable hysterics this early in the morning, either. So I grab a book from the shelf in my room and curl up on the couch in the living room. It's been so long since

I've taken the time to read anything for fun other than Julia's fashion magazines.

I'm into the third chapter of *A Tree Grows in Brooklyn*, a book I read at least twice when I was younger, when Levi steps into the living room. "Hey, Cass, there's someone here to see you."

I stifle a groan as I toss the book aside and follow Levi. "Please, tell me it's not Julia." Much as I love her, I know I can't handle one of her dramatic outbursts at only nine in the morning. I don't want to answer her million-and-one questions about what happened last night.

Levi's expression is enigmatic. "It's not Julia."

"Then who …" My voice dries up as we enter the kitchen and Ian rises awkwardly from one of the kitchen chairs.

"Hey, Cassie," he says softly.

My stomach plummets to my knees, and I remind myself to breathe. *Not now. I can't handle this now.*

Levi excuses himself, and, as soon as he's gone, Ian visibly relaxes. "I'm so sorry I didn't come sooner. I should've come last night, but Julia said that your brothers brought you here, and I thought …" He shrugs, his face flushing. "I thought maybe you guys needed some time as a family to … talk … or whatever."

"It was more like 'or whatever,'" I manage hoarsely. "Levi ended up whaling on Dad's face pretty hard. But we talked, too." I sound like such an idiot, babbling like this. Obviously he's here to break up with me; why am I prolonging it?

"Geez," Ian winces. He takes a tentative step toward me and rests his hand on my arm, as if he's afraid I'll run away. "How are you doing, sweetie? I mean, how are you really?"

"What difference does it make?" My voice comes out harsher than I intend it. "You're here to break up with me, so let's just get it over with."

"Break up with you?" Ian looks baffled. "Why would I break up with you?"

Has everyone around here gone crazy? Or is it just me? "Last night at the party … when Will, I mean, Oliver and I …" Now I'm the very definition of pathetic: my eyes are filling with tears in spite of my best efforts to keep them at bay. It feels like I've cried enough tears to fill an ocean in the past twenty-four hours.

"Hey, hey," Ian soothes, pulling me into his arms and ignoring how stiffly I stand there. "Don't cry. It's okay. I … well, I'm not going to lie; I was really hurt when Will first told me about you and Oliver. But when he said those things to you, and I saw how crushed you were … I'm not upset anymore, Cass. I swear, I'm not. I know you weren't trying to hurt me or anything; I know it didn't really have anything to do with Oliver, either. It was about you and your dad."

Now I'm crying in earnest. "Ian …"

"We don't have to talk about it, unless you want to. I just wanted you to know that what happened last night doesn't change anything about the way I feel about you. You're still the beautiful girl I love, the one I want to spend the rest of my life with."

"Don't say that," I whisper brokenly. "You don't know what you're saying."

He smiles that gorgeous smile that could melt granite. "Of course I do." He brushes the hair back from my forehead. "I love you, Cassie. I know I haven't really said that to you before, but, well, I knew you weren't over Will yet, and I didn't want you to feel like I was pressuring you or anything. But I fell in love with you on our first date, and I haven't seen or heard anything that would make me change my mind."

"But you don't … you don't understand. I'm not the kind of girl you should spend your life with, Ian. You deserve someone better than me. I'm—oh, just look at me, Ian! I'm a total wreck! You don't deserve that."

"You're not a wreck, Cass." He tilts my chin up so I'm looking him in the eye. "You're not. And I know things are really hard with your family and whatever's going on with your dad, so I don't want to rush you at all. You take all the time you need. But if you ever want to talk about it, I'm here to listen. And I promise you, whatever you tell me won't change how I feel about you."

"That's what Will said," I grimace. "Look how well that turned out."

"I'm not Will," he says quietly, and I can see in the darkening of his green eyes that I've hurt him.

"I'm sorry. I shouldn't have said that. I know that you're a much better guy than Will could ever hope to be; it's just that it may take me a while to be able to trust you enough to tell you everything. Not because of you, but because of me. What happened last night—the things Will said—was one of my worst nightmares come true. And I just … it's going to take me some time."

"I understand. I just wanted to make sure you knew that I'm going to wait for you, Cass. However long it takes; however much space you need."

"I don't … I don't know what to say," I admit, wiping at the tears that refuse to stop falling. "I don't deserve a guy like you. I really don't."

"You deserve one better than me. But you're stuck with me," Ian grins.

I can't speak past the lump in my throat. So I frame his face with my hands and kiss him, a kiss that's filled with all the things I can't say.

Peter

"Peter—what are you doing?" Marianne stands in the doorway leading to master bathroom, staring at me. Even after she's showered and applied her makeup, it's still obvious that she got virtually no sleep last night. I imagine that I look at least as awful, if not more so.

"I'm packing," I answer succinctly.

"Packing? What? Why?" she stammers.

I sigh. I love this woman more than my own life, but there are certainly times when she can try my patience. "You know why. After what happened last night, with the kids … I can't stay here. It's not fair to them. Or to you."

Her eyes are already filling. "No, Peter. Don't do this. We should talk about it …"

I laugh wearily. "What's there to talk about? I think Levi doing *this*," I point to my swollen face, still tender to the touch, "pretty much said everything that needed to be said."

"No, Peter, no," Marianne shakes her head fiercely. "Levi said he didn't mean to do it. He was just angry. He got carried away. It won't happen again."

"That's not the point, honey." I stop putting clothes into the suitcase on the bed and walk to the doorway, pulling her into my arms. "The point is that all of them are angry at me … and rightly so. If I stay here, they're never going to be able to get past it."

"But …" Her beautiful blue eyes are swimming with tears. "Peter …"

"Oh, honey," I whisper into her hair. "It's not forever. I just think that we need to show the kids that we value *them* more than …"

"More than our marriage?" Marianne interrupts.

"No, no." This is so hard. "You heard what Cassie said last night, about how she felt like they never came first? Well, now's our chance to show her that she's wrong. We need to put them first, Marianne. They need to *see* that we took them seriously last night, that we really heard what they said to us."

"And you really think that will make a difference, after all this time? You can't just move out for—however long—and expect that it will undo the damage of the past three years! And what about Jade?"

Jade.

My sweet baby girl is the one who stands to lose the most of any of us, except perhaps Cassie. Jade has no idea what really happened three years ago, and my absence now will probably throw her into a tailspin of confusion. So many times in the past three years I've wondered if we did the right thing in not telling her about what was really going on when I left home. "Maybe it's time for us to tell her the truth. When she's home from camp, I mean."

"Absolutely not," Marianne insists vehemently. "She's too young!"

"She'll be twelve in a couple months. That's old enough to understand, don't you think?"

"*No*! She's just starting to get over you leaving the first time; if we tell her *why* you left, she'll be devastated. I can't do that to her. This family cannot handle another out-of-control child. We just can't."

I sigh. "We're going to have to tell her sometime. I don't think it's a good idea to keep putting it off. What's she going to think when she finds out we knew about this for three years—or four or five—and didn't tell her?"

Marianne falls silent for a moment, and I hold my breath, hoping I've won this particular argument. But then she says, "After everything you've done to this family, is it really too much for me to ask you to just trust me on this?"

I flinch and pull away from her, turning back to the suitcase on the bed. I hate it when she plays the victim like this. Yes, part of me knows I probably deserve it, but at the same time, I know I've done everything I can possibly do to correct the horrible mistakes I made all those years ago. And yet she still brings up how I've "ruined" our family whenever it works to her advantage. It hurts, deeply.

"Peter, I'm sorry," she says now, touching my arm. I don't turn around to look at her. "Honey, I know that was a rude thing to say. I'm sorry."

I glance at her, sighing. "I know. You're always sorry."

She bristles and walks into the bathroom without another word. I sink onto the bed and rest my head in my hands. *Not again …*

The past three years have been an excruciating balancing act for the two of us as we've attempted to rebuild our relationship. I know Marianne has forgiven me for what I did to Cassie, but I haven't. I don't know if I ever will. And even though she's forgiven me, she still struggles with the emotional fallout.

If I had a dollar for every time I've wished to go back and change the decisions I made on those nights six years ago, I would be a millionaire. Possibly even a billionaire.

I'm nearly done packing when Marianne walks back into the bedroom and sits on the edge of the bed. "I'm sorry. I …" She looks down. "I'm just sorry, okay? I'm trying, Peter, but last night was one of the worst nights of my life and it's hard."

I sit down beside her and take her hand. "I know. I know."

"Last night when Levi … when he said that he didn't mean to attack you like that, and you said that now he understood how you felt—what did you mean by that?"

Tears spring to my eyes almost automatically. It's been three years, and I still get choked up whenever we talk about this. "I … I meant that that was how I felt after the first time I … touched Cassie. It was like I was on autopilot and then, all of a sudden, I realized what I had done to her and … "

"Oh, honey …" Marianne rests her head on my shoulder. "Don't do this to yourself. Don't torment yourself like this, Peter. It's not worth it."

I ignore her. I love my wife dearly, but she has no idea what it's like for me to wake up every morning and want to go back and re-do two months of my life. She doesn't know what it's like to be tormented with nightmares about what I did to Cassie, to see the shattered expression that was on her face that day in Dr. Morton's office. I see it nearly every time I close my eyes, and I hate myself for doing that to my baby girl. And after hearing Cassie say last night that she also has nightmares … My sense of guilt and self-loathing intensified about a hundredfold after everything I heard and saw in my children last night.

The ironic thing is that Cassie and I seem to have a lot in common in how we're dealing with everything that's happened in the past three years: the nightmares, the torment. But I'm the last person she'd ever feel comfortable talking to about all of it, even if I'm the one who would understand it the best.

"I need to go," I tell her. "Now. If I don't go now, I'll lose my nerve and I won't go at all."

Marianne bursts into fresh tears. "Then *don't*! You don't have to do this!"

"Yes, I do." Exhaustion presses down on me and I want nothing more than to sleep the rest of the day away.

"But I love you," she whispers in a broken voice.

"I don't think that's the issue here," I answer gently. "This isn't about you and me. This is about our children. This is about me accepting the consequences for what I did to our daughter. This is about me taking responsibility and putting them first for once. I've been so selfish the past few years—I never once thought to ask Cassie if she was comfortable living here with me, or if the boys were. Not *once*! And maybe you're right, maybe it's too late to fix anything with the three of them, but I want them to at least know that I tried."

She's openly weeping now. "Peter …"

I have to go. Now. If I stand here and watch her cry, I'll change my mind. I grab my suitcase and bend down to kiss her. "I love you. That's not what this is about, all right? Don't forget that. I'll call you once I figure out what we should do next."

And with that, I walk out the door. I force myself to walk past the kids' rooms without stopping, down the long hallway lined with their pictures. Their smiling faces stare down at me, mocking me and my mistakes and the grief and anger that's somehow become as much a part of this house as the wood and nails that hold it together. The atmosphere in this house is stifling, I suddenly realize, the tension palpable. *How did I not notice that before now?*

I walk out the front door and onto the lawn. I take a deep breath and let the clean air fill my lungs. Out here, it's easier to breathe.

TWO YEARS LATER

Jade

It's midnight, and I'm lying awake in bed, unable to sleep, when I hear my parents' voices from down the hall. I tiptoe to my door and crack it open just enough to be able to make out the words. I've heard several of these late-night tear-filled fights—or "discussions," as Mom likes to call them—in the past couple years, but usually I can only make out a word or two. Tonight, I can hear every word, and I lean against the doorframe, hungry for more. Maybe I'll hear something that will finally explain the way things are in this family ...

Dad's voice reaches me first. "Does it *always* have to come back to this? Are you ever going to let it go? I've told you over and over that I'm sorry! What more can I do?"

I can hardly hear Mom's voice; she's clearly crying and her words are jumbled. "I don't *know*, Peter! And yes, it is always going to come back to this because it's the one thing we can't get past! Can't you understand that? It's not something that I can just 'let go' and forget about! How can you even *ask* me to do that?"

Dad's voice rises in anger, and I shiver at the tone in his voice. "I'm not *asking* you to do anything! You've told me over and over again that you forgave me for what I did to her. Well, did you or didn't you? Because if you did, then why would you keep holding it over my head like this? It's like you've got me on a chain and you'll only let me get so far before ..."

"I've got you on a *chain*?" Mom shrieks.

"About this, yes! You *never* let me get past it! Any time we have an argument about anything that has to do with Cass, you always bring it up. Every. Time. And, you know, it's really starting to piss me off, Marianne. I made a mistake, I admit that. A huge mistake. A life-altering mistake. But I've done everything I know how to do to try to fix things—with Cassie, with you, with the boys—and it's good enough for everyone but you."

A huge mistake? What mistake? I don't know why I'm shaking so hard. It feels like I've stepped into a tub full of ice water, I'm so cold. My stomach turns in fear. *What are they talking about?*

"That's not true at all! I *have* forgiven you. But, while we're on the subject of being pissed off, it's completely unfair of you to expect us all just to forget about everything and move on just because you've said you're sorry and been to therapy and talked things over with Cassie. What you did—it's not something that I think I'll ever fully 'get over.' And you *know* that! I've told you that a thousand times! And you said you understood …"

"I thought I did. But you know, it's been five years. *Five years.* And call me crazy, but I guess I hoped that by now we could've gotten past this juvenile …"

"Juvenile? Oh, don't even *go* there with me, Peter! You sulk around the house for days every time I even *mention* …"

"Can you blame me? After five years of having it constantly thrown in my face, by you and sometimes even the kids? Can't you see how that would get a little old? It's not like I can do anything to change it. God knows I would if I could. But since I can't, I don't think it's unreasonable to expect you to start moving on from it. At the very least, you could have a little more grace for me, Marianne."

There's a long silence, which is good because my heart's beating so loud I couldn't hear much anyway. I don't know what my parents are talking about, but it feels like I've stumbled into the middle of a nest of spiders. Like I'm hearing something I definitely shouldn't be hearing—but I can't force myself to walk away from the door and crawl back into bed.

Finally Dad's voice cuts into my near-heart-attack. "Do you remember the first time I touched you after everything happened? You cried."

I nearly fall into the hallway, straining to hear Mom's response. I think she says, "I know." Or maybe, "I'm sorry."

"Do you have any idea how that made me feel? And every time since then, I've always been afraid that you're thinking about … what I did to her … and …"

"Oh, Peter." It sounds like Mom's crying again. "No, no. I don't think about that. I did the first few times, but not anymore. Don't torture yourself like that, honey."

If they're talking about having sex, I'm going to puke. But before I can think about that nauseating concept, Dad's voice rises again, his tone strident. "That's *exactly* my point! You're always telling me not to 'torment' myself, not to be 'too hard' on myself—and then the minute you're upset with me about something, *you* start saying all the things you tell me not to say to myself! How is that supposed to make me feel?"

"I'm sorry, Peter! I'm really, really sorry! Obviously this is all my fault! It clearly has *nothing* to do with the choices *you* made and the way that makes me feel! It's all my fault, and I'm sorry! Are you satisfied now?" There's the sound of a door slamming, and I hear Mom stomping downstairs. I practically vault into my bed and lie trembling under the covers, willing my heartbeat to slow back down to normal.

What was that about? What did Dad do? It must've been something pretty awful …

I lie there staring into the darkness for nearly an hour, racking my brain for clues about what my father might've done to my sister that would make Mom so angry. And later, when the pieces suddenly fall into place, like a trapdoor springing open, I don't think I can breathe. *Oh. My. God. But that … that can't be right. He wouldn't. He couldn't. Could he? No. No, that can't possibly be it.*

But I can't think of any other explanation. Tears squeeze past my eyelashes and nausea churns in my stomach. This can't be right. It *can't* be.

Maybe I should ask Cassie. She'd tell me, right? I bet she'll just laugh at me for even thinking up something so crazy. There's no way it can be true. If it was, they would've told me a long time ago, right?

I lie there, trying to stop the tears, wondering if the impossible really is possible.

****

"Hey, honeybunch," Cassie calls up the stairs. "You ready to go?"

I'm in the bathroom putting on the last of my make-up—which Mom *still* doesn't like me wearing, even though I'm almost fourteen—and trying to remember how to breathe normally. It's taken me three days to work up the nerve to call Cassie and ask if we can hang out for the day, so that I can ask her about …

I refuse to think about this right now. We're going back to her apartment for lunch; I can talk to her about it after we eat. Maybe if I wait a little longer, it'll be easier to ask her.

"Coming," I holler back. "Give me two minutes, okay?"

I hear her running up the stairs, and in thirty seconds, she pokes her head in the doorway. "Oooh, you look lovely! Eyeliner, huh? Does Mom know you're wearing that?"

I roll my eyes. "Yeah, but she'll probably still say something about it when I get home."

"Hey, you're lucky. I was fifteen before she and Dad let me wear *any* makeup! That's one of the perks of being the youngest, you know—you get to do everything way younger than the rest of us did."

"Oh, sure, being the youngest is *so* great!" Actually, it's not too bad. All my siblings are in their twenties now—Levi's twenty-three, Cassie's twenty-one, and Ben is twenty—and all my friends are jealous that my brothers and sister let me hang out with them almost whenever I want. They treat me like an adult, like my opinions actually matter to them, and I'm friends with a lot of their friends, too. Cassie says that's one of the "fringe benefits" of being the youngest by seven years. I have to say, she's probably right.

"I invited Ian over for lunch, too. Is that cool?"

"Um, sure. Yeah, no problem. Maybe … well, I need to talk to you about something after we eat, so could we maybe go for a walk or something? Like, just the two of us?"

"Absolutely." Cass narrows her blue eyes at me. "Is everything okay?"

I force my expression to remain neutral. "Oh, yeah. It's just, well, it's kind of a girl thing."

Her eyes light up with mischief. "Ohhhhh, I see! Is it about Collin? Did he ask you out?"

"Shut up," I mutter, hating the way my cheeks are turning red. I should never, never have told Cass that I had a crush on Collin. She teases me about it every time she sees me.

"Don't forget that I want to be matron of honor at your wedding," Cass calls over her shoulder as she drifts out of the room. I watch her walk away, envying her long tan legs and her nearly perfect figure.

"It's *maid* of honor, you moron!" I laugh.

"Not if you're married. And considering that you and Collin won't get married for another, oh, five or six years, I definitely *will* be married before you are. If you're married, you're the *matron* of honor, you moron," she teases.

"I am *not* going to marry Collin!" I shriek. "I don't even like him that much anymore!" That's a total lie, but since Cassie's not in the room and can't see my face, I can probably get away with it.

No such luck. She grabs me by the arm and propels me from the bathroom, even though my eyeliner isn't quite right yet. "You look fabulous, Jade. Now come on, let's go. You can tell me all about why Collin's out of favor with you." I can tell by the smirk on her face that she knows I still like him.

"You're awful," I grumble.

"I know," she answers lightly. "That's why you love me so much, right?"

I roll my eyes. The truth is, though, my sister is probably one of the best friends I've ever had. When I was younger, I hardly knew her—she's eight years older than I am, so it's not like we really spent a lot of time together when she was in high school. But in the past two years or so, we started going shopping together and things like that, and I realized what an amazing person Cassie is. She's gorgeous, of course, and she's smart and funny. I can talk to her about anything. *Until now …*

I stare out the window as Cassie drives over to her apartment, about twenty minutes away from our parents' house. Ian, her fiancé, has his own apartment but he spends a lot of nights over at Cassie's, even though my parents obviously think I don't know that. He never sleeps over when I do, though; I guess he and Cass are worried about "corrupting" me or something.

It's so ridiculous—all the things my family thinks I don't know and that they should protect me from. They probably have a file somewhere labeled, "Things Jade Shouldn't Know," and at least half of those things I bet I already know. *That* is one of the things that I hate about being the youngest—my parents always treat me like I'm still their baby. As if I don't know that Cass and Ian have sex, or that Ben was basically a drug addict until he got clean last year, or that my parents have almost gotten a divorce at least twice.

"You're awfully quiet today," Cassie interrupts my inner rant. "Any deep thoughts you want to pass over this way?"

I shrug. "Not really. I was just thinking about how Mom and Dad are always treating me like I'm five. They never …" I steal a sideways glance at her, trying to gauge her expression, "never really tell me anything about what's going on, you know?"

Cassie looks thoughtful. "What kinds of things do you think they're not telling you?"

She doesn't *look* upset or worried. *Hmmm.* I try to sound more nonchalant. "I think they still think I don't know that you and Ian are having sex. Or that Ben was, like, using drugs up until a year ago."

Cassie blushes. "Well, Ian and I aren't exactly setting a good example for you. I wish we were doing a better job of that, Jade. I mean, it's probably not good for you to see us living together."

I roll my eyes at her. "Why the heck not? I mean, geez, Cass, you guys love each other and you're *engaged*! What's so bad about sleeping together if you know you're going to end up together forever anyway? It's not like you're sleeping with a bunch of different guys or anything."

Is it my imagination, or does a faint shadow cross her face? "Yeah, but, I think it really is better to wait until you're married, if you can. I mean, look at Levi and Anna—they've been engaged for a year already, and I know they're committed to waiting until their wedding night."

I roll my eyes again. "*Duh.* He's a *youth pastor*, Cass! Of course he's going to wait till he's married! I mean, I think it's really cool that they're doing that, because I bet it's not easy, but … Well, I don't get why people make such a big deal out of whether you're a virgin or not when you get married. It seems like such a dumb debate."

Cassie smiles. "When I was your age, I was absolutely sure I was going to wait to have sex until I was married."

"And what happened?"

She shrugs, but once again I see that flicker of a shadow on her face. "Life happened. Waiting just didn't seem so important to me anymore, I guess."

I was going to wait until after lunch to say this, but the words are out before I can stop them. "Was it because Dad raped you?"

Cassie nearly runs the car off the road. She veers over into a parking lot and stops the car, staring at me. "*What*? What in the *world* makes you think that?"

Suddenly my eyes are filling with tears. "I heard Mom and Dad arguing a couple nights ago about … something bad that he did to you. They didn't say what it was, but Mom was really, really upset and saying she didn't know if she could ever forgive Dad for doing it. And I just … I thought about it for a long time and the only thing I could think of was that maybe he … maybe he raped you." So much for putting all that eyeliner and mascara on—my makeup is running like crazy now that I'm crying so hard.

"Oh, sweetie …" Cassie pulls me close to her—as close as you can get in the front seat of a car, anyway. "Oh, Jade … No, honey, Daddy never raped me. Never."

"Then what *happened*? I know he did something to you; why won't anybody ever tell me what's really going on?" I hate how desperate my voice sounds.

Cassie takes a deep breath. "Okay, okay. We'll drive back to the apartment, and I'll tell you everything."

Hearing her say that *should* make me feel better—after all, I wanted to hear the truth, right? But instead, my stomach sinks down somewhere near my knees, and I have a funny feeling that life as I know it is about to change. Forever.

Cassie

Promising Jade that I would tell her everything when we got to my apartment was a dumb move; I realize that as soon as my heart rate returns to normal and I stop shaking enough to be able to drive. I glance over at her in the passenger seat, tears still streaming down her face, and my chest constricts. *Oh, dear God, what have I gotten myself into?*

Thank God for small mercies: when we get to my apartment, Ian is already there with sandwiches ready. He takes one look at my face and mouths *What happened?* over the top of Jade's head. I shake my head at him, mouthing back *later*, and I tell Jade I have to make a couple phone calls before we can talk. "Eat your lunch with Ian, okay? I promise I'll tell you everything you need to know, after I ... I have to do a couple things first. Okay?"

"Okay," she shrugs, sounding much, much younger. I think I'll start crying if I look at her any longer. I practically run from the room, grabbing the phone off the kitchen counter and dialing Levi's number before the door to my bedroom even closes behind me. As his phone rings, and rings, and rings, I text Ben from my cell phone: *conference call with Levi if u can. NOW.* I give up on Levi's home number—the fact that I thought he'd be home this time of day shows how muddled my brain is right now—and dial the church. While I'm waiting for the secretary to transfer me to Levi, my cell phone vibrates with a text from Ben: *K, can do a conference call now. What's up?*

I don't bother to explain, just text back for him to call the church. As I snap my cell phone closed, Levi finally comes on the line. I nearly burst into tears at the sound of his steady, familiar voice. "Hey, sis, what's up?"

I manage not to cry, but my voice still shakes as I answer. "It's ... it's Jade. She came over about an hour ago and she asked me if Dad raped me when I was younger."

"*What?*" Levi sounds as shocked as I was when I heard her ask it. "Why … how did she … what … Wait, hang on a second, the secretary's buzzing me. Wait just one second, okay, Cass?"

Thirty seconds later, Levi sounds slightly more composed. "Okay, she said Ben called and wants to do a conference call with us. Can you hang on for a few more seconds while she sets it up?"

Five minutes later, I've explained the whole situation to my brothers. Both of them are quiet for a moment. Ben is the first to break the somber silence. "Well, we all knew this was gonna happen sooner or later, right?" He lets out a long stream of air in a protracted sigh. "Poor kid." I can picture him pacing around what passes for the living room in his tiny studio apartment, about an hour and a half from here, raking a hand through his dark hair. "That sucks."

"Thanks, Ben. *That's* helpful!" My voice is laden with sarcasm.

"Well, geez, Cass, what do you want me to say?" A hard undercurrent of anger runs through his tone. Ben has come a long way in the past year, but he still flares up at the slightest provocation when it comes to this issue.

"I wanted you two to give me some advice, you idiot! I *know* it's going to suck for her, and I *know* it's going to be hard to talk to her about it— what I wanted was for you to give me some advice about *how to do that!*"

"Okay, okay, calm down, you two," Levi interjects. "Look, this is just a really tense subject. Cass, I think you should tell her however much you feel comfortable with her knowing. I mean, I trust your judgment. You probably know Jade better than the rest of us, anyway. You know what she needs to hear."

"You should tell her everything," Ben commands. "That way, there are no surprises later on. You know, like there were for us that night Levi tried to kill Dad? When you just happened to mention that, *oh by the way, Dad apologized to me afterwards and told me not to tell Mom?*"

"Ben …" Levi warns. For some reason, he's still able to pull the "big brother" card with Ben every once in a while.

"I didn't mean that to sound ugly. All I'm saying is, Jade should know everything now, so that she can start dealing with it."

"So I should just overwhelm her with all this information, so that she can 'deal with it' all at once?" I'm fighting to keep the sarcasm out of my voice. And the tears.

"She thought Dad had *raped* you, Cassie!" Ben exclaims. "How much worse could it possibly get? Once you tell her what really happened, it'll probably be a huge relief to her, because it's not, well, you know, it's not as bad as what she was thinking. Not that it wasn't still awful," he adds hastily, "because it was. But you know what I mean, right?"

"So I go with full disclosure—then what? I'm trying to decide whether I should call Mom and tell her once I've explained it all to Jade. You know? Maybe … maybe Mom and Dad should know that I talked to her about it. I don't know, maybe not."

"I don't think you should," Levi answers. I close my eyes and envision him leaning back in the chair at his desk, arms crossed behind his head, our resident family expert on teenagers and their relationships with their parents. The vision makes me smile, just a little. "I think, once she knows everything, it's something she'll have to work out with Mom and Dad on her own. I mean, if she even wants to talk to them about it."

"Yeah," Ben adds, "I agree. We've all had to work it out with them on our own. I think we should let Jade have the same opportunity."

None of us says anything for a moment, an awkward silence descending. I think we're all remembering what "working it out with them on our own" has entailed over the past two years. For Ben, it meant fighting a nearly-losing battle with drug addiction. *What if Jade does something like that?* I worry.

"I'm worried about how she'll handle it," Levi echoes my silent musings. "Tell her I can fly her out here to Portland for a few weeks when school's over, if she wants to. She's got, what? Two weeks left of school? I'd be happy to have her for a little while, if she wants to come. And I'm sure Anna would love to hang out with her, take her shopping and stuff, maybe get her involved in the wedding plans. God knows I'm not much help in that department," he laughs.

I smile to myself. As much as Jade loves Levi, I know the prospect of spending a couple weeks with him, attending some sort of church function every night, is not going to appeal to her. "I'll definitely mention it to her, Leev. Thanks for the offer—that's so sweet. Especially since you guys are so busy right now."

"Only two more months until you're bound for life, big brother," Ben kids. "It's not too late to avoid the old ball and chain, you know."

Levi just laughs. "Oh, you just *wish* you had a girl as wonderful as Anna, Ben. I can't believe the wedding's only two months away; time's just gone by so fast."

"Well, *I* can't believe you guys are getting married before me and Ian," I tease. "It's not fair—we've been together almost two years *longer* than you guys, and you're still getting married first!"

"Have you and Ian set a date yet?" Ben asks. I roll my eyes, knowing I've told him the answer to this question at least twice. *Does he* never *listen?*

Levi answers for me. "April 29, next year. Come on, you *know* that!"

"Geez, cut me some slack, guys. I'm getting like four hours of sleep a night, if that. The Academy is kicking my tail, big time. If I'd known it was going to be so flipping hard I probably would've thought twice about becoming a police officer. "

I just laugh. Ben can grumble all he wants; I know he loves what he does. Deciding to drop out of college and join the police academy was one of the best decisions he's ever made; it probably saved his life. Now he has something to help keep him focused on staying clean and sober, just in case the thought of dying from an overdose in some alley or crack house isn't sufficient.

The three of us chat for a few minutes, helping me calm down and feel like I can talk to Jade without suffering some sort of breakdown. "Thanks, guys," I say before we say good-bye. "I think I just needed to talk through everything, before I talk to Jade. And I wanted you to know what was going on. Pray for her, please, guys. And for me."

"You know we will," Ben assures me. *That* is another major change from a couple years ago: Ben actually seems to be on speaking terms with God now. He's definitely not as dedicated to his faith as Levi, but it's there. It's another thing that I think has saved him from slipping completely away from us.

"Call us tonight and let us know how it went, if you can," Levi suggests.

I promise that I will, and we say good-bye. I stand there clutching the phone for a moment, just listening to the dial tone and praying for the strength to face my sister and answer her questions without falling apart.

The door opens a crack and Ian pokes his head in. "The native is getting restless out here."

I manage a small smile. "Tell her I'll be right out."

Instead of closing the door, though, he opens it wider and enters the room, pulling me into his arms. "You're going to tell her about your dad, aren't you?"

I don't say anything, just nod against his chest. He can read me so well, unlike anyone else.

"Do you want me to be there? I don't have to be, but if you want me to …"

"*I* want you to. I just don't know if Jade will."

As it turns out, Jade's so anxious for information that she doesn't seem to notice that Ian's even in the apartment, much less sitting on the sofa beside us. He takes my hand and doesn't let go as I take a deep breath and start the story. "Jade, when I was your age, something happened …"

****

Jade

The minute Cassie finishes telling me the disgusting story of what our dad did to her, I run. Literally run. I don't wait for her to say all the right things, the it-will-work-out-okay and the tell-me-how-you're-feeling. I just jump up from the couch and run out the door. I can hear Cassie calling after me, and maybe Ian, too, but I don't stop. I just keep going, tearing down the sidewalk toward the park that's about a mile from her apartment. *This is not happening.* The thought pounds through my brain in sync with my footsteps on the concrete.

Cassie will try to come after me, but there's no way she'll catch me. I may not measure up to my beautiful older sister in most areas, but I have it all over her when it comes to running. She was on the swim team for a couple years in high school, but I'm the fastest runner on the cross-country team at school. Running makes me feel alive in a way that nothing else can, and it's always a good stress reliever. At least, until now.

Even though the park is only a mile from Cassie's apartment, my body is coated with sweat by the time I get there. But even though I probably just set a personal record for fastest mile time, I didn't run anywhere near fast enough or long enough to drown out the echoes of what Cassie just told me.

"*… and then we went for an emergency session with Dr. Morton, and Dad basically confessed to sexually abusing me. That's when he moved out the first time.*"

I don't know why hearing the truth hit me so hard. After all, what I had suspected had happened—that Dad had raped Cassie—was much worse than what *did* happen, but ... I pace back and forth, trying to return my heart rate to something approaching normal. I feel nauseated and weak. *Oh God, oh God, oh God. Please make this go away.*

I'm still pacing near the entrance to the park and trying not to have a nervous breakdown when Cassie's car pulls up. Ian's with her, but he doesn't get out of the car. Cassie, on the other hand, nearly trips over her own feet in her rush to grab me by the shoulders and steer me toward a bench. "Talk to me," she begs. "Just talk to me."

I don't think I can, at first. All I can manage to say is: "Why? Why didn't anyone *tell* me?"

Cassie looks helpless. And panicked. "We should have. I know we should have. Levi and Ben and I all wanted to tell you a couple years ago, when Dad moved out for a couple months the second time, remember? We thought that would be a good time to tell you, but Mom ..." She shrugs, frowning. "Mom didn't think we should. She thought you were too young to really understand and that it would confuse you too much, what with Dad being gone and everything. She made us promise not to tell you."

"That's dumb," I object bitterly. "So there was no time in the past *two years* that you thought I might be old enough to understand?" My voice is nasty, unrecognizable, and I feel a muted flash of pleasure when Cassie flinches.

"I'm sorry, Jade. I'm really, really sorry. I should have stood up to Mom and *made* her tell you everything. Or told you myself. I wanted to, so many times. But then, well, I was worried about how it might affect you. You know about Ben and everything he went through? Well, a lot of that was because of this whole situation with Dad. And I was afraid that if you knew, you might—I don't know. I didn't *know* what you'd do."

"You still should have told me," I pout. "So now should I tell Mom and Dad that I know?"

"That's totally up to you, honey. Whatever you think you need to do, okay? And if you *do* want to talk to them, I can go with you, if you think that would help." It costs Cassie a lot to offer this, I can tell.

"Thanks," I answer feebly. "I don't ... I don't know what I want to do yet. I don't think ... talking to them would be such a great idea. I'm not sure I even want to *see* them, so talking to them is probably not smart."

"You can spend the night with me, if that'll help. I can call Mom and make sure she lets you."

I almost take her up on the offer, but then I take a good look at my sister's face. She's deathly pale, and I can tell she's trying to put on a brave front for my sake, but that she's about to fall apart herself. "I think I'll be okay. But thanks."

"Are you sure?"

No, I want to say. *I'm not sure about* anything *anymore.*

"Yeah, I'm sure. I think I just want to sit here for awhile. Can you stay with me?"

Cassie's eyes fill with tears. "Of course, sweetie. Of course."

Something inside me snaps, and I start to cry. "I'm sorry, Cass. I'm so, so sorry he did those things to you!" And then we're both crying, and Ian materializes on the bench beside us, putting an arm around me and pulling Cassie into his broad chest. Eventually, I glance at my watch and realize we've been sitting there for an hour. I'm suddenly so exhausted all I want to do is sleep. "Can I go home now?" I ask cautiously. Even though home is the *last* place in the world I want to be right now.

We drop Ian off at the apartment first, and before he goes inside, he sticks his head in my window on the passenger side. "Hey, Jade? You're a good kid. Don't forget that, okay? None of this is your fault. And if you need anything, Cass and I are always here. I mean it. Call me if you need me, got that?"

I can't speak for fear I'll start crying again, but I know Ian understands. He squeezes my hand and then gives Cassie a look that's enough to make *me* melt, much less her. *She's so lucky. Wait, did I really just think that?* My stomach turns. *What kind of sick person am I?* My whole life, I've been envious of Cassie—her looks, her popularity, her talent, the boyfriends she's had. And now it feels like God's playing some kind of cruel joke: now Cassie is the last person in the world I would envy.

"So …" My voice is reedy and thin; I clear my throat in an attempt to sound stronger, more in control. It doesn't work. "So … I mean … how did you … how did you *live* with Dad for three years knowing that he … like, did that stuff to you? I'm not trying to sound mean; I just don't get it. How could you do that? I think I would've never wanted to see him again." *I'm not sure I* want *to see him again and I'm not the one who was abused,* I add silently. But I don't think Cassie would appreciate hearing that right now.

She shrugs, a gesture so full of helplessness that I cringe. "I don't know, honestly," she answers. "It seemed like … well, it was like the only thing I could really *do* at the time. I mean, Mom really wanted him to move back home ... and so did you, because you were still so young and ..."

"And no one bothered to *tell* me what he'd done!" I interrupt, surprised at the hard edge of bitterness in my tone.

Cassie shakes her head impatiently. "Jade, you were in the third grade! There was no way we could've explained it to you at that age. It would've completely traumatized you. I agree with you that we shouldn't have waited for five years to tell you, but there's nothing you can say that would convince me that we should've told you when Dad first moved out. I will never apologize for that; you were just too young."

I'm hardly ever angry with Cassie but right now I feel like punching her in the face. "Whatever."

"Jade ..." Cassie sighs. "Never mind. What I was saying earlier, when you asked about it being weird around Dad when I lived at home? Yeah, it was. But, this will probably sound strange, but I guess I just got used to it after a while. I mean, it was one of those things that I just had to live with, you know? And I tried to stay away from home as much as I could, too."

I bite my lip to hold back another flood of tears. "It feels like they ... like everyone *lied* to me."

"Oh, honey. I'm so sorry. I know we should've told you sooner. And if it's too hard for you to be around them for awhile, you can always come stay with me."

I don't know if I want to be around you, either. I'm shocked by how angry and betrayed I feel, and furious with myself for feeling this way. Especially toward Cassie ... as if she even remotely deserves that. I clench my hands into fists so tight my knuckles turn white. *I hate you, I hate you, I hate you.* I'm not sure if I'm thinking of Dad or myself. Maybe both.

When we pull up at my house, Cassie hesitates before she parks the car. "Are you sure you want to stay here tonight? It's totally fine with me if you want to just crash at my place."

I dismiss the idea with a wave of my hand. "I'll be fine. Thanks for everything, Cass. I'm glad you told me."

Her blue eyes are filled with anguish. "I just wish I'd done it sooner. I'm sorry, sweetie. And ..." She hesitates, clearly battling tears. "Listen, I know this probably won't ever happen but ... if ... if Dad ever ... does anything inappropriate to you, or says anything, I want you to know you can always tell me. You don't ever have to feel like you can't talk to me about stuff, okay? So if Dad—if he ever does anything to you—just tell me, okay?"

The lie springs from my mouth fully-formed, before I even realize that I'm saying it: "He already did."

And in the horrible aftermath of those words and the guilt that I feel for saying them, I also experience a tiny flicker of an unfamiliar, addictive feeling.

Power. The desire for revenge.

Ian

I know something's wrong when, after two hours, Cassie still hasn't come back to the apartment. She won't answer her cell, and she's not responding to my texts. I'm considering calling the closest hospital when the door to the apartment slams open, nearly falling off its hinges, and Cassie stands in the doorway, looking like she's just been shot. I haven't seen her look this distraught since that night at Paul's party two years ago.

"Honey, what is it?" I pull her into my arms, but she fights back, so I let her go. If there's one thing I've learned in the past two years with this amazing woman, it's that when she needs her space, I have to give it to her if I want her to speak to me anytime in the next forty-eight hours.

I watch her pace around the living room, muttering to herself. I know the explosion is coming—and I'm right. After about five minutes of pacing, Cassie folds into herself, collapses on the couch, and sobs until she can hardly breathe. Then she lets me hold her, soaking the fabric of my T-shirt and breaking my heart in the process. How many times in the past two years have we sat like this, her breaking apart in my arms and me trying to help put the pieces back together? It kills me to watch her hurting this way, and in moments like these, it wouldn't bother me if I never saw Peter Wilson again. I wonder if he has any clue what he's *done* to his beautiful daughter, the love of my life?

I lose track of how long we sit there like that before Cass is able to speak. "Jade ..." she gasps. "Jade told me that Dad ... that he ... oh, God, Ian, I can't even say it!"

"She told you your dad abused her, too?" I finish for her.

Her body convulsing with sobs is all the answer I need. "Oh, honey," I whisper into her hair. "Oh, Cass." But warning bells are sounding in my mind. I would be willing to bet a large amount of money that Jade is lying—I love that kid like she was my own little sister, but I know that if

Peter had ever laid a hand on her, she would've screamed bloody murder and told *someone* right away. She's not nearly as passive as Cassie can be, and I know there's no way she would have kept quiet about something as devastating as that. Not to mention that the timing of this "confession" is just a little too convenient.

"I *trusted* him!" Cass shrieks. "I told myself he would never, never, *never* do something like that again, and now—oh, my God. Ian, how could he have done this *again*?"

I keep my doubts to myself and let her rage and scream and get it all out. I'm choking up just watching her suffer like this—I feel so helpless when this happens, like there's nothing I can do to make any of this better.

"Ian, it means the world to me that you'll sit through all of this and give me someone to hold on to," Cass always insists when the storm of emotion subsides. That doesn't stop me from wishing I could do more, however.

Today is different from the other times, though. Today is a flashback to the first few weeks after that disastrous night at Paul's party—it took her that long to tell me the full story about her dad sexually abusing her, and, once she did, Cassie changed into someone very different from the confident, strong, take-charge woman I'd thought I knew. Overnight, it seemed, she morphed into an emotional train wreck; it was unbelievable how fragile her emotions were the first couple weeks after she told me everything. She broke up with me at least four times in those weeks, but I ignored the "we're through" pronouncements and kept showing up at her apartment.

I knew she was only pushing me away because she had this ludicrous idea that I couldn't possibly love her after knowing what she'd been through. What she didn't understand—what she's never really understood—is that seeing her pain and realizing the hell she and her family had been through only made me love her *more*, not less.

Now, though ... I have a feeling that what's just happened with Jade is going to test our relationship more than all the tear-filled nights of the past two years combined. Cass won't even entertain the idea that Jade is lying. The tentative truce Cassie and Peter have reached over the past two years shattered the moment Jade accused him of abusing her. Much as I dislike Cassie's father, I feel for the man—he doesn't deserve to be dragged through the mud again. And I can guess it will be far worse this time.

It's getting dark outside by the time Cass calms down enough to be able to really talk about what's happened. She describes the conversation with Jade in the car, and she tells me that she panicked and called her mom, Ben, and Levi within ten minutes of the time she dropped Jade off at her parents' house.

"How did they take it?"

She shrugs wearily. "How do you *think* they took it? They all ..." She shakes her head. "It was a nightmare."

I choose my words carefully, feeling as if I'm treading on splinters of glass instead of eggshells. "Do you believe that Jade's telling the truth?"

She shifts so she's sitting beside me and looks me in the eye, shocked. "Of course! Why? Don't you?" Her blue eyes narrow and I realize I've made a terrible mistake even *mentioning* my doubts right now.

"I ... I want to," I answer honestly. "It just ... well, it seems a little convenient to me, you know what I mean? We sat in the park for an hour and she never said a *word* about your dad doing anything to her. And then you just mention it as she's about to get out of the car, and all of the sudden it's *oh, Dad abused me, too.* It just ... doesn't fit, Cass."

She launches her petite body from the couch and glares at me. "I cannot *believe* you just said that! She's a thirteen-year-old girl, for God's sake! She's probably so traumatized she didn't even know how to tell us!"

"Maybe so," I admit. "But Jade's not exactly the type to stay quiet about stuff, right? I think maybe she ..."

Cassie's face contorts with anger. "Shut up, Ian! Just shut the hell up! You have no *idea* what you're talking about! You're calling my sister a liar? As if you know anything about what it's like to wake up one night and find your dad in bed with you ..." Her voice cracks.

I start to say something—anything—but she holds up her hand to stop me. "Don't. I don't want to hear it right now. I ...just ... don't."

"Cass, honey, don't be like this. I just want to help. I don't want to see your dad get dragged through this stuff again if he didn't really do anything to deserve ..."

"What *he* deserves? Are you kidding me? What that man *deserves* is to spend the rest of his life in prison! Or worse! I can't believe you're trying to defend *him* of all people! Ian, how could you even ..."

"Okay, okay," I relent. "I'm sorry. Let's not fight about this now. We can talk about it later."

She softens just enough to let me hold her again. But I can feel the rigidity of her spine and the stiffness of her embrace, and it leaves me chilled. *This is nowhere near over.*

Cassie

It's only nine o'clock, but I'm already curled up in bed, wishing for the elusive narcotic of sleep. It's nearly summer and unseasonably warm, but no matter how many blankets I pile on the bed, I can't stop shivering. It feels as if the cold has seeped into my bones, as if I might never be warm again.

Thinking about what happened today is the last thing I want to do, but the images from today's conversations—confrontations, honestly—keep intruding. My brain freezes on the moment when Jade confessed that Dad had abused her, too. It was like a scene from a horror film—my worst fear realized. I literally stopped breathing for a minute; I just stared at her and it was a long time before I could make myself say, "What did you say?"

She fidgeted with the hem of her shirt, refusing to look at me. "Dad … he … he touched me, too. I didn't want to tell you, but …"

To say I freaked out would be the understatement of the century. I tried to keep myself under control for Jade's sake, but I failed miserably. I barely remember what I said to her, or how I managed to drive away from my parents' house and call Mom, Levi, and Ben without wrecking the car. Bits and pieces from those three conversations reverberate in my mind.

Mom: *"Cassie, what are you saying? Are you saying your father—that Jade—Oh, God!"* Then there was a dial tone.

Levi: *"Cass, Cass, slow down, I can't understand what you're saying. Wait … wait …* what? *What did she say happened? No, tell me* exactly *what she said!"* I remember him muttering some distinctly un-pastoral words and asking if he should book a flight back here immediately. I think I told him not to, but I can't be sure.

Ben was, predictably, the worst. Every third word was a curse word, after I managed to calm down enough to explain what had happened. *"I knew it; I* knew *this would happen! And we all believed him! Son of a …"* I begged him to stay at his apartment until he cooled down, to call his sponsor, anything. But he slammed the receiver down before I could get a fraction of the words out, and now I have visions of his car wrapped around a tree, or him overdosing somewhere. *Oh, God, please, please, no. Not after how far he's come, how hard he's fought. Don't let him do anything stupid.*

I curl into myself even tighter and realize that, as much as I want the release of tears, I cannot cry. My tears have all dried up. I certainly don't have any to waste on *him*—although, surprisingly, it is thoughts of my father that make me want to sob and wail the most. In the past two years, we've begun to build a fragile sort of peace and have achieved at least the semblance of a relationship. It's nothing like it was before, of course, and I know that it never will be, but it was something.

And to think that all the time we were navigating our way through awkward conversations, the occasional Sunday dinner, and birthdays and holidays spent together, he was *touching my sister*? Just the thought of it makes me want to vomit—or kill him. Before, on the night that Levi attacked Dad, and I was so afraid that he would try to kill him, I hadn't understood the depth of Levi's anger and hatred. Now I think I'm beginning to.

Why would he go to all the trouble of trying to reconnect with me—with all of us—if he thought we'd find out one day what he was doing to Jade? Did he honestly think she wouldn't tell us someday? Is he really that stupid? Was he addicted to porn again when he did it?

Jade didn't really tell me much about *what* Dad did to her—not that I remember, anyway. All she had said was that he touched her the way he had touched me, but she didn't mention how many times it occurred, or when. Once I calmed down a little, I realized that Jade hadn't actually told me much at all. But what she *did* say was enough to make my blood boil. *Didn't he learn* anything *after everything we went through the past five years? Is he just some sick pervert?* What *kind of person does that to* two *of his daughters?*

And Ian. I curl my hands into fists. Ian doesn't believe me. How could he doubt for one second that Dad might someday relapse, or whatever it's called, and touch Jade? Why is that such a huge leap of logic for him to make? He *knows* Jade—how could he ever think she'd make something like this up? *I can't believe this is happening.* The look in his eyes tonight when I yelled at him about not believing my sister—it was almost like he was irritated with me, tired of dealing with all this.

I *know* the past two years have been hard for him. I *know* it's been difficult to live with me at times, that I've been so emotional and needy and broken. But he always seems willing to hold me, to pick up the pieces after one of my meltdowns, to be there if I need someone to cling to—and he always insists that there's nowhere else he'd rather be than with me. If he *is* having a problem with it, why can't he just tell me, for God's sake?

I can hear him moving around in the living room, just beyond the closed bedroom door. I told him he didn't need to spend the night, but he was having none of it. "I'm staying," he answered firmly, his mouth a hard line. "I'll sleep on the couch, if you want, but I'm not leaving you alone tonight."

I struck back at him with my words. "What, are you afraid I'll slit my wrists if you leave me by myself?"

He didn't even flinch. "No, I know you won't. I just ... I'm worried about you, Cass. I don't want to leave my fiancée alone on one of the worst nights of her life, if that's not too inconvenient for you! In case you've forgotten, Cassie, we're getting *married*! No way am I leaving you here by yourself!"

I didn't even answer him; I just turned and stalked back to my room, my back tight with fury. Then I collapsed on the bed and sobbed, trying to stifle the sound so Ian couldn't get any satisfaction from it. *Why am I acting like this?*

About an hour later, as I'm still attempting to fall asleep and dreading the nightmares that will surely come when I do, there's a soft tap at the door. "I just wanted to take a shower," Ian says quietly. "Can I come in? I promise I'll be quick, and I won't bother you."

Just the effort of opening my mouth to answer him feels like pushing a load of bricks. "It's fine. Come in."

He cracks the door open just enough to slip in and closes it rapidly to avoid letting in too much light. His concern pierces me with a quick pang that I can't brush away. Ian doesn't speak to me as he heads into the bathroom, and the tears I thought had dried up come rushing back, forcing me to blink them away.

I listen to the whir of the fan clicking on and the rush of water from the shower. I hesitate a moment, then slowly uncurl myself and rise from the bed, padding noiselessly toward the bathroom door. It's unlocked, and I take a deep breath, pushing the door open.

Ian's scrubbing in the shower, his back to me. I try to move as noiselessly as possible and slip my pants and T-shirt off. Clad in only bra and panties, I tiptoe over to the shower's sliding glass door. "Want someone to help wash you?" I try to inject a lightness into my tone that is far from what I'm feeling.

Ian turns just slightly, glancing over his shoulder to look me in the eye. "Cassie ..." he sighs. "Not now."

Stung, I strive for false cheerfulness again. "I just ... I wanted to say I'm sorry for what I said earlier. I shouldn't have come at you like that; you were just trying to help."

Ian sighs again, heavier than before, a sound laden with regret. "Yeah. I was. That's kind of what I do, if you haven't noticed."

I take a step back, feeling foolish and shivering without my clothes but unwilling to take my eyes off Ian long enough to put them back on. "What … what do you mean?" I fight to keep my voice steady.

"Can we at least wait to do this until I'm out of the shower?" Ian snaps, an unusual current of exasperation in his tone.

"Sure," I mumble, my face flushing with more than just the heat of the steam from the shower. I grab my clothes and flee the room, gasping at the chill in my bedroom compared to the sauna-like atmosphere of the bathroom. I struggle back into my clothes and wait nervously for Ian.

He emerges from the bathroom fully clothed, hair slicked back—another small slap to my ego. Normally, he'd come out with just a towel on, if that. I wince and look down. "I'm sorry," I begin. "I know I've been all over the place today, and I shouldn't have taken it out on you. I … I know you don't believe Jade, but, baby, we can work through that. I know you'll believe her once you have a chance to think about it. She wouldn't lie to me, Ian. I know she wouldn't."

His voice is heavy. "Before that meeting in Dr. Morton's office five years ago, you would've said the same thing about your dad, wouldn't you?"

Anger sluices through me like scalding water. "How. Dare. You?"

"I don't know, Cassie," Ian erupts, yelling. "I don't know! I just know I'm sick of it—I am *sick and tired of always, always dealing with this*!" He swears at me, and I shrink back at the force of his fury. "It never ends, Cass—never! There's always something, and just when I think we're finally moving past it, your little idiot of a sister …"

"Shut up, Ian! Just shut *up*! You have no idea what she's been through! How dare you call her a liar?"

"I have no idea?" He swears again. "Haven't I lived through it with you for the past two years? You think I have *no* idea what it's like? Where do you think I've *been* for two years?"

I'd always thought anger was a hot emotion, but in that second, I decide my veins are going to freeze with the chill of it. "I didn't realize it had been such a burden for you."

He glares at me. "Don't start. Just don't. You know that's not how I meant it. But could you honestly blame me if I said that this whole thing between you and your dad gets a little old? I *know* what happened to you was horrible, and it kills me that you had to go through it. But, baby, you've got to start letting it go—and you have to just ignore Jade and whatever she's doing to try to get attention or one-up you or whatever the heck it is."

"You think she accused our dad of abusing her just so she could get *attention*?" My jaw nearly comes unhinged.

"Yes, I do. And it's working pretty well, isn't it? Never mind that your dad's life is probably going to be ruined because of it—Jade won't care. She's gotten it into her head that *she's* the victim in this situation because you guys didn't tell her the truth about your dad for all these years, so she's going to pay you back for it."

I stare at him, flummoxed. "Are you … Ian, have you lost your mind? I don't know *who* you think you're talking about, but Jade would never be that … vindictive. Ian, are you crazy?"

He shrugs, resigned. "Maybe I am. Or maybe I'm perfectly sane, and the rest of your family is nuts to believe her. But I'll tell you this, Cassie: your dad doesn't deserve to go through this. He made some pretty huge mistakes in the past, and I'm not saying we should just overlook them or that you two should be best friends now or anything like that. But I know he's sorry for what he did to you—*you* know he's sorry for it—and he doesn't deserve the hell that Jade's about to put him through."

"And what if you're wrong? What if Jade *is* telling the truth?" It takes all my strength to keep my voice steady.

"Then I'll be knocking down your parents' front door to beat the living crap out of him. But I'd be willing to bet my life's savings that he never came anywhere *near* her." His expression softens a bit as he looks at me. "But I know you don't believe that. So now what?"

My voice is lifeless. "What you said a minute ago, about me needing to let it go and move on? Is that really what you think?"

Ian sighs, raking his fingers through his hair. "I shouldn't have said that. I mean, I shouldn't have said it *like* that. I … I don't know, Cass. I guess I'm just getting tired of having to be the knight in shining armor all the time, you know? If … if things get as crazy with your family as I think they're going to, and you're not even willing to *consider* that maybe your dad is innocent, then …" He stops, pacing around the room.

"I just don't think I can stand here and watch your family fall apart again over something that's not even true. It's not that I won't support *you*—I would, you know that. But if you're just going to blindly agree with Jade … I don't—Cassie, I don't think I can stand by and watch that."

"So you're saying that I have to choose between the two of you?"

"*No!*" Ian exclaims, exasperated. "No, what I'm saying is that ..." He takes a deep breath and I watch anguish creep into his expression. "If you're not willing to at least talk to Jade about this and try to find out what the real truth is, if you just want to take her word for it ... well ... I think we need to take a break for a while."

The words are like a knife to my chest, but once I manage to speak, my voice sounds just as dull and flat as it did a few minutes ago. "Maybe you're right."

If he's surprised by my lack of emotion, Ian covers it well. "I love you, Cassie. You know that, right? I just ... I think we need some time to figure this out and ..."

"And you're tired of dealing with me. I get it, Ian. I totally get it."

"No, that's *not* what I said!"

"That's what you meant, and you know what? That's okay. I knew this would happen sooner or later. Remember after the night at Paul's party, when you came over to my parents' house, and I thought you were there to break up with me? Do you remember what I told you?"

"Cassie ..."

"I said," I continue, ignoring him, "that you deserved someone better than me, that I was way too much of a mess for you to have to try to fix. Remember that? Well, it took you two years to figure it out, but I guess you're finally listening to me."

Ian drops to his knees beside the bed and grabs my hands, squeezing them so tightly that it forces me to look at him. "No, that's *not* true! *I love you*! Everything I said to you that day about wanting to spend the rest of my life with you and how much I loved you—that's all still true, Cass. I just ... I think we both need some space right now. We need to figure things out. But I don't think you're a wreck or a mess or anything like that. You're not."

All the energy drains out of me. "Fine. Whatever. I think you should just go, Ian."

"I don't want to leave you here by yourself tonight. I told you ..."

"Fine, then go sleep on the couch. I don't care. Just go away."

He pauses in the doorway. "I'll call you in a few days, after we've both had some time to think about everything, okay?" I can hear the emotion in his voice and feel my throat swelling shut. "Good-bye, Cass."

Ian

I should've known that it wouldn't end as simply as that. I should've taken her at her word and left the apartment; I knew, deep down, that Cassie would be fine, and I was really just staying for myself, not for her. But did I listen to my instincts and get out of there? Oh, no. Of course not. And in the end, I have a feeling I'm not going to be the only one to suffer for it.

It's been a couple hours since Cassie and I talked, and I still can't sleep. After I said good-bye and closed the door behind me, I stood in the living room for a long time, just a few feet from Cassie's bedroom door, listening. I didn't hear her crying, but that means nothing. Knowing Cassie, she was probably stifling any sound in her pillow to keep me from realizing how deeply I'd hurt her.

As if I don't already know. Why she thinks I can see through her flawlessly sometimes and then imagines herself an impenetrable wall at other times, I will never understand. It's not as if I can read her mind, of course, but I *do* know her better than probably anyone else on the planet. And she can gauge my moods and thoughts equally well, so how did we find ourselves here—sleeping in separate rooms, taking "some time off"? Why is it so hard for her to understand *why* I'm not willing to instantaneously condemn her father on simply the word of a thirteen-year-old girl?

On the other hand, I don't fully understand the way I've acted tonight, either. How is it possible for things to change so completely in just a day's time? *Yesterday, I would not have been able to imagine saying those things to her.* All right, that's not completely true. The things I said about Cassie needing to move on from the past and how I'm getting tired of being the "knight in shining armor" all the time have been niggling at the back of my mind for weeks. I've tried to push them down, tried to distract myself and ignore them, but when this situation with Jade came up, it was like all of it came flooding out, even though I didn't say half of what I was thinking.

I guess I've sorted through what I *do* think, after lying awake for a couple hours. Here's the thing: I *love* Cassie. When I say I want to spend the rest of my life with her, and I can't imagine my life without her, I mean that with all my heart. But it's been a rough two years and I'm just getting tired of it. Tired of watching her suffer—tired of the tears, the nightmares, the sleepless nights, the days and weeks of her pushing me away and the fragile, awkward truces we always reach when she finally decides to let me back in. And it makes me angry—all of it makes me angry. I guess that's the real problem: I'm angry, but I know I shouldn't be angry at *her*, after all she's been through. So who *should* I be angry with? Who *should* I blame in this scenario?

Peter is the obvious choice—except for two factors.

First of all, I've seen the way he looks at Cassie—at all of his kids, but especially her—when he knows she's not looking, and I can tell you, that man is tormented over what he did to her. Sure, there are moments where I conveniently forget that, but when I'm in a rational mood—when I'm not in the middle of trying to help Cassie through yet another flashback or nightmare or breakdown—I feel little but pity for the man. He made a horrible decision, but it's clear to me that he's more than paying for it now.

The other thing that keeps me from being angry at Peter is that he's not the only one who deserves some of the blame for Cassie's emotional fragility. Marianne's done her share of damage as well. And the worst part about Marianne is that she doesn't seem to understand *what* she's done; I think she prefers to think of Peter as the villain in this family saga. I guess it's easier than facing the fact that she emotionally abandoned her children when they needed her.

Maybe what angers me most is the fact that there's no one person *to* be angry with: I'm angry at all of them—even Cassie. This realization inundates me with guilt, but the truth of it resonates all the same.

As if on cue, Cassie's bedroom door cracks open, and she slips out, wearing the nightgown I bought her for Christmas. The see-through nightgown. *Oh, boy. Here we go.*

"Cassie," I sigh, turning my back on her and hoping she'll get the message. She doesn't—I feel her perch on the edge of the sofa, and I try to suppress the flash of irritation that shoots through me.

"Can we just ... talk?"

I still refuse to look at her. "If you'll put some real clothes on first, sure."

A tinge of hurt creeps into her voice. "If that's what you want ..."

I ignore her, because I know if I try to answer her, I'll explode. *I shouldn't be this angry. What is* wrong *with me?* But I don't move from my position on the sofa, and I hear Cassie walk back to the bedroom. A few minutes later, she returns, her voice heavy with sarcasm. "You can look now."

I roll over and see that she's changed into a pair of shorts and one of my T-shirts. "What do you want to talk about?" I'm fighting to remain unemotional and detached, but god, I *love* this girl, and I hate to see her hurting. How is it possible to feel that way and still be angry with her? *Maybe I need therapy as much as she does.*

"I just … I know you're right that we probably need some time apart, but, Ian …" She starts to cry, but I can tell she's attempting to stop. "Ugh! I told myself I wasn't going to be emotional like this. Sorry." She wipes her eyes, sets her jaw in determination, and resumes in a calmer, stronger voice. "I know this whole thing with Jade is … hard. And I'm sorry that I didn't listen to you earlier; I shouldn't have freaked out like that. So. I'm going to listen now. If you want to tell me why you don't believe her, I'll listen."

I feel myself softening. *I do owe her an explanation.* But I keep the hard edge to my tone as I answer: "Are you sure you want to hear it? Are you going to *really* listen?"

Cassie stares at her hands. "Yeah. I … I want to hear what you have to say."

I take a deep breath, steeling myself. "Okay. It's pretty simple, really. I think your sister is lying."

She rolls her eyes. "I know. You already *said* that. What I don't understand is *why* you think that. I mean, since when has Jade been a liar? She talks to me about everything …"

I groan inwardly. "I know, I know. But, come on, can you honestly tell me that you don't think the *timing* of this is just a little odd? Not to mention the fact that I don't believe your dad would ever do that to Jade. He learned his lesson after …"

"After he came into my room six different nights and sexually abused me?" she interrupts, eyes flashing.

This, I realize, *is why I'm angry with her. It* always *comes back to this. She* always *has to play the victim.*

"Fine. If you're going to bring it back around to that, then this conversation is over."

If I had slapped her in the face, I don't think I could have shocked her more. "*What?*"

"I'm tired of it, Cassie! Okay? And maybe that makes me the bad guy, but I'm just … I'm sick of it always coming back to this. At some point, you're going to have to start moving on with your life."

Cassie simply stands there, as if she's been poleaxed.

"I'm not sick of *you*. I'm just tired of … all this. All the drama and the craziness. It's … we just need to take a break so you can sort all this out, Cass. And … I need to figure out how I feel about it, what I should be doing to help you. Right now, I don't think I'm helping you at all by… by letting you…" I stop. I've simply run out of words.

"You're right," she whispers. "I know you're right." Tears slip down her cheeks, but I doubt that she realizes she's crying. "I just … I just hoped maybe … we could try …"

Forget staying detached; I get up from the sofa and pull her into my arms. "I know. I know." I should know better, but I kiss her tears away, finding that my own eyes are misting over as I do. She wraps her arms around my neck and kisses me, soft and slow, the tears on her cheeks mingling with my own. When she pulls back, desire smolders in her eyes. "Ian, please …"

Everything in me is screaming *Leave. Now!* "Cassie …" My voice is rougher than I'd intended it. "Not now. We shouldn't … it'll just make it harder when I leave in the morning. "

She kisses me again, and part of me wants to hate her because I know what she's trying to do. The other part of me knows that she's succeeding, and I don't care. "Please," she repeats.

I feel my defenses crumbling, and I kiss her back. Hard. When she leads me toward the bedroom, I don't resist. The tension that hangs in the air makes speech impossible; the moment is too fragile, too transient. Too painful.

Afterward, she lays immobile in my arms, her long hair splayed out over my chest. "I love you," she whispers, just before she falls asleep.

I should say it back to her; I know I should. It's true, after all: I do love her. Instead I whisper, "I know." I wish it were that simple; I wish it were true that all you need in the end is love. But it's not—not this time.

I don't sleep at all the rest of the night. Instead, I lie there and watch Cassie sleeping. And, as soon as dawn begins to break, I slip out of bed, throw my clothes back on, and kiss her forehead, careful not to wake her. Then I take the coward's way out and leave, unwilling to face her one more time. I'm afraid that, if I stay until she wakes up, I might never go.

I try to imagine how she'll feel when she wakes up and realizes that I'm not there. I wonder if she'll hate me as much as I hate myself.

Peter

For the third time in my life, I'm standing in the doorway of an inexpensive hotel room, holding the bits and pieces of my life that will fit into a suitcase in one hand—and wondering how I ended up here. The first time, I knew beyond a shadow of a doubt that exile from my family was the least of what I deserved, and I was bracing myself for the fact that I might never be with them again. The second time, I'd had noble visions of making the sacrifice for my children—a notion that dissipated in about two days, when I realized that the only person I was really looking out for was myself.

I know I'm not a perfect person, but I believe that I've come a long way since the last time I moved into a hotel room, two years ago. I stayed away for two months, and during that time, I started going to therapy again. I still see Dr. Morton about twice a month, and I believe that my sessions with him have uncovered the real issues that caused me to make such a colossal wreck of my life. And, for the past two years, I've tried my best to become the husband and father I know I should be, to get myself right with God and my family. I've tried to make up for the past, to the extent that that's even possible.

And that's what makes this trip to yet another hotel so excruciating—this time, I don't believe that I deserve what's happening to me. This time, when I say I'm doing this for the good of my children, I really mean it. Even if the child I'm doing it for is breaking my heart ...

Shakespeare once said, "Hell hath no fury like a woman scorned." With apologies to Mr. Shakespeare, I'd have disagree. I would say that hell hath no fury like a woman who believes that her husband has sexually abused their daughter for the second time. I can honestly say that, except for the night Levi attacked me, I haven't been as terrified as I was this afternoon when Marianne got the phone call from Cassie ... I shudder involuntarily, remembering.

Jade had been home for only ten or fifteen minutes when the phone rang. I was in my office, catching up on some paperwork, since Jade had been visiting Cassie and Marianne had just come in from working in her flower garden. I had promised Jade that, as soon as I finished up in the office, we could go rent a movie and order pizza for dinner. That's become a sort of Saturday night ritual for us, since she's usually home. I know the days of her *wanting* to be at home on a Saturday night, much less wanting to spend time with her parents, are fleeting, so I treasure our tradition all the more.

When I heard someone coming up the steps a few moments after the phone rang, I assumed that it was Jade. "I'm almost done, honey. Give me three minutes, and we'll go pick out a movie, okay? What kind of pizza do you want tonight?"

There was no answer, so I looked up from my desk to see Marianne standing in the doorway, as white as a sheet. "Honey, what's wrong? Did something happen to one of the kids?" *Ben. It has to be Ben. Oh, God, please don't let him have relapsed and gotten into an accident or something!*

"Oh, yes, *something* happened to one of the kids!" Her tone was icy. "How *could* you, Peter? Did you honestly think I would never find out?"

I shook my head, bewildered. "What are you talking about? What happened?"

"Cassie just called." Marianne's composure was beginning to slip; I could sense her fury rising. "She and Jade had an interesting conversation this afternoon. Jade told Cassie about what you've been doing to her."

The words landed like a punch in the stomach. "No, no, that's not true! I would never ..."

Instantly, my wife changed into someone I could barely recognize, her normally serene and lovely face contorted with fury. I've rarely heard her swear in all the years of our marriage, let alone the string of obscenities that came out of her mouth. "*Don't lie to me, Peter*! I *trusted* you with Jade, and you do this? What kind of sick person *are* you? Get. Out. Now."

My head was spinning; everything was happening too fast. *Wait ... Jade said I touched her? Why would she? Does she know about what I did to Cassie?* "Why ... why would Jade say something like that? I swear to you, I've never ..."

"I said, *get out*!" Marianne screamed. "And this time, you are *not* coming back, do you understand me? *Ever*! You will never get within ten feet of Jade if I have anything to say about it! Thank *God* Cassie told her about what you did to her and Jade felt safe enough to admit what you've been doing to *her*! How long has this been going on, anyway? Never mind. I don't want to know. Just pack your things and get out! You have ten minutes and then I'm calling the police. *I mean it, Peter!*"

The pieces began to fall into place. *Cassie told Jade this afternoon, and Jade. Oh, my poor baby.* I realized what she was doing, and I knew just as clearly what I had to do in response. "All right. I'll go."

Marianne paused, deflated, clearly having anticipated more of a fight. "So you're admitting it?"

"*No*! I *never* touched her! But if you want me to go, I'll go."

"Oh, of *course* you never touched her! Of *course,* our thirteen-year-old made something like that up! Especially since you've *never* done anything like this before!" Her face twisted in an ugly sneer, and I flinched at her sarcasm. "Excuse me for not believing you, Peter! You're lucky I'm not forcing you out at gunpoint."

Another string of obscenities chased me down the hall, as I stumbled toward the master bedroom in a fog. *Oh, Jade ...* I packed my things hastily, pausing in the hallway to look one last time at all the pictures lining the wall. *Maybe this is the last time I'll see them ...* I pushed the thought away and trudged down the stairs, coming face-to-face with Jade, who was lingering in the downstairs hall.

"Jade," I whispered, barely able to speak past the lump in my throat. "Honey, I don't know why you're doing this, but ..."

Before I could say anything more, Marianne barged into the hallway. "How *dare* you try to talk to her?" she hissed.

Jade looked impossibly small, much younger than thirteen; fear and an emotion I couldn't place flickered over her face and stripped the years away. It was like looking at the little girl she had been when I returned home the *first* time. "Mom, don't ..."

"Jade, go to your room!" Marianne ordered. "I don't want your father anywhere *near* you!" When Jade hesitated, glancing in my direction but refusing to look me in the eyes, Marianne turned on her. "I said *go to your room*, young lady!"

Jade scurried away, taking a large chunk of my heart with her. I ignored Marianne's tirade and simply walked out the door. It wasn't until I was behind the wheel of my SUV that I realized the emotion that I'd seen on my daughter's face was, in fact, a very familiar one.

It was guilt.

And that's what has led me to this hotel room, where I unpack my things and attempt to get my bearings. If Cassie really did tell Jade the story of how I abused her and what's been happening in our family the past five years, it makes perfect sense to me that Jade would react by saying that I abused her, too. I know Jade well enough to know that she hates to be left out of anything, especially when it involves the people she loves. To her, the knowledge that she'd been kept in the dark about all of this for five years would have seemed like the ultimate betrayal. And in some ways, I suppose she's right. *We should have told her a long time ago.*

So I won't try to convince Marianne or the rest of the children that I'm innocent—I know they'll never believe me anyway. I'll just hope and pray that Jade eventually comes to her senses and admits the truth.

Even if our family will never be the same again.

Ben

Score one for the home team, I tell myself wryly, keeping my hands steady on the steering wheel. I know Cassie was terrified when I hung up on her earlier, after she told me what happened this afternoon with Jade. But she'd be proud: I slammed things around my apartment for a few minutes and contemplated how much I needed a hit, but in the end, I called my sponsor and talked things through with him. Once I did, I realized that there was really only one option.

So now I'm heading back to my hometown, the place I fought so hard to escape. Not that I'll be there long this time—what I need to do tonight will take an hour, tops. I should be back at my apartment by midnight at the latest. If everything goes according to plan, that is.

I'm fighting to keep from thinking about my dad. *Peter,* that's what I'm calling him from now on. Not Dad. Not ever again. *And to think I was actually starting to have a* relationship *with him again. How could that… okay, okay, stop. Just breathe. Think about something else.*

But what else is there to think about that's not going to make me equally furious? Jade? Oh, no … I can't even go there right now. Cassie and how she's probably in the middle of a nervous breakdown or something? At least she has Ian; thank God she found a guy who will stand by her through all this. Mom? My fingers tighten involuntarily on the steering wheel. *Okay, that's not a good topic, either.*

I take a deep breath and fiddle with the dial on the radio. I need something hard and fast, something that makes the bass pound through my chest and helps me forget. No such luck. I flip the radio off and swear softly. *God, where are You? I really need Your help here …*

A year ago, if someone had told me I'd be *praying,* much less about this mess with my family, I would've laughed in the person's face. Now, though, I find myself checking in with God at least a couple times a day.

That's how I like to think of it: checking in with God. I can't stand the overly religious hypocrites in most churches, but I definitely know that I can't stay clean and sober without God. I've learned that much in the last year, and I never want to try to do it on my own again.

But right now, even checking in with God isn't making me feel much more settled. *Am I doing the right thing?*

I'll know soon; forty minutes or so and I'll be at my parents' house. I haven't been there since Christmas. *Was Dad abusing Jade then?* I try to push the thought away, can't, and try the radio one more time. Nothing. Frustrated, I drop my favorite death metal mix into the CD player and crank the volume. I roll the windows down and lose myself in the music.

Even with the music to distract me, my stomach is in knots as I pull up to the house forty-five minutes later. *God, am I doing the right thing? Just—could you help me out here, please?* I take a deep breath and head up the sidewalk.

The minute I put my key into the lock, anger hits me like a tidal wave. I try to remind myself not to give into it, but that's useless. I push the door open so hard it slams against the wall, the sound reverberating through the house like a gunshot. Mom appears at the top of the steps a few seconds later. "Ben?" Confusion etches itself across her face. "What are you doing here?"

I ignore her and start up the steps. "Where is he?"

"Ben, honey, listen to me."

I'm facing her now, at the top of the stairs. "Mom. I'm trying really hard to stay calm here, but I am *this* close to losing it. So *where is Peter?*"

Mom looks older than the last time I saw her. "He left. I … I threw him out." She holds her head up defiantly. As if I'd ever tell her do anything *other* than throw the scumbag out. "It was the right thing to do."

"Yep. Now where's Jade?" I don't wait for an answer; I just stride down the hall to my sister's room. "Jay? Get your stuff together, baby. I'm taking you to my house for a couple days."

Her door is open, and she jumps up from where she'd been sitting on her bed. She looks like a deer caught in the headlights—eyes wide and a startled expression on her face. "Wh-what? Why?"

I'm normally not this short with her, but I simply jerk my head toward her closet. "Get your stuff. We're leaving in ten minutes."

Mom practically pounces on me the moment I step out of Jade's room. "*What* do you think you're doing, Ben? You can't just take your sister away like this! She needs to be *home*, where it's safe."

I merely raise an eyebrow at her. "Oh, yeah, I'd say it's real safe here, Mom."

Her face flushes. "Well, then *you* can come and stay *here*. There's no need to take Jade back to your place. I can promise you, your dad won't be coming anywhere *near* this house—or your sister."

"I don't really want her around *you* right now either, Mom. She needs to get away from here. She's *not* safe here, and if you can't see that, then you've got to be one of the blindest people I know."

"Ben, that is completely unfair! Your father …"

"You didn't *listen* to me!" My voice is rising despite my best efforts to remain calm. "I warned you—we *all* warned you that this might happen and you *didn't listen*! So why in the world should I trust you with her now? I'm sorry, but Jade needs to get away from this house. And since Levi's too far away and Cassie's probably too much of a mess to take care of Jade right now, I'm going to."

Mom's mouth is hanging open. "Ben …" she sputters.

I realize that I need to get away from her fast, before I say some things I'll regret. Things like *How could you have let this happen again? Weren't you paying* any *attention to what Dad was doing?* I turn on my heel and almost jog down the hall toward Jade's room. "You ready, kiddo?"

"I guess so. I packed enough stuff for three days. Is that good?"

"Yeah, that's okay for now. If you're going to stay longer, we can always come back and get whatever else you need."

She's still so young, even though she'd hate me for saying so; it breaks my heart to look at her and know that Peter did something like this. Again. *What was he* thinking? *How could that selfish …*

"Why are you doing this?" Jade's voice interrupts my inner raging. "I mean, I don't mind staying here with Mom. Dad went to stay at a hotel, so I think I'll be okay here."

"No," I shake my head at her. "No, you won't. Trust me."

She looks genuinely confused. "Why *not*?"

My throat closes as I look at her. I'm remembering what Cassie told us that night two years ago, about the nightmares and flashbacks that haunted her almost every night. Does Jade have them, too? I'm almost afraid to know the answer to that question.

"Ask Cassie," I answer gruffly. Then without waiting for her answer, I walk out of the room, down the hall past my confused mother, down the stairs, and out the front door. The air is cool for this time of year, and I lean back against the porch railing.

This is the right thing to do. I know it is.

I couldn't protect Cassie from him, and I guess I'm also too late to protect Jade. But I *can* make sure that Jade doesn't have to go through what Cassie did—sleeping in the same room where he touched her, living in the same house where she should've been protected and wasn't. I can at least save her from that.

Jade

I am going to hell, for sure. I know it. I think about it sometimes late at night, when I can't sleep—which is most nights. I imagine that, whenever I die, I'll stand in front of God, and He'll shake His head at me and say, "I'm sorry, there's no room here in heaven for a person like you." And the thing is, I wouldn't blame God if He *did* send me to hell for this; I would, if I were Him.

So why am I still lying to everyone about this? Am I really willing to let my family fall apart over this web of lies I've concocted in the past couple weeks? Yes. No.

Maybe.

I guess you could say it's complicated.

For one thing, I never in a million years would've thought that everyone would take me so *seriously*. I don't know *why* I thought no one would believe me or that it wouldn't be a big deal—looking back, I know that was about the dumbest thing I could've thought. But that moment, when I lied to Cassie and she flipped out, I was honestly shocked that she got so upset. Sometimes I fit the stereotype of a dumb blonde: how could I have been so dense?

The smart thing to do would have been to immediately admit that I lied—right then, while Cassie was still in mid-freak-out. But did I do that? Oh, no.

And I didn't admit the truth when my mom came barreling into the living room fifteen minutes after I got home, jerked me up from the couch where I was watching TV, and shook me by the shoulders so hard that my teeth rattled. "Is it true?" She demanded, not looking a bit like my mother. The woman in front of me was some type of crazy person. "Did your father touch you? *Did he?*"

I knew, even then, that my next words were going to change all of our lives. And I said them anyway: "I'm sorry, Mom. I'm sorry I didn't tell you."

I knew what I was doing was wrong—I *knew*. But in a way, it felt so good. Watching Cassie and then Mom absolutely flip out over a single sentence from me, when I'd spent my entire life doing whatever *they* wanted, hanging on every word *they* said, idolizing *them*? That was an incredible power rush; I wonder if that's how Ben used to feel when he did drugs.

The rush evaporated like morning mist when I saw my dad come down the stairs with his suitcase a few minutes later. And that was the moment when I almost, *almost* told the truth. I came so close—Dad and I were alone in the hallway for a few seconds, and I caught one glimpse of his eyes before I had to look away. I've never felt so guilty in my whole life. Or so angry.

He stood there in front of me and started to speak. My dad. My hero. The person I've looked up to the most for probably my entire life, the guy who made Saturday nights "our" special time, who made me chocolate-chip pancakes on the weekends and taught me how to ride a bike and swim and ice skate. The one who's come to all of my cross-country meets and school plays and, when I was little, dance recitals and T-ball games.

And he's also the person who sexually abused my sister. My best friend. Not just once, but six times. *Six times.*

Standing there in the hallway for those few seconds, staring at him, I couldn't make those two images fit. My dad, the hero versus my dad, the child molester. I couldn't look him in the eyes, because I knew if I did, I would blurt out the truth. But inside I was screaming, *Don't you understand? Don't you see why I have to do this?*

Maybe he would've understood. Probably not, though. It's been two weeks since that day, and I'm not sure I even understand it myself. When I first told the lie to Cassie, it was automatic—I didn't think it through, and honestly, I just wanted to see what would happen. When I lied the second time, to Mom, I knew exactly what I was doing, and I did it because I was angry. Because I wanted revenge. Because I wanted them all to know how it felt to be lied to, to be stabbed in the back. I guess I still feel that way, and that's partly why I've kept lying for the past two weeks.

But the main reason I've continued to lie is because of that moment in the hallway with my dad, when I changed my mind about admitting the truth. In that moment, it was as if everything Cassie had told me about what happened to her crashed down on me—as if her words became a living, physical weight. I could hardly breathe. I looked at my father and thought, *You hurt my sister. You hurt her so bad that it's been five* years *and she still cries when she talks about it.* I thought about all those Saturday nights that Dad, Mom, and I have eaten pizza and watched movies, and nausea swept over me. *All that time, you* knew *what you had done to her, and you* never *told me! I told you everything, and you told me nothing.*

I stared at my father, those brief seconds feeling like hours, and realized that I did not know him at all. And I also realized that I didn't *want* to know him. I didn't *want* to understand him or feel sorry for him or forgive him. What I wanted was for him to leave and never come back.

So I haven't told the truth. I'm afraid, now, of what will happen if I do. Things have changed drastically in only two weeks. Ben only stuck with the idea of me living with him for about two days, then he realized that his apartment was too tiny for another person and, besides, he knows basically *nothing* about girls. So I went back to my parents' house, and Ben moved in, too.

Except I guess it's not our *parents'* house anymore—they're probably going to get a divorce; Mom is refusing to talk to Dad except through a lawyer. It's only a matter of time, according to Ben, until they "make it official." My mom put me into therapy, like, thirty seconds after Ben and I moved back in. And I had to have a meeting with some people from Social Services, and a medical exam, just like Cassie did. All of it sucked, but I guess I was convincing enough for the experts to believe me.

The worst thing that's happened, though, is Cassie and Ian breaking up. I didn't find out until a few days later, but they broke up that night when Ben came and basically kidnapped me. Cassie pretended that it wasn't my fault, but I know she was lying. They broke up because of me, because of what I accused Dad of doing to me. I know that as surely as I know my own name.

I'm watching my family splinter apart around me, and it's all my fault. If I had just told the truth, even once, none of this would've happened. Ian and Cassie would still be together, my parents wouldn't be divorcing, and Ben would still be living at his own apartment, instead of sleeping down the hall from me in his old bedroom. Dad and I would've had our pizza-and-movie night that Saturday night just like always, and I would be looking forward to the last couple days of school. Maybe I'd even be able to sleep at night.

But if I *had* told the truth, Dad would have gotten away with what he did to Cassie. He would still be living here, still living a lie right in front of me. Until I accused him of abusing me and Mom decided to divorce him, he never really had to accept any consequences for abusing my sister. Now he has to. Now he's lost everything. Now he'll pay for what he did. Now maybe he'll realize how much he hurt Cassie—and all of us.

Doesn't that make what I've done worth it?

Cassie

I thought I knew what it was like to have a broken heart. I thought I learned that when Will broke up with me four years ago, when it took me months to be able to get through a day without thinking about him. Now I know that I was a fool to believe that I knew what it was to have my heart broken. Now I know what it's like to have my heart *shattered*, the kind of pain that embeds itself under your skin, like shards of glass that pierce with every breath.

That's what it's been like for the past three weeks, since Ian left. Waking up that morning and realizing that he was gone left me reeling; I could not believe that he had simply *left*. Even though I knew it was the right thing; even though I'd *told* him I knew it was the right thing—I didn't believe he'd actually do it. I was an absolute wreck for days.

I still am, according to Julia. She has her own apartment across town now, but she still stops by once or twice a week to see how I'm doing. Today when she arrives, I'm still in my bathrobe, having called in sick to work. Again. I'm curled up on the couch watching some sappy romance movie on TV when Julia lets herself into the apartment.

She puts her hands on her hips and glares at me. "Cassie, this has got to stop. It's been *three weeks*! You have to pull yourself together!"

I want to tell her that she has no idea what she's talking about, since she and Paul are perfectly happy together, but I can't muster up the energy to even glare back at her. She marches over to the TV and turns it off. "Get up," she orders. "Get up, get dressed, and we're going to clean this place up. Have you eaten today?"

I try to remember and can't. I shrug.

Julia rolls her eyes. "Cass, it's almost three in the afternoon! What have you been *doing* all day? Never mind. I don't want to know."

Walking into the bedroom is a chore; I feel like my legs have turned to concrete. I try not to look at the bed, made up so carefully on one side, as I throw on some clothes. I brush my hair and shake my head at the lifeless eyes that stare back at me from the mirror over my dresser.

"Have you talked to him?" Julia asks when I come out of the bedroom.

I shake my head. So far, I haven't said a word to her. My tongue seems glued to the roof of my mouth.

Julia heaves another sigh. "*What* is wrong with you two? You have to *talk* about this! Or you need to do what he asked you to do, and get some help—*then* talk to him. Something, Cass! You can't keep going on like this. You look horrible. And you're going to lose your job if you're not careful, and you know you can't afford that."

"Gee, thanks for all the advice, Mom," I reply sarcastically.

Julia softens. "Look, Cass, I know this is hard. Breakups suck. I know. I get that. But, come on, you and Ian have something special. Isn't that worth fighting for? Isn't it worth it to do whatever you can to get him back? I mean, from what you told me, it's not like he's left you for good. It sounds like he's willing to work things out, if you'll get some help dealing with, well, all the issues."

Julia knows about my dad and the sexual abuse, but we rarely discuss it. I told her about the situation with Jade when I called her, hysterical, the morning after Ian left. She was about as understanding and supportive as she ever is, but I know that she's uncomfortable talking about the sexual abuse issue with me. Not that I blame her; it's a little awkward for both of us.

"Look, Cass," she continues when I don't say anything, "I know I don't understand everything you're going through with your family, and especially your dad. I know I *can't* understand it since I haven't been through it. But, well, it seems to me that you should do whatever you can to work things out with Ian. And maybe getting some help dealing with the family issues will be the best thing for you right now. I ... I know the past couple years have been really hard for you, and I just hate to see you suffering like this, honey."

"I know," I sigh. "Thanks, Julia. You've been a great friend. I know I need to get some help. And I will; I promise. I just ..." I choke up, fighting to keep the tears at bay. It seems like all I've done the past three weeks is cry nonstop. "I just miss him so much."

Julia stays with me for a couple hours, forcing me to eat something, helping me clean up the apartment, and trying to distract me from the ever-present ache in my chest. *Ian …*

Once she leaves, I take a deep breath, pick up the phone, and dial the number Dr. Morton had e-mailed me. It's a phone number that I've had on my refrigerator for a week and a half, but I couldn't seem to get up the nerve to call. The conversation takes less than two minutes, but when I hang up the phone, weariness floods my veins, and I lean against the refrigerator to stop the room from spinning. *At least I did it. Finally.*

Three days later, I have my first appointment with my new therapist, a woman named Trisha Rogers. Dr. Morton recommended her when I e-mailed him and said that I'd prefer to work with a female therapist who had experience dealing with clients who'd been sexually abused. He promised to forward my file to her, as well, to save me a couple sessions worth of "re-plowing the same field." Getting ready for the session, I realize that it's the first time in three weeks that I've put on makeup or worn nice clothes outside of work. *Julia's right. This has to stop.*

Driving to Dr. Rogers's office, I remember with a pang that I haven't called Jade in a day or two. Despite the wreck I've been since Ian left, I've spent whatever emotional strength I had on my sister. I went with her and Mom to the hospital for the medical exam, and I made sure to stay with her. I didn't want her to go through the ordeal of shivering alone on an exam table, confused and frightened. She hasn't wanted to talk much about what happened, and I've tried to give her space so she doesn't feel pressured, but I'm sure, if she's anything like me, she's going to want to talk about it all eventually. And when she does, I never want her to feel that there's no one there to listen. Like I did.

I'll call her once I'm done with my session, I promise myself. Then I check my hair and makeup on last time, grab my purse, and head into Dr. Rogers's office. *Please, God, let her be able to help me. Please,* I beg silently. *I need Ian to come home. He has to come home. Please, God.* I doubt that He's listening, but it can't hurt to ask, can it?

Dr. Rogers doesn't keep me waiting; promptly at four, she comes into the waiting room to greet me and usher me back to her office. "Cassie, what a pleasure! I've heard so much about you; it's wonderful to finally meet. I'm Trisha Rogers." She offers her hand and shakes mine with a surprisingly firm grip.

"Nice to meet you, too," I reply, assessing her. She's a petite woman, probably about my mom's age, with short dark hair and vibrant green eyes.

She also has a slight British accent, and I'm tempted to ask where she's from as I follow her into her office.

"Please," she gestures around the room, "take a seat wherever you feel comfortable." Once I do, she picks up a stack of papers on her desk and waves them at me. "Richard—oh, I'm sorry, Dr. Morton—forwarded me the notes from his sessions with you. He said he'd cleared that with you ahead of time. And after reading them, I have a question for you, Cassie."

I brace myself inwardly, but I try for a polite smile. "Only one question?"

"Only one. What was your life like before all this shit happened to you?"

I laugh out loud, caught completely off-guard by her directness. It's perhaps a crude assessment, but the most accurate one I've heard in the past five years. "I'm sorry; I don't mean to laugh. I just—that's such a *perfect* description of what it's been like!"

She smiles. "Well, I suppose I phrased it in a less-than-professional manner, but the whole time I was reading Dr. Morton's notes, that's what I was thinking."

I blush. "I'm sure you see lots of clients who've been through much worse."

Dr. Rogers holds up her hand to stop me. "No, no, my dear. That's not how this works—one never compares her experiences to someone else's while in my office. Your experiences are *your* experiences; it's not possible to accurately measure them next to someone else's. Is it true that what happened to you could have been much worse? Of course. Situations like these can nearly always be worse. However …"

She pauses, picking up a piece of paper from my file and skimming over it. "From what I can gather, your family had not had significant problems prior to the discovery that your father had sexually abused you. Now, I know your parents were having some marital issues—that's apparently why all of you were in therapy, according to Dr. Morton. So I'm not trying to say that you had a flawless family before this. What I *am* saying is that it seems that this issue with your father has come to define your family in many ways. So I'm curious to hear what you think life was like before all of this happened."

My mouth is suddenly dry. "Well …" I hesitate a moment, remembering. I don't often allow myself to look back on the years before that awful day in Dr. Morton's office; it's simply too painful. I swallow hard. "I would say things were perfect."

"All right," Dr. Rogers replies, scribbling something on the paper in front of her.

"I mean, not *perfect*, perfect," I add hastily. "I know nothing's ever really perfect. My parents fought sometimes and stuff, and you're right, we *were* in therapy, so it can't have been 100 percent great or anything. But when I think back on it, I mostly remember us just being … happy. We were …" I start to choke up, and Dr. Rogers pushes a box of tissues my way.

"Take your time," she says gently.

"We were a family," I manage finally.

"And how about now?"

I roll my eyes derisively. "I'm sure my mom would say that we still are. She never likes to admit how much things have changed; I think she's in denial in a lot of ways. And she's not completely wrong—things were kind of getting better for a while. Over the last year or so, we were starting to have real relationships with each other again. But never like it was before. And now, I don't think there's any chance of us being a family again."

"Is that because your sister has accused your father of sexually abusing her? You believe that that's destroyed any chance for family relationships?"

"Relationships with my dad, yeah," I sigh shakily. "I mean, none of my siblings and I were *close* to my dad since … you know, we found out that he'd abused me. Well, Jade was always really close to him, but she didn't know what he had done until a few weeks ago. But the rest of us were starting to have a relationship with Dad again, and I was hoping that maybe …" I shrug, unwilling to cry again.

"What were you hoping, Cassie?" Dr. Rogers prods.

"I just wanted … I wanted things to be like they were before. I *knew* that wouldn't really happen; I knew it probably wasn't even possible. But I still wanted it. I miss us being a family, the way we used to be. And I miss …" Now I'm crying in earnest. "I miss my dad. I miss being able to trust him. I miss being able to *talk* to him! I miss … I just miss *him*. We were really, really close before, before …"

"How does it make you feel," Dr. Rogers begins after giving me a few moments to compose myself, "to know that in spite of the closeness you had with your father, he chose to take advantage of you in a sexual manner?"

I flinch. "I don't … Do I have to answer that?"

"Of course not," she answers pleasantly. "But if you're ever going to get to the bottom of this, and, I hope, get past it in some measure, you're going to have to face the hard questions at some point. It doesn't have to be today. But you will need to answer this someday—you'll at least have to admit it to yourself, if not to me."

I stare at my hands and watch them disappear in a blur of tears. It feels like an eternity before I can speak around the knot in my throat. "Honestly?" I look straight at her, not bothering to wipe away any of the tears streaming down my face. "When I think about that, *really* think about it, I feel like I'm being ripped into pieces."

"Well done, Cassie," the therapist says softly. "Well done."

*****

When I get home, I feel like a sponge someone's squeezed dry. I should've remembered that I used to feel that way after my appointments with Dr. Morton—at least when I was actually being honest with him about how I was feeling and what I was thinking. By the time we ended our sessions together, I'd become an expert at faking my way through the one-hour time slot each week. I'm going to try not to let that happen with Dr. Rogers; I already feel much more at ease with her than I ever did with Dr. Morton. Maybe it's simply because when I was seeing Dr. Morton, I wasn't quite ready to face what was going on in my family and how I felt about it all. And now I am.

Or I'm attempting to be; I shiver involuntarily, remembering my admission in the therapist's office this afternoon. *Ripped into pieces.* I hadn't intended to be quite so honest and vulnerable in only my first session. *Is that* really *how I feel?*

"I can't think about this now," I announce to the empty apartment. But what is there to distract me? I'm sick of TV, and I'm too full of restless, nervous energy to even begin to concentrate on a book or a magazine. I tried to call Jade on the way home, and Mom said she was out with friends.

"She seems to be doing better," Mom enthused. "She's been spending more time with her friends the past couple days, and the other night, a *boy* called for her! I only let her talk to him for ten minutes, of course. I think his name was Collin? Well, anyway, she definitely seems like she's turned a corner! She's still sleeping in one of your dad's shirts, but I don't hear her awake in the night as much as I did a week or so ago. I'll get her to call you when she comes home, all right?"

She seems to be doing better now, *but what about later?* I wonder, a wave of sorrow crashing over me. *What if she ends up in some therapist's office in five years saying the same thing I just said today? What if she never gets over this? What if neither one of us does?*

There's only one thing left to do. I grab my cell phone and, almost without thinking, dial. When he answers, the sound of his voice—oh, his voice—nearly knocks me over. "Cassie... hey ... what's up?"

"Ian," I manage through tears, hoping that I can keep my voice steady enough that he won't realize I'm crying. "I just ... I just thought I'd call and tell you that I had my first appointment with a therapist today."

"Really?" He sounds genuinely surprised. "Wow! Well, that's awesome, baby! How, um, how did it go?"

It only took her thirty minutes to get me to admit something that I've tried not to think about for the past five years. *It was awful. It was awful enough that I'm calling you like some pathetic creature.* "It was good."

"That's great." An awkward silence descends between us, and I realize how desperate I must seem to Ian. Calling him out of the blue like this, after not speaking to him in three weeks.

"I'm sorry," I fumble. "I shouldn't have called you. I just ... I just needed to hear your voice." Now I *know* he can tell I'm crying; there's no point in trying to hide it.

"Hey, hey, don't apologize. I'm the one who should apologize to *you.* That night, at your apartment ... I shouldn't have left you like that, Cass. I'm sorry. It was a really crappy thing to do."

"No, no, it's okay." I swipe at the tears. "It was probably better that you did, anyway." Another lie. To say that I was shattered when I realized he had left me in the middle of the night is a massive understatement. But he doesn't need to know that.

"Yeah, well, I'm sorry I haven't called, either. I just ... I knew we both needed some space, and I thought if I heard your voice, I'd ..." His voice trails off.

"I miss you," I blurt out. *Dear God, can this get any more embarrassing? Shut* up, *you fool!*

"I miss you, too," he says simply. "More than you know. But I know we're doing the right thing here. We are. And it won't be forever." He doesn't sound entirely convincing.

We fumble through a few more minutes of excruciating awkwardness and then the conversation finally ends. But the steady *beep beep beep* of the dial tone makes me burst into tears all over again. As difficult as that conversation was, at least I could hear his voice for a few minutes. *Ian.* He's been my lifeline for two years; how am I ever going to make it through this therapy stuff without him?

His words echo in my mind: *it won't be forever.*

What if it is? How can I ever survive this without him?

Marianne

When the envelope arrives with Peter's handwriting scrawled across the front of it, I almost toss it into the trash can without even opening it. After all, I haven't talked to him since the day after I threw him out, and it's been nearly six weeks. But something makes me pause, my hand poised over the trash can, ready to hurl the envelope inside and forget about it.

Read it. You should read it. Peter's been extremely respectful of the boundaries I've set for him—for us—in the past six weeks; I suppose the least I can do is hear what he has to say. I brace myself as I open the envelope, unfold the letter inside, and begin reading. The salutation makes me cringe: *dearest.* Fury surges through me. *How dare he call me that? Does the man not realize we are in the middle of a* divorce? I tamp the thoughts down and force myself to continue reading.

Dearest,

I know you're refusing my calls and probably not even listening to my voice mails, so I thought I'd try to reach you via mail. I understand why you don't want to talk to me; I don't blame you, given what you believe has happened between me and Jade. But I also feel that it's unfair that you have never given me the chance to respond to Jade's accusations. When I first left home, I was determined not to defend myself—I was sure that Jade would admit the truth within a few days. But clearly, she's not the girl I thought she was, and I cannot let you end our marriage over a bunch of lies.

You have to believe me: I never, ever touched Jade. I never did or said anything inappropriate to her in any way. I would never do that, Marianne; I'm honestly angry that you would even believe that I could have. Don't you think I learned anything from what happened to Cassie and our family after what I did all those years ago? If I had for one second *felt tempted to do anything like that to Jade, I would have left before anything could happen. I promise you that. I would never have put another daughter at risk.*

I don't really understand why Jade is lying about this, but you have to believe that she is *lying. If you truly want a divorce, I won't fight you, but I'm begging you to reconsider. Talk to Jade. I'm sure she'll tell you the truth.*

I will never stop loving you or fighting for what we have together.

Peter

I roll my eyes at the last line and try to convince myself that my husband is merely being pathetic. But there's a niggling doubt at the back of my mind, one that persists for the rest of the day and into the night: *what if? What if he's telling the truth? What if Jade* is *lying?*

That night, I sit in my room trying to read before going to bed, but the words from Peter's letter keep echoing in my mind. After reading the same paragraph five times with absolutely no idea of what it said, I put my book aside and close my eyes, thinking back over Peter's letter and the events of the past six weeks. *Why,* I ask myself, *would Jade have lied about something so serious in the first place? And even if she did, why on earth would she* keep *lying about it for this long? And the medical exam and the interview with the lady from Social Services, not to mention all the therapy I've forced her into—why would she go through all of that if she didn't have to?*

It makes no sense. But I also know Peter, and the initial blind rage that consumed me the afternoon I threw him out has subsided enough that I can tell the tone of his letter is genuine. That doesn't mean I believe he's telling the truth, of course; I'm not sure *what* to believe anymore. On the one hand, there's my husband of almost twenty-seven years, whom I still love, deep down, despite everything. On the other hand, there's my daughter, my precious baby girl, who says her daddy sexually abused her. I don't want her to feel that I've abandoned her the way Cassie believed I did, the first time around.

I know that my children—the older three, at least—still think that I'm in denial about how much our family has changed, and I know they also feel that I've never realized how badly I abandoned them all, especially Cassie, when they needed me most. But I know that I comprehend a lot more than the three of them give me credit for—perhaps what they see as denial is just my attempt to put on a brave face for them and try to save some semblance of a childhood for Jade. Or perhaps I'm just trying to make myself feel better about my horrendous shortcomings as a mother.

Either way, I don't believe that I have my head in the clouds anymore. Not like I used to.

Someone is obviously lying in this situation: either Jade or Peter. But no matter which of them it is, I'm fully aware that our family as a whole is going to lose either way. If Peter's lying and he did abuse Jade, our marriage is over and Jade's life is altered forever. But if Jade's lying—well, our lives are never going to be the same in that case, either. How could I ever trust her again? Even the thought that my thirteen-year-old could lie so convincingly for so long sends chills racing up my spine.

I glance at the clock: Jade should still be awake. *I'm going to ask her now. No point in spending half the night awake because of this.* I pad down the hallway to her bedroom and tap softly on the door. "Can I come in for a minute?"

She's curled up in bed reading, wearing one of Peter's T-shirts. She's practically swimming in it; she's so petite, and she's kept up her running regimen even though school's out. She keeps reassuring me that her coach ordered the team to stay in shape over the summer, but I worry that she might be developing some sort of eating disorder. Yet another concern that keeps me pacing the floor at night.

"What's wrong, Mom?" Jade's nervous voice breaks into my thoughts, and I realize that I've been staring at her.

I swallow a lump in my throat, remembering how Cassie slept in one of Peter's shirts, too, during the two months he was gone the first time. But back then, I could occasionally hear Cassie crying late at night. Jade never cries, at least not that I ever hear.

"I need to talk to you." I shake myself free of the memories—and the guilt that trails them—and sit beside her on the bed. "Your dad wrote me a letter today."

"Like about you guys divorcing?" Her eyes are wide and childlike, betraying nothing.

"No ..." I choose my words carefully, suddenly questioning the wisdom of taking such a direct approach. "He says that, well, I don't want to upset you, and I want you to know that I will always believe you, always. But your father is saying that he didn't do anything to you. He says he thinks you're ... well, that you're lying for some reason."

Her eyes are filling. "And you believe him? Mom, how could you think that I would lie to you about something like that?"

"No, no, Jade," I soothe, stroking her long blonde hair and putting an arm around her shoulders. "No, I'm going to believe whatever you say is the truth. But I wanted to be fair to your father, too, and at least *ask* you. If … if … there's anything you've told me in the past month or so that's *not* true, you can tell me. I won't be angry. I just want to be sure I have all the facts. Do you understand what I'm saying?"

She nods once, leaning her head on my shoulder. Her voice is little more than a whisper. "I would never lie about something like this. I promise."

When I get up to leave the room a few minutes later, Jade stops me. "Hey, Mom? I just … I wanted to say I'm sorry that you have to go through all this. It must totally suck that the guy you've been married to for, like, ever turned into such a sicko. I mean, isn't it kind of weird that Dad … you know … had sort of a *relationship* with us *and* you? Me and Cassie and you, I mean. Dad's, like, *done stuff* to each of us. Isn't that weird?"

I sense the color leaching from my face, and for a moment, I cannot speak. It's not that her exact words were inappropriate; it was more the way in which she said them. In a single sentence, my daughter has managed to pierce my heart with the one arrow that has found its mark countless times in my own thoughts. But I never would've expected to hear anyone say those words aloud, much less Jade. I stare at my daughter as if she's a stranger and wonder, just for an instant, if she said it specifically to hurt me. *She wouldn't do that. She wouldn't be deliberately cruel like that, would she?*

I tell her to go to bed and all but flee from her room. *She is thirteen years old, for God's sake! What is she doing even* thinking *like that?* But in my next breath, I chide myself for not being fair: *after what she's been through, how can I expect her to think normally about sex, even at such a young age?* Then I peruse Peter's letter one last time before going to bed and feel all my doubts resurface.

I lie in bed, trying to fight off the recurring question of *what if*? It is a long time before sleep claims me, and around midnight, I hear a noise I haven't heard since this drama began six weeks ago. It is the unmistakable sound of my daughter's weeping. As my eyes drift closed, I tell myself that that settles it: of course Jade wouldn't be crying like that if she had just lied to my face about the situation with her father. *Peter is the one who lied. He is the one who's ruined our family. My sweet little girl has done nothing wrong.*

Jade

When I was a kid, I was terrified of thunderstorms. I wasn't afraid of anything else that kids my age were normally scared of—the dark, monsters, things like that—but if there was ever a thunderstorm, I would literally hide in my closet or under my bed until it was over. Obviously, I've grown up some since then, but I still hate thunderstorms. But a few weeks ago, when I was out running, I got caught in one.

I knew it was going to storm soon when I left the house, but I figured I could at least get in an hour's run before the storm hit. I was nearly right. The sky got darker and darker the longer I ran, but up until the last ten minutes, there was nothing more than the wind and the nearly-black sky to worry me. Then the thunder started, and suddenly the entire sky opened up over my head. I was soaked in seconds—and that's when a crack of lightning split the sky, way too close for comfort.

At first I was absolutely freaked out. I had to keep running to make it back home, and, even though I *knew* I was only a few minutes from home and the storm wasn't really that close, my heart was still pounding double-time. But I made myself keep going, and before long, I realized that it wasn't actually so bad. Running through the rain like that was amazing, and the thunder and lightning receded a little more with each minute, as I got closer to home. It really wasn't so scary once I relaxed a little bit.

Once I *did* get home, my mom flipped out, of course. She already thinks I run too much, anyway; I think she thinks I have some kind of eating disorder or something because I've kept running even though it's summer. And I run a *lot*. Of course, what Mom doesn't understand is that the only time I can turn my thoughts and feelings off is when I run. When I'm pounding the sidewalks or the trails at the park and my body is coated with sweat, I'm not thinking about anything except the rhythm of my feet and the music on my iPod. But as soon as I step back inside the house, everything comes rushing back.

Anyway, back to the thunderstorm. When I got home that day, despite Mom freaking out, I felt invincible—it was like I had just faced one of my biggest fears and won. It was an incredible sensation.

That's kind of how I felt tonight, when I was able to convince Mom that I was telling the truth about Dad abusing me. When she came in and asked me, point-blank, if I'd been lying, my stomach sank. *There is no way I can pull this off,* I told myself. But amazingly enough, I did. She believed me. And honestly, I felt a twisted sense of pleasure watching her face go pale when I said what I did about Dad having all three of us. I bet I'm the only one in this family of liars and fakes who's ever had the guts to actually *say* that to her face. *She* probably hasn't ever said it out loud before. But you can bet they've all thought it. I know they have. How could they *not*?

See, that's the confusing thing about all this lying stuff that I've been doing lately: part of me feels like I'm an awful, horrendous person, and I'm practically eaten up with guilt. And that part of me—the old Jade, the good little girl I used to be, the one my family thinks I still am—knows that I *deserve* to feel guilty. That was the part of me that cried over everything a couple hours later. That's the part of me that's keeping me awake right now.

But there's also a part of me that feels like I *have* to do this—that I'm the only one in my family who's being *really* honest, even though I sort of had to lie in order to get anyone to listen in the first place. It's difficult to explain, and sometimes it doesn't make sense even to me. If I hadn't lied and accused Dad of abusing me, everyone in my family would've gone on pretending that things were normal again or that what he had done to Cassie was somehow not as big of a deal because he was sorry for it and was trying to change. But when I said he abused me, too, *then* everyone acted the way they should've acted the first time around, when it was Cassie and not me. *Then* they basically all told Dad, through their actions if not their words, what they should've said all along: *you're sick. You don't deserve to be a part of this family anymore because of what you did. It doesn't matter if you're sorry: you can never repay Cassie for what you did to her.*

In the beginning, when I first started lying, all of this made perfect sense to me. Now it's not as clear. It's been six weeks since Dad left, and Levi's wedding is only two weeks away. Dad *will* come to the wedding, since not very many people know yet that my parents are getting a divorce—although most of our friends know that they're separated—and Mom and Levi both decided that it would only fuel more gossip if Dad didn't show up to the wedding at all. So that will be the first time any of us have seen him for two months. And I'm afraid I might lose my nerve and admit everything the second I see his face.

It's hard enough not seeing him or talking to him at all for this long; the shirt of his that I've been sleeping in doesn't really smell like him as much as it used to, and that makes me want to cry. I miss him. Or at least, the good-girl part of me misses him. The other part of me—the evil, twisted, lying part of me—hates him. Sometimes, when I try to think about all this and figure out how I *really* feel, what I *really* think about my dad, it feels like my brain has been put into a blender. It's just too confusing. All of it.

But I'm pretty much stuck now, I guess. There's no way I can confess the truth after all this time, not without ruining everyone's lives. More than I already have, I mean. It's kind of like the other day when I was caught in that thunderstorm: I have to just keep running. Maybe what I'm doing is wrong and dangerous—but if I just stop, if I just give up? That feels infinitely more risky.

Maybe I'm just going insane. Or maybe I'm really an evil person, deep down, and it took this happening for me to realize it. Maybe I'm just a coward. Or all three?

This will get better once Levi's wedding is over. Anyhow, that's what I keep telling myself. Once the wedding is over, I won't have to see Dad ever again, if I don't want to, and he and Mom will get a divorce, and he'll be out of our lives. Once that happens, I won't have to deal with these two parts of me: the good girl, the one who feels guilty and horrible all the time; and the evil girl, the one who knows exactly what she's doing and *likes* it.

Two more weeks. That's all I have to do: get through the next two weeks, handle the wedding, and everything will be fine.

It has to be. It just has to be. I can't keep living like this much longer.

Levi

This should be the happiest time of my life—in a little over a week, I'll marry the love of my life and start the first chapter of *our* lives. Together. I should be walking on air right now, but instead, I'm pacing around my office at the church, trying to distract myself from the fury that's been building inside me for the past seven weeks.

After that disastrous night two years ago when I attacked Dad, I promised myself that I would never let myself get *that* angry again. I promised myself that I would never react the way I did that night. I've been mostly successful. Even when Cassie first called me in a blind panic and told me what Dad had done to Jade, I managed not to completely lose it. Oh, I was angry—you bet I was angry. I contemplated hopping on the next plane and flying across the country just for the pleasure of planting my fist in my father's face one more time.

But I held it together and turned to the people I knew I could trust to help me through it: Anna, of course, and Ron, the senior pastor here at New Covenant Church and also, incidentally, my boss. The two of them have been amazing the past seven weeks, praying for me constantly and making sure that I know they're available if I ever need or want to talk.

So far, I haven't, at least not in any great detail. Anna has gently suggested, more than once, that I should go back into therapy. After all, it seems to be helping Cassie a lot—she's even started going back to church. Before this nightmare with Jade happened, I never would've envisioned Cassie back on speaking terms with God. "There's nothing wrong with needing some extra support and prayer, Levi," Anna insists. "And if it's helping Cassie so much, there's no reason to think it won't help you, too."

Something in me resists the idea, even though I know, deep down, that Anna is probably right. I'm a youth pastor, for heaven's sake: *I'm* the one who's supposed to be counseling the kids in my youth group. I'm not supposed to be the one *needing* counseling. It infuriates me that, after all this time and all the progress that I thought I had made over the past few years, I seem to be right back where I started, if not further behind. It's as if I'm frozen in the two moments, five years apart, where I first learned that my father had sexually abused my sisters. I just cannot get past the thought of him hurting Cassie and Jade like that. And while I know it's awful of me to ever compare my sisters this way, I also find myself far angrier over what he did to Jade.

I was such an idiot. I trusted *him and I honestly never thought he would do something like this again. How could I have been so naïve?* Sometimes I can't decide who I'm angrier with: my dad or myself.

For the past seven weeks, I've done a fairly good job of keeping my rage in check, pushing down the murderous thoughts that try to creep in late at night and burying my feelings about the whole sordid mess under my hectic work schedule and all the plans for the wedding. But now that there's less than ten days until I'll see my dad face-to-face, it's becoming harder and harder to tamp down my anger. I manage to remain composed in public, distracted by the kids in our youth group and the small dramas of their lives, but when I'm alone with Anna and my guard is down, my real feelings begin to show through the cracks in my armor. She's been nothing but supportive, just like she's been throughout the entire two and a half years I've known her. Sometimes, I feel a flash of resentment toward her because of it. Does she *never* get impatient with me and my moodiness? How can she be so calm and composed about all of this, all the time?

As if on cue, Anna appears in the doorway of my office. She sees me pacing, and her whole expression softens and her large blue eyes fill with sympathy. "Hard day?"

I shake my head, rolling my eyes. "You could say that."

"Well, I'm pretty much done for the day. You want to go grab some dinner, and we can talk about it?"

I hesitate a moment, just looking at her, drinking in the sight of her. "You're really beautiful, you know that?" It's true—she's tall and willowy, with a smile that captivates my attention, and my heart. At the risk of sounding too clichéd, what makes Anna truly stunning is her inner beauty. Her sense of humor. Her intelligence. Her compassion. Her absolute commitment to God, to me, and to the kids we've been called to teach, mentor, and serve.

Anna blushes. "I was *asking* about dinner."

I pull her into my arms and kiss her, thinking back to the conversation I had with Ian a couple days ago. I had called to ask him if he would consider being my best man, since my dad obviously isn't going to be able to fill that role. That had naturally led to us talking about him and Cassie, since she's going to be one of the bridesmaids. Ian had sighed and said, "I don't know what's going to happen with the two of us, man. I don't want to end things, and I don't think she does, either, but … I just don't know. I wanted to ask you something, while we're on the subject of relationships and all that: has it been hard for you and Anna to stay virgins until you get married?"

I had laughed outright. "Of course it's hard! But we've tried really hard to give ourselves boundaries and stick to them. And honestly, at this point, it's less than two weeks away, and if we gave in now, I would probably never forgive myself. We've waited this long; we can definitely wait a few more days."

Ian sounded subdued. "That's really awesome, Levi. I think it's great that you guys have stuck to your convictions like that, especially since it hasn't been easy. I wonder if … Maybe things would've been different for me and Cass if we had done that. Waited to have sex, I mean." Then he gave a sharp, bitter laugh. "Although who am I kidding? For the first few months we were together, before that party at Paul's house, that's all our relationship *was*. I definitely couldn't have done what you and Anna are doing. You should get some kind of medal, Leev."

Anna's hands framing my face bring me back to the present. "It seems like maybe you need some time alone tonight. We can do dinner tomorrow, or Friday, if you want."

"I'm sorry," I sigh heavily. "I think I just need some space. Not because of you. It's just this whole thing with my dad. It's … it's really getting harder to deal with all of it, Anna. And I don't want to put you in the middle of all of it. That's so unfair to you. You didn't ask to be dragged into all this crap."

"Hey," she stops me with a hand on my arm. "Don't talk like that. I'm here because *I love you*. Because I *want* to be here for you. I understand if you need some space; that's fine. But if you need me, I'm *here*, Levi. Don't push me away or shut me out, okay? You had to go through this on your own for three years. You don't have to do that anymore. All right?"

I kiss her again, long and slow, as my answer. *God, how did I ever end up with such an incredible woman by my side?* "Thank you, Anna. You're amazing. You really are."

She ruffles my hair. "Not as amazing as you."

"I know," I tease.

She rolls her eyes at me and turns to leave. "Levi?" She turns back to face me, leaning against the doorframe. "Just remember that none of what happened to Jade was your fault. It wasn't. Don't forget that, okay?" Then she's gone, leaving me alone with my tortured thoughts and that rising current of rage that I feel powerless to combat. I'm tired of fighting it. *Look where that got me the first time.*

So, instead of trying to distract myself from the burning sensation in my chest, I surrender to it. At first, it seems as if I'm simply angry with myself and Dad; but as I ride the current of emotions to the center, I'm confronted with a stunning realization. A realization that sends me practically running to my car and peeling out of the parking lot, desperate to escape the crushing weight of the truth. But, as I've learned so well over the past few years, some truths cannot be outrun. This is one of them.

I drive around aimlessly for as long as I can, wishing there was somewhere secluded to go. My mind keeps returning to the story in the Bible where Jacob wrestles the angel, and to the book of Job, where Job argues with God after everything precious to him is taken away. I wonder what it would be like to actually wrestle with God, to force Him to answer your questions. *As if a mere human could ever try to hold God accountable.*

I shouldn't even be *thinking* these kinds of thoughts; I'm a pastor. I'm supposed to be the one who counsels people through these types of questions. I'm not supposed to be wondering what it would be like to wrestle with God, to scream in His face, to have it out with *Him* because, after all, *He's* the one I'm really angry with. Even though I know I shouldn't feel this way, even though it goes against everything I believe in and everything I stand for, it's true. Beneath the surface of my anger at my dad, my mom, even myself, pulses a steady rhythm of anger toward God.

I guess, deep down, I've always known I was angry with Him. I just didn't want to admit it. There are a lot of things I haven't been willing to admit, and the weight of those unspoken truths is slowly dragging me down. Even though I promised myself that I wouldn't ever get as out-of-control as I was on that night three years ago when I tried to beat Dad senseless, as I speed over the wet roads toward my apartment, I can feel myself getting close to that level of rage. The dark clouds and pouring rain suit my mood perfectly.

I manage to hold it together until I get back to my apartment. It's raining so hard that I'm drenched by the time I get inside, a trail of water marking my footsteps as I pace through the house.

I can't stop thinking about my sisters, as if a movie reel of my memories of them from over the years is playing in my mind. I see Cassie at her swim meets; Jade learning to ride a bike without training wheels; Cassie and me playing basketball in the driveway for hours on autumn weekends; Jade at her ballet recitals when she was little. I remember how innocent both of them were, especially Jade. Cassie was my best friend growing up, but Jade was everyone's baby. She was the one I always wanted to protect, the one who could melt me with just a look, the one who had me wrapped around her little finger. I let the memories roll over me and then I think of my father touching both of my sisters. I allow myself to imagine it in a way I haven't before—what the girls must have thought at the moment Dad first came into their rooms, how terrified they must have been.

Then I break my promise to myself.

I grab the closest heavy object I can find, a paperweight off the desk in my tiny office, and I hurl it at the wall, feeling a twist of pleasure at the sound it makes as it crashes through the cheap wood. "Where are You?" I scream. "*Where are You?* Why are You letting this happen? How could You have just *let* him do those things to them? Didn't You *care?* Didn't You care that they were alone? That they were scared? Why didn't You stop him?"

I scream my questions at God until my throat is raw and my face is soaked with tears. Some rational part of my mind is horrified by this display; I'm supposed to *trust* God, not question Him. But I'm so tired of faking it, of running, of pretending that things are fine. I'm done lying and pretending. I give full vent to my anger and let it exhaust me.

Once it's all over, nothing's different—on the surface, nothing has changed. And yet, everything has. I pick up the phone and call Ron. "I think I might need some help dealing with all this family stuff. You know, like therapy. Can you recommend anyone?"

When the conversation is over, I hang up the phone and lean against the wall, closing my eyes. It feels as if a huge weight has been lifted from my shoulders, despite the lingering confusion and guilt.

Where are You?

Cassie

Somehow, before I even had time to blink, June and July flashed by, and now it's the middle of August, the day before Levi's wedding. It's amazing how quickly the past two months have sped by and how much has changed. How much *I've* changed. My twice-weekly sessions with Dr. Rogers have opened up a whole new world for me. Even though it has been grueling to relive the memories and face some of the truths about myself and my choices over the past five years, it has also been incredibly liberating. It's as if a light bulb came on, and I can finally understand the person I've become. After all these years of attempting to merely survive the storm of emotions unleashed by what my father did to me, now I'm beginning to hope that, soon, I'll be able to *live*, not just survive.

I started going back to church, too, a few weeks ago. And just like my therapy sessions, I'm amazed at the change that's occurring in me as a result of it. I can't really explain *why* I decided to go back to church after almost five years of making only occasional appearances there to placate my parents, but I think it had something to do with the things I was uncovering in my sessions with Dr. Rogers. I knew I couldn't handle the emotional fallout of those sessions on my own.

I don't quite have the level of faith that Levi and my parents have, but I've been praying daily and going to church with Mom and Jade. At first, I felt pretty hypocritical for deciding to turn back to God only when I was truly desperate. I didn't even know where to start the first few times I prayed; it had been so long since I'd prayed anything other than generic *"God bless my family and friends and keep them all safe"* kinds of prayers. But it has been surprisingly easy to fall back into the type of relationship I had with God when I was younger, before my faith splintered along with my family. I regret running away from Him for as long as I did. I'm nowhere near where I probably should be yet, but at least I'm trying.

This weekend is going to test the fragile peace and stability I've achieved to the absolute limit. Watching my older brother get married would be a little bit emotional anytime, but given the current situation in our family, I'll be lucky to make it through this with my sanity intact. It seems like Mom and Levi have lost theirs, though; I don't know *what* makes them think it will be acceptable for Dad to come to the wedding. How is Jade supposed to handle seeing him there, not to mention all of us pretending that things are still somewhat normal in our family? How are *any* of us supposed to handle it, for that matter?

And Ian ... My stomach somersaults at the realization that it's only four hours until I'll see him at the rehearsal tonight. I'm determined to keep my composure—I will not cry or make a fool of myself. This is Levi and Anna's big weekend; I'm not going to ruin it for them. Maybe Ian and I will have a chance to talk after the wedding. Just the thought of hearing his voice, seeing him face-to-face and being close enough to touch him makes me weak-kneed. *Get it together, girl. You can't act like this.*

The door to the hotel room flies open, and Jade bounds in, throwing herself onto the bed where I've strewn the contents of my suitcase in an effort to unpack and reorganize. "Oh my *God*, Cassie! This is so exciting! Only four more hours!"

I can't help but smile at her. "Someone needs to switch to decaf."

"Are you kidding me? Aren't you so excited? Levi's getting *married*! And we get to be bridesmaids together!" She squeals and starts jumping on the bed like a five-year-old.

"You're just a junior bridesmaid," I remind her with fake condescension.

Jade sticks her tongue out at me, but she's too pumped up to be annoyed. "I. Am. So. Excited."

"Really? Gee, I never would've guessed."

"You are *no* fun! Aren't you excited? Geez, Cass ..."

"I am, I am," I insist, laughing at her craziness. "I just ... I'm a little nervous, I guess."

Jade stops jumping and sits on the bed. "Because of seeing Ian tonight?"

"Yeah, that's part of it," I sigh.

"Oh, you guys are going to get back together this weekend. I know it. You *have* to, Cass! You guys are, like, perfect together. I can't believe you haven't even talked to him in all this time."

"It's a little complicated," I stammer.

"Do you miss him?" Jade's completely calm now, lying on her stomach and staring at me intently.

A few weeks ago, that question would've made me burst into sobs. Now, there's just a slight ache in my chest as I answer, "Every day."

"Do you miss having sex with him?"

I whirl around and stare at her, feeling my cheeks redden. I cannot believe she just said that. "Jade!"

"I'm just *saying*, if you're used to having sex a lot, it's probably hard to not have *any* for two months. Is it?"

I stare at her for a few seconds before I'm able to answer. She's changed at least as much as I have in the past two months—and not exactly in a good way. A few months ago, she never would have asked a question like that. *What's happening to her?* "Jade, that's a completely inappropriate question. I'm not going to answer that."

She rolls her eyes. "Whatever. Sheesh, Cassie. You're so uptight lately."

I bite my tongue to keep from retorting with something sarcastic. I should cut her some slack, after all; the kid's been through so much lately, and isn't it *normal* to wonder about sex at her age? "Maybe I am. But I'm not going to talk about me and Ian. If you have a specific question about sex you want to ask me, I'll answer. But I'm not talking about personal stuff like that. Sorry."

Jade rolls her eyes again. "Fine."

That's another change: normally she would've apologized for saying something so rude. *Maybe she's just nervous about seeing Dad tomorrow at the wedding.*

As if she read my mind, Jade asks, "So, you worried about seeing Dad?"

My stomach tightens. "Yeah. I'm glad we don't have to see him tonight at the rehearsal dinner, at least. How about you? How are you doing with all that, anyway? We haven't really had much of a chance to talk lately."

She shrugs, staring at the floral pattern on the bedspread. "I'm fine. I'm nervous about seeing him, but it's going to be so crazy tomorrow, I probably won't even have time to think about it, you know?"

"Are you sure you're doing okay? I mean, just with … everything? Not just seeing him tomorrow, but all of it."

She looks up at me, her blue eyes snapping. "I *said* I'm fine. Jesus."

I flinch. "You don't have to swear."

"Oh, that's right, you're a holy roller now. I forgot," she sneers.

"Why are you acting like this?"

"Like *what*? I say one little thing, and you jump all over me!"

"Jade, come on. You never used to talk like that. What's going on?"

"*Nothing* is going on! I'm acting the way I always do. *You're* the one who's changed. You're no fun anymore. Ever since you and Ian broke up, you've been such a Goody Two-shoes. It *sucks* to hang out with you now."

"You're not much fun yourself," I shoot back. "Seriously, Jade, what is going on with you lately? I know everything with Dad has been hard, and I know I haven't really been there for you like I should have. I'm sorry for that. I was just … such a mess after Ian and I broke up. But I'm here now. If you need to talk or scream or cry or whatever, then I'm here for you. But you can't keep acting like …"

"Like such a bitch?" She supplies.

"*Stop* it! You're a good kid, Jay, and you can do better than this. You and I both know that."

She holds my gaze for a minute, her eyes showing nothing of what she's thinking. Then the corners of her mouth tip in a smirk. "Or maybe I've always been like this deep down, and you just can't handle it. And besides, you have a lot of room to talk."

A chill sweeps over me. "What is that supposed to mean?"

She continues to hold my gaze, still smirking. "Collin told me there's a bathroom stall in the guys' room at the high school that's devoted exclusively to you."

No. No. No! She's not supposed to know about that yet. I'm supposed to get another year to figure out how to tell her. "Jade, I …"

"Forget it. Just forget it." She flounces out of the room, only to reappear in the doorway a few seconds later. "You said I could ask a question about sex if I wanted to? Well, I have one, since you're obviously an expert. When you have sex with … well, whoever's the guy of the moment, do you think about him while you're doing it? Or do you think about Dad?" She smiles—a cold, calculating smile—and darts away.

I stand there for a moment after she leaves, unable to move or speak and not entirely sure that I'm even breathing. Then my stomach heaves, and I stagger toward the tiny bathroom and vomit. I lean back against the wall until the room stops spinning. I don't know when my sweet little sister morphed into some sort of vixen, but I never would've thought her capable of saying something so heartless to me.

What is going on with her? God, please, please help me here. If this is what the rest of this weekend is going to be like, I don't think I can handle it.

Jade's question haunts me the rest of the afternoon, whispering in my ear as I get ready for the rehearsal. *Do you think about Dad?*

If she only knew.

Three hours later, as I'm getting ready for the rehearsal, I'm so nervous my hands are trembling. I can barely hold steady long enough to apply my makeup. The confrontation with Jade earlier left me shaken, and the thought of seeing Ian again and figuring out what in the world I'm supposed to say to him reduces me to a mass of nerves. *God, please, please, help me tonight. I don't know if I can do this.*

Before I know it, it's time to leave for the church. Ben and I ride in one of the rental cars, while Mom and Jade take the other. Jade and I still haven't spoken since our argument earlier, something that even Ben comments on as we drive to the church. Once we get there, Levi comes out to meet us.

I blink back tears when he hugs me; I didn't realize how much I'd missed him until I saw him. He hugs each of us, holding Jade the longest. I look away, unable to bear the sorrow on Levi's face and my sudden surge of anger toward our sister. The tension is so thick you could slice it with a butter knife, and the air around the five of us practically hums with the things we're not saying.

Thank God for Anna; she comes out to greet us and relieves some of the strain. I love Anna, and I think she and I would be close friends if she and Levi lived nearby. As it is, I've only met her in person once, at Christmas last year, and I liked her instantly. She's perfect for Levi—not nearly as high-strung and intense as he can be. Anna helps to balance him.

And suddenly there he is. Everything seems to be moving in slow motion. *Ian ...* I'm fully aware that the rest of my family is watching me, waiting to see how I'll react, but pretending not to.

Ian comes to stand beside Levi and Anna, nodding to me. "Hey, Cassie."

"Ian," I nod back.

He's four feet away; it takes all my restraint to keep from jumping into his arms and begging him to take me back. I look away, feeling myself start to blush as I remember Jade's question from earlier: *Do you miss having sex with him?* I try to think of something, anything, else, but images from the past three years with him keep intruding. All those nights come rushing back and I can't possibly look him in the eye.

Anna comes to my rescue, grabbing my arm and propelling me into the church, chattering about the rehearsal. As soon as we get inside, she stops and studies me closely. "You okay? I'm sorry that was so awkward."

I wave her concern away. "No, no, I'm fine. It's just ... a little hard. But it's okay. I'm thrilled to be in your wedding, and I know Ian is, too."

Anna smiles sympathetically. "You're such a wonderful person, Cassie. Levi and I both really appreciate what you're doing for us; we know it's not easy."

She's mostly right. As the night wears on, though, it becomes easier to ignore Ian. Right before Ben and I are heading out the door to go back to the hotel, Ian corners me. I've managed to avoid him all night, but now there's no way to escape without seeming rude.

"Hey." Ian runs a hand through his hair, his signature gesture when he's nervous. "I ... Can we talk sometime this weekend? I mean, not now. I know it's late and we have a big day tomorrow. But maybe—maybe at the reception tomorrow?"

Breathe. My voice is surprisingly steady. "Yeah, of course."

His relief is palpable. "Thank you. Well, I'll let you go. I know Ben is waiting." He starts to leave, then glances over his shoulder at me. "Cass? I ... I really miss you. More than you probably know."

As I'm getting ready for bed back at the hotel, I'm still rolling Ian's words—*I really miss you*—over and over in my mind, trying to make them last the way I used to do with Jolly Ranchers when I was a kid. It's well after midnight by the time I crawl into the queen-sized bed, trying to stay as far from Jade's side of the bed as possible. To my astonishment, she breaks the silence just as I'm about to drift off to sleep.

"Cassie? You still awake?"

"Barely," I yawn. "What do you want?"

It's impossible to see my sister's face, but her voice is trembling. "I wanted to apologize. For what I said earlier. What I said about Dad, and what Collin told me ... I shouldn't have said those things."

I'm wide awake now. "No," I agree, "you shouldn't have. And you shouldn't have asked about my personal relationship with Ian, either. I know I always tell you that you can talk to me about anything, but, Jade, there are some things you just *can't* ask me, okay? And asking questions about my sex life is one of them. I'm just not going to go there with you. It's not fair to Ian."

"I know," she answers in a small voice. "I know I shouldn't have asked you. I'm sorry."

"It's okay. I forgive you." I grope for her hand in the darkness, find it, and squeeze tight. "Friends again?"

Jade squeezes back, and I expect her to launch into some crazy story about the rehearsal dinner tonight, but she's silent for several minutes. Just when I think she's fallen asleep, she clears her throat. "Do you believe that God can forgive you for anything?"

Taken aback, I fumble for a response for a moment. "I ... Yeah, I think so. You mean like if I killed somebody or something awful? I think if you're truly sorry for whatever you did, and you're willing to change and never do that thing again, then of course God will forgive you."

Tears fill her voice. "What if ... What if you do something really bad over and over again, and part of you isn't sorry for it? Do you think God will forgive you then?"

I prop myself up on one elbow, trying to get a glimpse of her face. "Honey, what's wrong? What's this really about?"

"Nothing. Never mind. It's late; we should go to sleep."

"Are you crying?"

"I'm fine. It was a stupid question anyway. I'm going to sleep now."

I know she's not fine, but I also know that if I push her we could end up in the same situation we were in earlier today, and I'm not willing to risk that. I lie back down and try to sleep. Just before I drift off, Jade's voice floats over me one more time.

"Cassie? If ... if I told you something about me, something really bad that I did recently, would you still love me?"

My eyelids feel like they're weighted with concrete, and I'm having difficulty concentrating on what Jade is saying. "Hmmm? Of course I'd still love you. What did you do?"

"Never mind." Her voice is very far away. "It doesn't matter, anyway."

The last thing I hear before sleep claims me is the sound of my sister starting to cry.

Jade

Any normal girl my age would be thrilled on a day like this—getting to be a junior bridesmaid in a wedding, complete with tons of professionally-applied makeup and a gorgeous hairstyle. The dress is beautiful, a form-fitting strapless gown in a dark shade of peach. Cassie squeals when she sees me. "Jade, you look *amazing*! You look like you're at least eighteen! Oh, my gosh!"

I should be happy. I should be *thrilled*. Instead, it's all I can do not to burst into tears when I look at my reflection in the mirror. Because I can see what the rest of my family can't: I'm a fraud. An imposter. A liar. A fake. And a coward, because I came so close to telling Cassie the truth last night and chickened out. I stare at my reflection menacingly, as if I could shoot darts with my eyes. *I hate you, I hate you, I hate you.*

Once we get to the church, I plaster on a smile as my family oohs and ahhhs over me and Cassie. Mom takes about a million pictures of us with Levi and Ben, her eyes already misting. "My babies are all grown up." But the camera *finally* stops clicking, and Cassie and I hurry off to see Anna.

She's breathtaking. "Oh, I *so* want your dress when I get married!" I exclaim before I can stop myself. Anna laughs, blushing. Her dress is simply gorgeous. For the first time that day, I feel a flutter of the excitement I felt yesterday afternoon, before Cassie and I fought. *Levi's* really *getting married!* I can't wait to see the look on his face when Anna walks down the aisle and he sees her in her dress for the first time. *Maybe this will be an awesome day, after all.*

My happy mood vanishes when I excuse myself to go to the ladies' room about thirty minutes before the ceremony is supposed to start, and I run into the one person I hoped that I wouldn't see here. Emotion slams into me like an oncoming train, and the room spins crazily. I hadn't expected the sight of him to impact me this way; I thought I'd be able to walk right by him with my head held high, ignoring him the way I know my siblings are planning to do. I was so wrong.

"Jade," he stammers. "Honey, I've missed you."

Daddy. I can't speak past the lump in my throat, and tears prick at the corners of my eyes. I don't know what I'd imagined: that he'd look different, morphed into some type of monster just because that's the way the rest of my family sees him now. But of course, he looks just the same as he always has, except that he's noticeably thinner. Standing face-to-face with him like this, it's suddenly hard to remember why I feel so justified in lying about him the way I have.

"Sweetheart, we need to talk. And I think you know why." Dad lowers his eyebrows at me, the way he always used to do when I got in trouble as a kid. "I don't know why you've been lying to your mother and everyone else, but it needs to stop."

One of the tears I've been fighting to hold back escapes, and Dad's expression softens when he realizes I'm crying. "We don't have to talk about this now. I don't want you to ruin your makeup. You really do look beautiful, Jade." He runs his finger down the side of my face. "My little girl is growing up."

"Daddy …" I choke out, unsure what I should say but knowing I have to say *something*.

"Shhhh. It's okay. Don't cry. We'll work this out. I'm not angry at you, honey. And I know that you'll do the right thing. I love you, you know that, right?"

I just nod. It's only after I hurry away that I realize what I should have said was this: *I love you, too. And I'm sorry.*

I don't know how I make it through the ceremony without passing out or bursting into tears or doing something equally embarrassing. The wedding is beautiful, as we all knew it would be, but I can hardly focus on it at all. I'm too distracted by the sight of my parents sitting in the front row, pretending to be the perfect couple, and the noxious combination of guilt, fear, anger, and betrayal churning in my stomach. I honestly think I might throw up.

Somehow, I make it through the ceremony without getting sick, but when the pastor says, "Ladies and gentlemen, may I present, for the first time, Mr. and Mrs. Levi Wilson," I lose it. All my makeup is ruined in moments by the tears streaming down my face, and, to my utter humiliation, I can't seem to stop crying. Not when Anna's cousin, one of the groomsmen, escorts me down the aisle. Not when my family gathers in the back of the church and embraces, all stiff arms and tight smiles, putting on a good show for the congregation. Not when all the guests file by us and head downstairs for the reception in the church fellowship hall.

"Awww, honeybunch, don't cry," Cassie pulls me aside, smiling. "It's not like you'll never see Levi again. And besides, you're going to ruin your makeup for the pictures."

When I still can't stem the flood of tears, Cassie's brow furrows in concern. "Jade? What's wrong?"

Everyone crowds around me, trying to calm me down and figure out why, exactly, I'm crying so hard. I pull away from them and break through the little circle they've formed around me, walking straight to Dad. He's been hanging as far back as he can ever since the guests departed; and with the looks my siblings and Mom have been giving him, who can blame him? His eyes widen as I approach him, and he glances around wildly at the rest of them, obviously bracing himself for some type of fight.

"I have something to say to you." I'm crying so hard that my words are barely intelligible. "I'm sorry. I'm so, so sorry that I lied."

Mom shoves herself between me and Dad. "Jade, *what* are you talking about? This is not the time and place for a discussion with your father." She leans close enough to hiss in my ear. "You are going to *ruin* your brother's big day. Whatever this is about, it can wait, young lady!"

"No," I shake my head at her. "No, it can't." I turn around to face the rest of my family. Ian has slipped into the back of the room sometime, when I wasn't looking. The expression on his face is enough to wilt me. *He knows. He's always known.*

"I have something to say to all of you," I announce, slightly more composed even though the ground might as well be crumbling beneath my feet. "I ... I lied. About everything. I lied. I'm sorry." My composure is swept away in another flood of tears. "I'm so, so sorry."

Then I do what I do best: I lift up the hem of my pretty dress and run out of the church. There's a beautiful garden near the back of the church's property with a gazebo in the center of it. I sink down onto one of the benches in the gazebo and bury my head in my hands. *What have I done?*

Cassie

After Jade runs out, it's as if a bomb has been dropped in the center of the church. At first, we all stand there staring at each other, shell-shocked. Within moments, that numbness begins to wear off and a rising tide of anger begins to build inside of me.

Levi is the first to break the silence, his joyful expression from minutes earlier replaced by one of pure bewilderment. "Pet— I mean, Dad ... was ... was Jade saying that she lied about ... you touching her?"

For the first time in months, I truly look at my father. I'd avoided his gaze all during the wedding, and I'd been determined to not even talk to him today if I could help it. But now I look straight at him. His face is lined with a mixture of emotions: anguish, a little bit of anger, and profound relief. "Yes," he answers simply, sighing heavily. "I'm so sorry that she's ruining your big day, son. But yes, it's true: she lied to all of you."

Beside me, Ben swears under his breath and Mom gasps. "Peter ..." she whispers, her face stricken. Levi clenches his fists, and Anna appears just as shocked and speechless as Mom.

She lied to me. All this time, she lied. The thought drums in my brain like a mantra. The tide of anger is shifting into a flood, powerful enough to suck me under. I don't fully know what I'm planning to do when I run out of the church after Jade, ignoring the rest of my family's cries behind me. *She lied, she lied, she lied.*

It's not difficult to find her, and she doesn't try to run away when she sees me coming. She merely stands up, wipes her eyes, and appears to brace herself.

I've barely come to a stop in front of her when I backhand her as hard as I can. The sound of my hand connecting with her face seems to echo in the tiny space between us, and the momentum pushes her backward. She grabs her face, staggering. "I guess I deserved that," she manages weakly, once she can speak again.

"And you deserve this, too." I hit her again. And again. I'm raising my hand to hit her a fourth time when someone grabs my hand from behind.

Ian. "Cassie, don't!"

I ignore him and glare at Jade as she cowers on the bench in front of me, sobbing. "I'm sorry, Cassie," she begs. "I didn't ... I didn't mean for all of this to ... I thought I could stop it ..."

"Shut up! Just shut up! I cannot *believe* you did this! What kind of sick person does something like this? What is wrong with you?"

"I know, I *know*," she sobs. "I'm sorry."

"Do you have any *idea* what you've done to all of us? To *Dad*? Mom was going to divorce him over your little lie! Didn't that *matter* to you? Ben moved back home and has been practically killing himself with the commute back and forth to work. He would never have done that for anyone but you. And Levi—congratulations, Jade, you just managed to single-handedly ruin his wedding! How do you think he and Anna are feeling right now? Or do you even care?"

"I *said* I was sorry. I know …"

Only Ian's grip on my arm keeps me from punching her in the face again. "I don't want to hear about how sorry you are. I don't want to hear *anything* from you, do you understand me? I really don't care if I never speak to you again after today."

All the color leaches from her face. "Cassie …"

"I mean it. We're done, Jade. This is the last conversation you and I will have for a long, long time. Maybe ever."

Her lips are white. "You don't mean that."

"Don't you get it?" I explode. "Don't you understand what the past few months have *been* like for me? It was hell to watch you go through all of the stuff with Social Services and the doctors and the therapist, but I came to every appointment and did everything I could to be there for you because I didn't want you to feel alone like I did when it happened to me. It almost killed me to relive all of that, but I did it. And you know what's even worse?" Tears are streaming down my face, the words spilling out from some dark corner of my heart. "I lost Ian because of you. I gave up *the love of my life* because I *believed* you were telling the truth about Dad. You have no *idea* what it's like to lose someone that you love that much. So yeah, Jade, I do mean it: I really don't care if I ever speak to you again."

"Cassie, wait!" Jade pleads.

"You came within an inch of destroying our *entire* family, Jade! Think about that for a while—I mean, *really* think about it. Let that sink in. You were willing to let Dad's life be ruined, just so you could get back at him or whatever you were trying to do? You make me sick."

With that, I yank my arm out of Ian's grip and walk out of the gazebo and into the surrounding garden. Ian follows me, silent for a few moments. "Cassie?" he says tentatively.

I can't risk looking at him. I know I'll burst into tears again and make a complete fool of myself if I do. "I'm not going to apologize for hitting her. She deserves a lot worse than that."

"No, that's not what I was going to say. I think you did the right thing. I just didn't want you to beat the crap out of her right before the reception. That might not look too good. No, I … I was going to say that—what you said back there? You haven't lost me, Cass. Wait, wait." He lays a hand on my arm, bringing me to a stop. "Look at me."

He gently raises my chin so that I'm looking him in the eye. "You haven't lost me," he repeats. "I'm here." My own eyes are so full of tears that his face blurs, but I'm pretty sure he's crying, too.

"Can we … Do you think we can start over?" My voice is trembling. "I know … I know we have a lot to talk about, and I still have a lot of stuff to work through, but if you're willing to take a chance on a crazy girl like me …"

He reaches over and slips the engagement ring off of my finger, and my heart plummets. I hadn't been willing to take it off, even weeks after we broke up; I kept hoping he would come back. Now I have my answer.

Ian drops down on one knee. "I know I've already asked you this, but … Cassie, will you marry me?"

I'm sure my mouth is hanging open, and I couldn't stop crying even if I wanted to. "Yes, baby. Yes, of course I'll marry you!"

He adjusts the ring on my finger again and pulls me close. When he kisses me, everything in me starts to settle. It feels as if I am falling back into place. It feels like coming home.

Levi

How could the best day of my life turn into such a nightmare? This is the thought that's running through my mind after Cassie tears out of the church after Jade. Beside me, Anna stiffens. "Someone has to stop her," she whispers just loud enough for me to hear. She squeezes my arm. "*Levi!*"

But I can't make myself move. I can't force myself to chase after my sisters and be the hero this time. I just can't. Right at this moment, all I can focus on is how deeply Jade's hurt me and Anna on *our* day. Somewhere in the back of my mind, I'm aware that the rest of my family is suffering just as much, if not more, but I don't care. This is my wedding day, and my selfish little sister ruined it.

While I'm wallowing in self-pity, the rest of my family is looking at each other. It's as if they're all thinking the same thing, but no one wants to make the first move. Ian catches my eye. "I'll go. I think I can calm her down." With that, he's gone.

"Kick Jade in the tail for me while you're at it," Ben mutters as the front door slams behind Ian.

"Levi?" Anna whispers. "Honey, are you okay?"

No, I'm not okay. I'm not even on the same planet *as okay.* I just shake my head at her and pull her into my chest. "Baby, I'm so sorry this is happening."

She swallows hard. "Me too. But it's not your fault. None of this is your fault."

"I should never have invited Dad. If he hadn't been here, Jade probably wouldn't have said anything. I'm so sorry."

"Levi, he's your *father*! And after … what just happened—I'm glad you *did* invite him. I mean, can you imagine how hard the past two months have been for him?"

An ugly surge of anger twists my stomach into knots. *If it's been so hard for him, why didn't he say anything two months ago? Why did he let Jade get away with this? The past two months have been hard for all of us, and it's at least partially his fault. If he had just told somebody …*

Just then the photographer pokes his head in the door leading to the sanctuary. "Anna? Levi? Are you two ready for pictures? Or am I interrupting something? I'm sorry … I can come back later."

And just like that, I'm plunged back into reality. No matter how much I want to get away from here and just talk to Anna, there's no chance of that for the next several hours. She squeezes my hand. "We'll get through this," she whispers. "It's only a few hours. We can do it." Then she turns her million-dollar smile onto the photographer. "It's no problem. We can do pictures now."

Thank God for small mercies: all the pictures except the ones of Anna and me together were done before the ceremony. And since Cassie and Jade may very well be pulling each other's hair out somewhere outside, that's probably a very good thing. Not to mention that the rest of my family looks completely dumbstruck.

"Can you give us two minutes?" I ask. The photographer nods and retreats into the sanctuary. I inhale deeply, hoping to pull courage from somewhere, grip Anna's hand a little tighter, and walk across the foyer to my father.

"Dad." My voice cracks and I clear my throat, praying that I can speak without breaking down. "Dad, I just … I'm sorry. I'm sorry she did this to you, and I'm sorry I believed her. I …" *Great, now I'm crying.* "I'm glad you came today. You should've been my best man. And I'm sorry."

Beside me, Anna's weeping, and I can hear Mom softly crying behind me. Dad's eyes are full of tears. "Son …" His voice trails off and he simply embraces me. We stand like that for what feels like an eternity—both of us crying. "I'm so proud of you, Levi. I'm so proud of the man you've become."

Once Dad and I finally step away from each other, I pull Anna into my arms and kiss her as long and slow as I can. "How many wedding days are we going to have in our lives, huh?" I tease with a levity I'm far from feeling. "Let's enjoy it."

Jade may have just ruined all our lives for the foreseeable future. But I'm not going to let her ruin this day—I can't do that to my beautiful wife. So I plaster on a smile and follow Anna into the sanctuary, praying for calm and a grace I don't feel. Even without looking back into the foyer, I know that by the time the rest of my family goes downstairs for the reception, the smiles will be in place, the makeup fixed, hair smoothed, and all traces of tears removed. We can make it through the next few hours—after all, pretending is what we do best in this family.

Peter

It's been a long time since I've felt the mixture of emotions that are flooding me now: pride and joy for my oldest son and his wife, profound relief, a large dose of anger, and a layer of sorrow and grief so thick that I'm not sure I'll be able to pull myself together before the reception begins. Marianne starts to say something, but I hold up a hand to stop her. I can't speak past the lump in my throat. I *should* feel vindicated, but that's all swallowed up in the realization that our family has been altered forever. Again.

When I'd imagined this scenario in the past two months, I had never envisioned it playing out quite like this. I never believed Jade would be so foolish and insensitive as to blurt out the truth on Levi's wedding day. What I'd *hoped* would happen was that she would confess to Marianne within a few days of the time I moved out, and I was willing to give her space to do that. But when that didn't happen, and the weeks dragged on, I could feel everything that was important to me slipping through my fingers.

That's when I began to get angry: *who does Jade think she is?* Obviously she felt deeply hurt and betrayed over what I did to Cassie, coupled with the fact that we hadn't told her about it for five years, but did she really think she had the market cornered on suffering in this family? Did she concoct this web of lies just to get back at me for what I had done? Was it all just a plea for attention? *Why, why, why?*

The first week or two after she lied about me sexually abusing her, I kept telling myself, *She's young. She doesn't understand what she's doing. She's just scared to tell the truth. And she's angry at me for what I did, and all of us for not telling her about it sooner. She'll come around soon.* But by the time a month had gone by, I was glad that I wasn't allowed to communicate with her at all—I was afraid I'd lash out and say things I'd regret. Something along the lines of, "You are hurting this family far worse than I ever did."

Not that that's true. Deep down, I'm fully aware that nothing Jade has done or attempted to do even comes close to what I did to Cassie. But it's tempting to think otherwise, mainly because Jade's been calculating the whole situation. What I did to Cassie was reprehensible, of course—but it was never something that I intended to happen. It was a series of bad choices and stupid mistakes that I would give anything to take back. But Jade has deliberately lied for *months*. It chills me to realize how little I actually know my daughter—if someone had asked me six months ago, I would've said that I knew her better than any of my other children. But now … Now, I wonder if I really ever knew her at all.

Marianne's voice breaks into my tortured thoughts. "I should go get the girls. We need to go downstairs; people are going to wonder where we are."

"Let me do it," Ben interrupts. "Cassie's probably with Ian, anyway. I want to talk to Jade."

"Just don't … .please, honey, don't make a scene. This is *not* the time for …"

"I know, Mom, I know. I won't. I'll just go get her and bring her down for the reception. Don't wait for me. It might take awhile to convince her."

I bite my lip to keep from telling him to just leave her outside. *God, help me,* I beg silently. *I don't like this anger I'm seeing in myself. Help me forgive her.*

As soon as Ben leaves, Marianne turns to me, her eyes anguished. "I don't guess saying 'I'm sorry' will really cover it, will it? But I'll say it anyway: darling, I'm so, so sorry I didn't listen to you. I'm sorry I just condemned you unheard."

Again with the anger: I wait for the momentary flash of heat in my insides to subside before I answer her. "I understand why you did." Which is true—in her place, I would probably have done the same thing. For the first couple days, not for two months. "I wish you had tried harder to find out the truth, though. I wish ..." I stop, not wanting to turn this into a fight.

"What?" She presses. "You can tell me; I won't be upset. I know you're probably angry with me, and I deserve it."

"I just wish you had fought to save our marriage and to keep believing in me. It felt like you just... gave up, right from the beginning. Like you weren't even willing to *consider* that maybe ..." I take a deep breath, reigning in my emotions. "We shouldn't do this now. I do want to talk, but not here. Levi and Anna have been through enough today. I don't want to make their day even worse."

A shadow of hurt crosses her face, but she nods. "You're right. Maybe ... maybe tonight you can come over to the hotel and we can just talk about all this. We need to decide ..." A sob catches in her throat. "We need to figure out what to do about Jade. Peter, what are we going to do? How could she have done this?"

I sigh. "You were right: this is the wrong time and place to talk about this. But we can discuss all of this later tonight."

"You could ..." Marianne hesitates, clearly trying to keep the hopeful expression off of her face. "You could check out of your hotel and stay with me."

"So I guess that means you're not divorcing me anymore?" I can't keep the sarcastic edge out of my voice, and I hate myself for it when I see her wince.

"I'm sorry," she whispers. "I know I could say that a thousand times and it wouldn't be enough, but I really am. Of course I don't want a divorce—part of me never did. I still love you. I've *always* loved you, Peter. If you can forgive me, I just want to start over."

I fight the urge to respond with another angry comment. Deep down, I want all the same things she does; the problem is that I also want to hold onto my anger and resentment for a little while longer. I take a deep breath. *God, forgive me. Please change my attitude about this. I know I have no right to hold any type of grudge. Help me to forgive my family.*

"Starting over sounds like a good idea," I finally say. I can't manage a smile, not yet, but Marianne looks thrilled enough for both of us. She wraps her arms around me, and I allow myself to relax.

"It's going to be okay," she reassures me. "We'll get through this. I know we will."

Then she takes my hand and leads me down the stairs into the reception hall, where we smile and chat with the guests as if nothing is wrong. It's a performance so flawless I almost believe it myself.

Ben

When I was in high school, a kid in my grade named Josh Winters lost both his parents in a car accident. They were driving home from the grocery store one night, just a few miles from home, when a drunk driver slammed into their SUV. They were both killed instantly, and Josh and his younger sister were orphans. Just like that. I didn't know him well, but I went to the wake anyway. That was the day that I realized that there will always be someone out there who has it much, much worse than I do.

I'm trying to remind myself of that as I walk to the gazebo searching for Jade. I think about Josh and his little sister, try to frame their faces in my mind and focus on the utter devastation that painted their expressions that night at the wake. *Okay, our family's definitely screwed up, but at least we're all still alive. At least we still have each other. Things could be a lot worse.* The thought rings hollow, despite my best efforts to convince myself otherwise.

Maybe I'm just a selfish, spoiled punk, but I don't see even a glimmer of light in this situation. The past two months have been a nightmare, but I'd hoped that after the wedding, things would calm down—Mom would divorce Dad, I'd move back to my apartment and get on with my life, and I wouldn't have to see Dad ever again if I didn't want to. Sometimes, the only thing that kept me sane the past few weeks was constantly reminding myself that, once the wedding was over, things could get back to some semblance of normal. But now? Thinking that things could ever be normal in this family again? What a joke.

Rage begins to simmer in my stomach, and I force it down. *Josh. Think about Josh. Think about what it would be like to lose both your parents like that. Think about how much worse things could be. Think about how lucky you are, Benjamin Michael.* I take several deep breaths as I step into the gazebo. Jade is huddled on a bench, her back to me.

"Hey," I say softly.

She whirls around, clearly startled. "I … I didn't hear you coming," she stammers. Then she crumples into tears, and for a fraction of a second I hesitate. Her hair and makeup are disheveled, and chill bumps are rising on her arms despite the heat. That, combined with the tears streaking her cheeks and the haunted look in her eyes, makes me pause. She looks so much younger, almost like the scared, lost little girl she was five years ago—the day that Dad moved out. For just a moment, I realize how much Jade still *is* that little girl, and a wave of pity washes over me.

But only for a moment. As soon as she flings herself on me, sobbing, I stiffen and shove her away, anger and disgust churning in my stomach again. *Ignore it, ignore it. You can scream at her later. Mom said not to make a scene. Come on, just get her inside.* "Cut that out, Jade. I mean it. I'm not in the mood." I use my best stern-police-officer tone, my mouth in a hard line so she'll realize that I mean business.

She flinches as if I'd slapped her, her eyes widening before they pool with tears again. "I'm sorry," she chokes. "I thought ... I thought maybe you'd understand. You've been there for me so much in the past two months, and I thought maybe I could ..."

I snort derisively. "The past two months? Right, when I moved home, the last place in the entire world I'd *ever* want to be, and drove an hour and a half each way to work every day—and practically wore myself out doing it— just so that I could be around if you needed me? The past two months when I've tried to protect you, even though it was already too late because the worst thing that could've happened to you already happened? The past two months when I worried about you all the time, and I was scared you'd never get over what Dad did to you? Except ... oh, wait, that's right ... he didn't really do *anything* to you, did he?"

"Why ..." she hiccups. "Why are you being so mean to me?"

I'm not sure whether to laugh or scream. I'm afraid I'll say something I'll regret so I turn to walk back to the church. Who cares if Jade misses the reception? The state she's in, she shouldn't go anyway. But she grabs my arm, her fingernails digging in.

"*Wait!*" she shrieks, her voice desperate. "Ben, please, please, listen to me!"

I yank my arm away from her and fix her with a glare that should fry her. "Keep. Your. Hands. Off. Me."

"I didn't mean for this to happen!" Jade wails. "I just wanted ... I wanted him to pay for what he did to Cassie. I tried to tell her that, and she ..." Her lower lip quivers. "She said she never wants to talk to me again. She ... she *hit* me!" Jade touches a trembling hand to her cheek, and I notice the bruise that's already forming. Cass must've packed quite a punch. I can't keep the ghost of a smile from flitting across my face. *Way to go, Cass.*

"You poor baby," I comment dryly. "Excuse me for not feeling very sorry for you. You'll be lucky if she *does* ever talk to you again. And that goes double for Dad. What were you *thinking*, trying to ruin his life like that? Even if you thought he deserved it, how in the world ..."

I stop myself, holding up both hands to silence Jade, since she's already starting to speak. "Never mind. We are not going to talk about this now. Here's what's going to happen: you and I are going to walk back into the church, and you are going to clean yourself up. Then we're going downstairs for the reception, and we're going to try to make it as good as we can for Levi and Anna. You can cry and explain everything to Mom and Dad once we're back at the hotel. If they'll even speak to you. But no crying at the reception. Do you understand me?"

Jade nods meekly, swallowing hard and obviously trying to hold back a fresh flood of tears. "I really am sorry," she whispers. "Do you hate me?"

I sigh. *Remember, she's only thirteen,* I tell myself. *She's still just a baby, really.* "No, I don't hate you. I'm very, very pissed off at you, but I don't hate you. Now let's go."

Just before Jade slips into the ladies' room next to the church sanctuary, I grab her arm. "Hey. It'll be okay. And Cassie doesn't hate you, either. She might think she does, but she'll come around. Okay?" She nods wordlessly, her eyes filling yet again. *How can she possibly have any tears left? Great. Nice job, Ben.*

I head downstairs before I can allow my emotions to catch up with the rest of me. I attach a cheek-splitting grin to my face, grit my teeth, and wish fervently that this reception featured an open bar. After a day like this, I'm more than ready to say "screw you" to sobriety and drink myself into total oblivion. So maybe it's a good thing that there's no alcohol available for the next several hours.

As soon as my feet touch the floor of the reception hall, Mom corners me. "Is everything okay?" she asks smoothly, her expression betraying nothing to the guests surrounding us.

"Yep," I answer, hoping my own expression is equally blank. "Jade's coming down in a few minutes. She just needed to clean herself up a little. What about Cass?"

"She's with Ian, as far as I know. I'm sure they'll be in soon."

I nod and walk away from her, mingling with the guests. Most of the people here are from Levi and Anna's church or friends of theirs from college here in Portland, so I don't know many of them. A few of our cousins and close family friends from back home flew out for the wedding, though, and soon I'm lost in a series of meaningless conversations with them. It's awkward because I can tell they're trying to ask, in the most politically correct, sensitive way possible, if I'm drinking or using again, or if I have my life "straightened out." I smile and nod and manage to convince them that everything's fine, great, wonderful, never better.

I'm such a great liar. Maybe it's genetic.

The afternoon and early evening pass in a blur of small talk with strangers and family friends who might as well be strangers. And thank God for a good DJ—this reception may not feature alcohol, but there is dancing, and that helps distract me. After Levi and Anna's first dance, the DJ opens the floor for a couples' dance. Cassie and Ian are the second ones on the floor, and I smile my first genuine smile of the afternoon and give Ian a thumbs-up. I'm definitely not a relationship expert, but even I can see that those two were made for each other. I guess it only took them two months of torture to figure it out for themselves.

After about three hours, Levi and Anna have left for their honeymoon and most of the guests are gone. Mom's visiting with Aunt Janice, Dad's sister, and Jade's hanging out with a couple of our cousins and managing to look surprisingly composed and calm. No sign of Ian or Cassie, and I'd be willing to bet they've gone back to Ian's hotel. *We probably won't see her for the rest of the night. Or tomorrow,* I smirk to myself. But the humor falls flat, and I quietly slip out the side door of the reception hall and walk outside, feeling like there's a fifty-pound weight hanging from my neck.

I didn't realize how much effort it took to keep smiling and acting cheerful until I let the smile fade, and exhaustion sweeps over me. I can't remember the last time I wanted a drink this badly. Or a hit. *Anything.* I walk to the gazebo and pace restlessly. *Just one drink. Just something to take the edge off. This has been such a crappy day, and maybe if I just had one drink ... No, no, come on, Ben, you know you can't think that way. Call your sponsor. No way, I'm not going to call him! I don't want to talk to anyone; I just want one little drink. Why is that such a horrible thing? Why can't I at least ...*

I swear softly under my breath. *God, please, a little help here?*

The voice behind me nearly makes me jump out of my skin. "What can I do to help you, Ben?"

I jerk around, convinced for a heartbeat that maybe God was actually *talking* to me. But my father is standing in front of me. "It's been a hard day, huh?" He says sympathetically.

I shrug. "I guess that's one way of putting it."

"Would you like to go for a walk? Sometimes if you keep moving, it helps. It always does for me, anyway."

"How would you know?" I mutter, still caught in the grip of longing for what I know I can't have. It's so intense I can practically feel the warmth on my tongue, the fire searing the back of my throat.

Dad merely raises an eyebrow at me. "I've been sober twenty-seven years now. It *does* get easier, I promise."

"Wait, wait," I sputter. "*You* were an alcoholic? Why am I just now hearing about this?"

Dad shrugs. "You never asked. And … it's not something I like to talk about very often."

"You could've mentioned it sooner. It would've really helped me when I was first trying to get clean."

"I could've done a lot of things differently, Ben. If there's one thing I've learned in the past two months, it's that I've made a lot of very serious mistakes in how I raised you kids. I should've done so many things differently. And I'm sorry for that." His voice trembles, and I look away, uncomfortable with the sudden emotion.

"It's okay," I answer roughly. "I'm sorry I was such a jerk to you when … you know, Jade …"

"Oh, son, I don't blame you one bit for that! If I'd been in your place, I would've done the exact same thing. Your mom and I haven't had much of a chance to talk yet, but she's told me a little bit about how much you did for her and Jade while I've been gone." He lays a hand on my arm, stopping to look me in the eye. "Jade couldn't ask for a better brother, and your mother and I couldn't ask for a better son. I'm so proud of you."

My throat tries to swell shut, but I force the emotion out of my voice. "What, me a better son than Levi? You sure you're not high or something, Pop?"

He holds my gaze. "No, no, listen to me. *You* are the one who's sacrificed so much the past eight weeks to be there for your mother and your sisters. *You* are the one who's making the right choice right at this moment, by standing here and talking with me rather than drinking yourself into a coma at the nearest bar. *You* are the son I was afraid we were going to lose, and here you are. To be very honest, a year ago, I would never have believed you'd step up and be a man as much as you have the past few months. You're a better man than I am, Benjamin. I know you struggle with some of the same issues I did when I was younger, but you're going to succeed far more than I ever did."

I look away from him so he won't see me blinking the moisture out of my eyes. How did he know that some part of me has always been terrified that I'm going to turn out like him, to repeat all of his mistakes? I've never admitted it out loud, not even to myself. How did he know?

"Dad," I croak. "I …"

"It's okay. I know. I'll just … leave you to your thoughts for awhile, all right? If you need anything, come and get me. I'm sure your mom and Janice will be talking for another hour," he adds with a smile. He squeezes my arm and walks away.

I walk back to the gazebo as if I'm stumbling through fog. I sink down onto the bench and lower my head into my hands. *You're a better man than I am, Benjamin.* It hits me with a jolt that I still love my dad very much, even though I tried for months to convince myself that I hated him. And just as jarring is the realization that some part of me has wanted all along to hear him say the things he said tonight. For those few moments, it felt like all the father-son talks he used to give me and Levi when we were kids. It felt like it used to, before everything changed. I would give anything to get that back. I would give anything to go back to the days when my dad was my hero.

I wish I understood why that realization makes me cry.

Jade
Six Weeks Later

"Jade, where are you going?" Mom stops me at the door, her mouth set in a frown the way it always seems to be when she looks at me these days.

"Running," I glare at her. Is she *blind*? I'm wearing my workout clothes, and have my iPod like I always do when I go running. "Where else would I be going?"

Her frown deepens. "Don't you sass me, young lady. Didn't you run yesterday? Do you really need to go again today?"

I grit my teeth. I turned fourteen two weeks ago, but you'd never know it by the way my parents treat me. They act like I'm about six. "Today's Saturday. Coach said we have to keep running on the weekends and take one day off. Since we have *church*," I try hard not to spit the word, "tomorrow, that's going to be my day off. Call this a school project, Mom." Normally, I would just push past her with that and head out the door, but

I've learned my lesson in the past six weeks. If I ignore her, I get grounded for a week or more.

That frown stays cemented to her face, but she steps back from the door a couple inches. "All right," she relents. "Be back in … an hour, at the latest. And don't go far; stay in the neighborhood. Do you have your phone with you?"

"Yeah, yeah," I grumble, opening the door and escaping into freedom. Running and school are my only means of escape now, except for the rare times I get to hang out with my friends. All two or three of them. I didn't realize, until Cassie shoved me out of her life, that I really didn't have many friends my own age, and none of them were as close to me or understood me as well as she did.

Don't think about that now, I order myself. I try to lose myself in the music, in the rhythm of my feet pounding the sidewalk, in the crisp, cool air and the sight of the leaves starting to turn on the oak and maple trees in our neighborhood. It's hard to believe it's the first week of October already; it's been six weeks since Levi's wedding.

The wedding … Ugh, is there nothing *I can think about that doesn't lead back to all of this?* There's no point in fighting it; I might as well go with it. The music blasting from my iPod becomes merely background noise as I let my mind drift.

It's been six weeks since I finally admitted the truth to my family. Six weeks since Dad moved back home, and he and Mom started going to marriage counseling again. Six weeks since Cassie and Ian got back together, although they're not living together anymore. My sister's such a holy roller now that she thinks they should wait to live together again until they get married in a few months. I mean, I *think* that's what she thinks; it's not like she's talked me about it or anything. I haven't spoken to her since she slapped me in the face after Levi's wedding.

Just thinking about our fight that day makes me run as fast as I can, trying to combat the anger surging through me. For the first day or two after it all happened, I was so devastated by how much I'd hurt my family that I didn't much care that Cassie had slapped me and basically cut me out of her life on the spot. At first, it seemed like something I deserved, and I almost wanted to call her and tell her she could come over and hit me again if she wanted, since I deserved it. But now, it's been six weeks, and I don't feel nearly as understanding. I feel like I'll probably punch *her* in the face whenever I see her again.

How could she treat me like this? I blink back tears, furious at myself for letting it get to me. If she wants to forget about me and act like I don't exist, why can't I do the same thing for her? I can't. I just can't. She wasn't just my sister; she was my best friend. And maybe I'm just naïve, but that day at the wedding when I finally told the truth, I thought Cassie, out of all of them, would understand why I did it. I thought she would be mad for a couple days, sure. But I really believed she would understand why I'd lied about everything.

But she didn't. Not only did she not understand it, she made it sound like I was some manipulative, conniving brat who did it all for attention. *That* is what makes me angry at her now: the way she didn't even give me a chance to explain it to her, but just shut me out of her life without even glancing back. If Ian hadn't been there that day, she probably would've beat the crap out of me and enjoyed doing it.

She thinks she's so much better than me. They all do. Mom and Dad put me in therapy and grounded me as soon as we got back from Portland, and they've both acted like they're doing me some huge favor to forgive me and try to "move on," as Mom likes to put it. I've never had the guts to say this to her face, but if it weren't for the two of them, I would never have lied about anything in the first place. I never would've had anything to lie *about* if it weren't for them. So, if they're looking for someone to blame for all this, they could both start by looking in the mirror.

Ben and Levi have barely talked to me, either. Ben moved back to his apartment, and, even though he's visited several times since, he's said only a handful of sentences to me. Levi called me once, just to tell me he and Anna have "chosen to forgive" me for ruining their wedding day. How sweet of him.

At first, I was truly sorry for what I did and how much I hurt each member of my family, especially my dad. He didn't deserve that—well, not totally. He deserved some of it. I should never have kept the lies going as long as I did; I admit that. I should've told the truth after a few weeks, not two months. But as the weeks have gone by since then, I've gotten angrier and angrier with all of them and the way they've shut me out of their lives. They're all such hypocrites.

"This anger you have is just eating you up," my therapist told me last week. I'm seeing the famous Dr. Morton, the one I wasn't allowed to see back when the rest of my family was having sessions with him almost six years ago. I actually like him for the most part. If I *have* to be in therapy, I could definitely have a worse therapist.

"Wow, *that* was profound," I shot back at him. "What exactly do you think I should do about it?"

He didn't miss a beat. "You need to talk to your sister. Tell her how you're feeling, and try to explain your side of the story."

I snorted in derision and rolled my eyes. "She'd hang up on me the second she heard my voice."

"I don't think so," Dr. Morton shook his head. "Cassie has had plenty of time to cool down and think about what happened. Plus, from what you've told me, she's back together with Ian now, and she's a lot happier than she was just a few months ago. I think she'll be more willing to listen to you now."

Needless to say, I haven't done that yet. But I can't stop thinking about it. Even though I'm angry with my sister—and the rest of my family—I also miss her like crazy. I hadn't really realized how close we were until she did a disappearing act from my life overnight. We used to see each almost every other day, or at least talk on the phone, and now it's been six weeks since I've even heard her voice.

It takes me a minute to realize that tears are dripping down my face, mingling with the sweat from running. *I just miss her. I mean, yeah, I'm pissed at her, but I miss her so much. She forgave Dad for doing something way, way worse, so why can't she just forgive me?*

I look at my watch and groan, picking up my pace. Only thirty more minutes 'til I have to be home and face another nearly-silent dinner with my parents. Dad always tries to start a conversation, but it never lasts. We really have nothing to talk about after he asks me how school was and how running's going. I know he's forgiven me for what I did to him, but our relationship is never going to be the same. I can't stand losing that closeness with him, but then again, maybe it was never really there in the first place. Not since he abused Cassie. Maybe it was all in my mind: I thought we were so close, but if that were really true, wouldn't he have told me the truth a long time ago?

I slow to a walk and try to stop the tears. I'm a complete mess of contradictions these days: missing Cass but also sort of hating her, too; angry at my entire family for their hypocrisy but wanting more than anything for them to just forgive me and let things to go back to normal; hating my parents for dragging me to church every Sunday but also wishing I could believe in God the way I did when I was a little kid. I'm not sure *what* to believe anymore, about anything.

Are you sorry for what you did, Jade? Are you sorry for the way you lied to your father and me? Do you realize how close you came to completely destroying this family? I was ready to divorce *your dad and never let him see you again, do you understand that?*

Those were some of the things Mom screamed at me when we got back to the hotel that night after Levi's wedding. I nodded and cried and begged for forgiveness. Of course I couldn't say what I really thought: *Yes, I'm sorry. And no, I'm not.*

I barely manage to stop crying by the time I make it home, on time right to the minute. Mom is, of course, waiting right by the door with her watch in her hand. "You were almost late," she points out. I just start up the stairs to take a shower, ignoring her completely.

It's not until I'm under the soothing hot water that I let myself really cry. I scrub as hard as I can and wonder if I'll ever feel truly clean again, if I'll ever be able to fully wash away the guilt, anger, and shame that haunt me every day. *I just want this to all go away. I'm sorry, okay? I am* sorry! *What more do I have to do to fix this? I just want this to stop. Please, please make it stop.*

No one hears me crying, of course. And half an hour later, I sit through another stilted, awkward dinner with my parents and try not to remember how things used to be and how much we've lost.

Cassie

You can do this. You've come such a long way in the past few months. You know you need to do this—it may be hard at first, but you can get through it. Just breathe. In, out, in ... I look out the window at the leafless trees, trying to focus on something else. It's one week before Thanksgiving, and winter is about to descend with a vengeance.

Dr. Rogers looks across her desk at me and smiles. "You've done such a terrific job the past few months, Cassie. You've really given your all in our sessions, and I can tell what a difference it's made in you. I know you're probably nervous about today, but trust me, this is going to be a huge step in the right direction for the healing process. I'll be right here the whole time, and if you need to stop at any point, just say so. All right?"

I swallow hard. "Okay. I'm ready."

And then my dad walks into the room. *Here we go.* If someone had told me six months ago that I would be having a joint therapy session with Dad, I would've laughed in their face. Now that he's here, ready to listen and promising not to say anything until I'm done, I have no more excuses. I get a second chance to say all the things I should've said that day in Dr. Morton's office.

Dad sits in one of the chairs across from me, with Dr. Rogers sitting behind her desk, between us. "Before we start," Dad glances at Dr. Rogers as if he's afraid she'll immediately tell him to be quiet, "I just had one thing I wanted to say, if that's all right."

Dr. Rogers raises an eyebrow at me, and I nod. "Sure, Dad."

Dad looks like he's already fighting tears. "I just … I know I've said this a million times and maybe it doesn't mean much to you to hear it, but … I'm so, so sorry for what I did to you. I would go back and change it all if I could. And if you … if you feel like you need some time away from me, or if you just want me to stay out of your life, I accept that. I deserve it."

My palms are clammy, and my stomach twists into even tighter knots. "Thanks. I definitely don't want to shut you out of my life …" *Like I'm doing to Jade.* The thought springs unbidden to my mind, and I force it away. *Not now.* "I just had some things I thought I should say to you."

I take a deep breath. It's time. I reach into my purse and pull out the notes I jotted down for this session. It's my one chance to do this right, and I didn't want to blow it by forgetting any of the things that need to be said. I smooth the paper out on my lap and look up at Dad.

It's the first time I've looked at him, *really* looked at him, for months, maybe even years. Instead of seeing him as he is right now—red eyes, obviously bracing himself for whatever I'm going to say to him—I'm transported back to my childhood and see him as the daddy I knew as a little girl. My hero. My protector. The look in his eyes now is the same as it used to be back then, despite the tears he's trying to hold back in this moment. It's the look that says, *You're my precious Princess, and I love you no matter what. I'll always be here for you.*

I close my eyes to prevent my own tears from spilling over. I let my notes slip to the floor and reach back into my purse for the one other item I brought for today. It's a photograph, and I don't let myself look at it until I slap it down on Dr. Rogers's desk, where we can all see it plainly. It's my favorite picture of my dad and me, one that I managed to sneak out of one of the family photo albums one day when no one was home.

I slap it down on the desk with a little more force than necessary, and I let them both just look at it for a few moments before I speak. Not that I could speak around the lump in my throat, anyway. The photo is of me and Dad when I was about three, maybe four. I'm sitting on his lap, and we're wearing matching baseball caps and huge smiles. Even at a glance you can tell I was a Daddy's girl, that I felt completely loved and happy there in his arms. It's the expression on my face, that look of utter joy and love, that always makes me want to cry when I look at that picture.

"That," I begin, my voice cracking and the tears starting to fall despite my best efforts to stop them, "is what we need to talk about today."

I turn to Dr. Rogers, swallowing hard and forcing the tears down. "Remember, at our first session you asked me what my family was like … before? Well, this picture is my answer to that. This is how I remember my relationship with my dad back then."

I don't look at him, but I can hear Dad starting to cry. "I remember when I was little, all I wanted was to be like you. All I wanted was to spend time with you and do everything you did and show off for you and make you proud of me. I wanted to *be* you when I was a kid."

I take a deep, shaky breath and grab my page of notes off the floor. I skim them over and the words blur together as tears fill my eyes again. There were so many things I thought I wanted to say: *Do you have any idea what it was like those nights you came into my room? Do you have any idea how scared I was? You said you thought I was sleeping or you never would've done it, but that is a load of crap! You had to know I was awake; my heart was beating a mile a minute because I was so terrified. You knew I was awake, and you did it anyway. Over and over and over again.*

And: *Did you know how much I hated myself because of what you did? I honestly thought it must have been my fault. I thought there was something horribly wrong with me that made you do those things to me, and I hated myself for years. I still do, sometimes, deep down. It's been almost ten years since the abuse occurred, and I'm just now starting to realize that it wasn't my fault and I'm not some worthless human being.*

So many things I thought I wanted—*needed*—to say to him. But it really all boils down to two things, two things I never wanted to admit out loud. I crumple the papers into a ball and toss it into the trash can underneath Dr. Rogers's desk. I don't even bother trying to stem the flow of tears this time. I just look straight at my father and pray that he truly hears me this time: "Daddy?" I never call him Daddy anymore; not since that day in Dr. Morton's office when everything fell apart. It seems like a lifetime ago. "I really … I really wish you hadn't done those things to me."

I reach for the photo on Dr. Rogers's desk and hand it to Dad. "Did you …" I stop. These are some of the hardest words I've ever had to say. "Did you really … Did you really love me, Daddy? Because …" *Come on, girl, you can do this.* "When I look at that picture, I remember how close we were when I was little and how special our relationship was and I just… I don't understand how this could've happened if … if you really loved me as much as I thought you did. I mean, I was basically just a kid and you came into my room all those nights and … you *stole* my childhood from me. So if I didn't do anything to cause it, like you keep telling me, then … did you really love me?"

Dad just stares at me, tears cascading down his face. And I realize, looking at him, that I'm never going to get an answer to these questions. Not the way I want them to be answered, anyway. He *can't* answer them because there just isn't an answer that makes sense, that makes all the puzzle pieces click into place to form a neat, tidy picture. An answer like that doesn't exist.

I guess I've known this all along. I'd just hoped that somehow, he would be able to explain it all to me in a way that made sense, that made everything okay again. "All I really wanted," I say softly, looking at the picture in his hands, "was for us to go back to the way things were. I wanted *that*," I point at the smiling three-year-old in the picture, content and happy in her daddy's arms, "again. And I know we can't … we can't get that back, but maybe, maybe we can just try to—I don't know, start over?"

Dad swallows, tries to speak, and can't. He tries again and, after a moment, finds his voice again. "I've always loved you, Cassandra. I understand why you doubt it, after what I did, but please just … just know that I was selfish, I was stupid, I made mistakes that I will regret for the rest of my life, but I *never* stopped loving you. I guess it wasn't so much that I didn't love *you*; it was that I loved *myself* more. I chose to do what I wanted and … and ignore the consequences to you, to our family. But none of this, none of it, is your fault. Please, please believe me when I say that. There was absolutely nothing you did to cause the abuse, honey. Nothing. I will regret it for the rest of my life, and I doubt I'll ever forgive myself, but …"

I can't wait another second. I get up from my seat and cross the room to hug him. "*I* forgive you. I forgive you, Dad. I really do. And I want us to start over, okay?"

Even though I'm crying as I say it, and we both continue crying for several minutes, I feel as if a two-ton weight has been lifted from my back. It's as if all the barriers have come crashing down and there's nothing left standing in the way of me and the life I've dreamed about for years. There's me and my dad, with nothing left unsaid that needs to be said, ready to start over again after all these years. *Why didn't I do this years ago?* I wonder. *It wasn't so terrible to tell him the truth after all.*

Does that mean everything's completely fine now? Of course not. I'm not an idiot—I know I'm never going to forget the sexual abuse and the loss of my childhood relationship with my dad. I know that there's always going to be at least a little bit of distance between us because of it. But it feels like I'm finally, *finally*, ready to start living again, instead of just existing like I have been for the past six years.

Something niggles at the back of my mind, though. *Jade.* I ignore the thought; today is about me and Dad fixing our relationship. Jade can wait.

When I get back to my apartment about an hour later, Ian's waiting for me. He visibly relaxes when I walk through the door. "How did it go?"

Instead of answering, I just wrap my arms around him and hold him. "It was amazing," I whisper into his chest. "I feel like I can finally close that chapter of my life."

Ian laughs out loud. "Wow. I *never* thought I would hear you say that! That's so amazing, Cass. You deserved that closure with your dad. So—is he going to walk you down the aisle at the wedding?"

The wedding's only a month away. Back before we broke up during the summer, we'd planned to get married in April of next year. But after we got back together and worked through some of our issues in premarital counseling with Dr. Rogers, we decided to get married the week before Christmas. Christmas has always been my favorite holiday, and there's nothing I want more than to be married to the love of my life in time to celebrate it this year.

I can't keep a smile out of my voice as I stand on tiptoe to kiss him. "Yes. My dad is going to walk me down the aisle."

"Oh," Ian says when he finally pulls back for air, "I forgot to tell you, your mom called. She wants you to stop by the house as soon as you can. She said she has something to talk to you about, and it's pretty important."

I frown, confused. "I wonder why? She knew I was having the session with Dad today. Maybe I'll just go over there now."

Ian grins sheepishly. "I should've probably called you while you were still in the car so you could just go over there, but I really wanted to see you in person to hear how it all went. I'm so happy for you, baby."

On the drive over to my parents' house, I'm so giddy I nearly laugh out loud. *Thank You, thank You, thank You, God!* I asked Him for His help today and He certainly gave it to me. It feels like I have a whole new lease on life—amazing that just one fifty-minute therapy session could accomplish all that. Of course, it took months of grueling weekly sessions to get to the point where I was able to even consider having the session we did today, but still, I'm shocked by how much better I feel now that's it over. I hadn't expected anything to really change, but clearly, I was wrong.

I park my car in the driveway, noticing that only Mom's car is here, and I practically skip into the house. Mom meets me just inside the door. "How did it go with your dad?" she asks, breathless.

"It was incredible!" I gush for five minutes straight about everything that happened, but Mom doesn't seem too interested. "Is something wrong, Mom?" I ask finally.

She crosses her arms and shifts her weight from one foot to the other. "I just … I don't understand why you're willing to make things right with your dad, after everything he's put you through, but you're not going to give your sister the same chance."

My chest tightens. "It's not the same thing. It's a totally different situation, and it's taken me *years* to get to the point of talking about everything with Dad. It's not like …"

"Cassandra Elizabeth!" At that, I stop, speechless. I can count on one hand the number of times she's called me by my full name. "This is just ridiculous, young lady! Your sister should never have done what she did, and I don't blame you for being angry at her. But you haven't spoken to her for *three months*, Cass! You two were best friends up until Levi's wedding, and after that, you completely cut her out of your life. She's fourteen years old! Do you remember what it was like to be fourteen? Do you have a *clue* how difficult it has been for Jade to lose you like this?"

"Mom, I didn't …"

"I'm not trying to butt into your relationship with her, but I *am* still your mother, and you need to listen to me. Your sister is suffering. I should've said something to you a long time ago, and I apologize for not doing that. But Cass, you're an adult—you need to take the high road here and fix things with Jade."

I feel my face flushing with embarrassment at her rebuke. "But, Mom, she was so ... so vindictive about the whole thing. She lied for *months,* and she made me relive some of the worst months of my life, and the whole time, she *knew* she was lying—and she kept doing it. And then when she finally decided to tell the truth, she acted like all she had to do was apologize and we'd just forget about it. Don't you *get* it, Mom? She was willing to wreck our entire family over that stupid lie! So why should I fix things with her? She deserves to feel guilty. She *should* suffer a little bit after what she did!"

Mom doesn't say a word, merely lets my emotional tirade hang in the air for several moments until I'm embarrassed by how childish I sound. I blush, stammering, "I just ... I don't think I can fix our relationship right now."

Mom drills me with one of her famous "Mom looks." "If not now, when? At your wedding? If you even decide to invite her? She was supposed to have been your maid of honor, and I don't think I have to remind you how excited she was about that. You have no idea how hurt she is to have been left out of all the wedding plans."

Part of me is furious at Mom for scolding me like a five-year-old. Another part of me realizes how much I deserve it. Haven't I been thinking about apologizing to Jade for weeks now, and I just keep putting it off? I look down, embarrassment mingled with anger turning my cheeks red.

Mom lays a hand on my arm, softening her tone. "Honey, I don't blame you for being angry at Jade. I was angry with her, too, for a long time. But, as time has gone on, I've realized that she's really sorry for what she did, and she's still angry at us for not telling her about everything that happened with your dad. She has a right to be angry; we should've told her years ago."

Should've, should've, should've. I'm so tired of that word.

"She needs you, Cass. Jade needs you to help her through this. You don't want her to struggle to deal with what your dad did to you and not have someone there to support her. I know you. You don't want Jade to have to go through what you went through, dealing with all of this grown-up stuff alone."

I stare at her, amazed that she's basically admitting, after all these years of denial, that she left me alone to deal with the implosion of our family. "I wasn't completely alone," I protest weakly.

"Oh, honey," Mom laughs, a brittle sound. "Don't try to pretend that you don't know what I'm talking about. It's one of my greatest regrets as a mother, the way I left you on your own to deal with everything that happened. I don't want Jade to feel the same way, even though I'm really trying to make sure she knows I'm here for her. I'm her mother, and she's just not going to open up to me the way she would to you."

"Okay," I sigh reluctantly. "I don't know if she'll listen to me, either, after the way I've ignored her lately. She's probably furious at me."

Mom shakes her head and starts to speak, but before she can, the door opens.

"Jade!" I gasp involuntarily. I haven't seen her in over three months, and the girl slouching in the doorway, looking like she's ready to bolt, doesn't look at all like my sister. She's thinner and paler and has dark shadows under her eyes. *Oh, Jade.*

Her eyes dart from me to Mom and back again, clearly terrified. "I… I didn't know you'd be here. I can come back later or something. I'll just …" She starts to back out of the room, but I grab her arm before she can.

"Hey, wait." I swallow hard, suddenly on the brittle edge of tears. I clear my throat and try to push the emotion down. "I … Could we talk?"

A flash of anger sparks in her eyes. "We haven't talked in three months. Why start now?"

"Jade," Mom warns.

Jade rolls her eyes. "Fine." She pushes past me and starts upstairs, apparently not caring whether I follow her or not. *God, help me. Please don't let it be too late for me to fix things with her. I know it was wrong of me to stay away from her this long; I'm sorry.*

Once we're in her room, Jade and I just stand there looking at each other for a few minutes. She's put up some new posters since the last time I was here, and there's a lot more makeup scattered over the top of her dresser. I nod toward it. "Is Mom finally letting you wear as much as you want?"

"I got all of that for my birthday." The statement hangs in the air; I completely ignored her birthday this year.

"Um … Mom told me you're doing really well in cross-country. And she said that you …"

"Why are you here?" Jade interrupts, turning to face me with her hands on her hips. "Did you just come over here to make small talk? Because if you did, I have a lot of things I need to get done, and I really don't have time for this."

"No," I sigh. "I came over to say I'm sorry. I'm sorry for the way I've been treating you. I never should've shut you out like this. It was a horrible thing to do and I need to ask you to forgive me."

She looks steadily at her feet, refusing to meet my gaze. I step a few feet closer, and she stiffens. I reach out and touch her arm, hoping she won't shove my hand away.

"Look, I know you're probably angry at me, and I guess you have a right to be. But you also need to understand that what you did—lying about Dad like that—It was not even remotely okay, Jade. I know you were angry that we didn't tell you about the abuse stuff sooner, but you shouldn't have ..."

"Don't you think I know that?" She jerks her head up and glares at me, but tears are forming in her eyes. "Don't you think I've had that drilled into my head for the past three months? I *know* it was wrong! I *know* I shouldn't have done it! I think I'm pretty freaking clear on that, Cassie!" She swipes angrily at the tears trickling down her cheeks.

I take a deep breath. "Okay. So. I think we need to get together soon to talk about the wedding plans."

"Wedding plans?" she repeats blankly.

"Well, you're going to be my maid of honor, right? And the wedding's only a month away, so we have some serious work to do."

"You ... you still want me to do that?" she asks in a small voice.

"Only if you want to. I know you're angry at me, and you should be, after the way I've treated you. We've both done things we shouldn't this year. But you're my sister, and I love you. Of *course* I want you to be my maid of honor, if you want to."

"Really?" Her voice is a thread about to break.

I can't stand to watch her trying to be brave like this; I wrap my arms around her and hold her tight. That's all it takes for her to start crying. "I thought you hated me," she sobs. "I missed you so much but I was so mad at you ..."

"I know, I know," I whisper. "I'm sorry. I'm so sorry."

We have so many things to talk about, to apologize for, to explain. But I have my baby sister back. For now, that's enough.

Peter

It's finally here, the day I've both anticipated and dreaded ever since my daughter was born. Today, Cassie will change her last name and start her own family with Ian. Marianne joins me at the bathroom sink as I finish shaving. "Where did the time go?" she asks wistfully, echoing my thoughts. "It seems like just yesterday …" She stops abruptly. "I can't start crying yet. Good grief, I should at least wait till we get to the church!"

I smile as she walks away. She'll cry her way through a whole box of tissues today, I guarantee it. But what a difference between Cassie's wedding today and Levi's a few months ago! *Thank You, God, for giving my family back to me.* Of course, things aren't like they were before I abused Cassie; they never will be. But for the first time in years, I'm forging real relationships with each of my children, and Marianne and I are working through our issues, one by one. Our marriage is stronger now than it's been in years. Maybe ever.

It's a bittersweet feeling to know that I'm going to walk my little girl down the aisle in a matter of hours; I may wipe away a tear or two when I give her away, but this is a day for celebrating. No one outside of our family, except maybe Dr. Morton and Dr. Rogers, can truly understand what this day means to all of us. In those first dark days and weeks after I confessed to abusing my daughter, I believed I would never get the chance to walk her down the aisle—or to be a part of her life at all.

At the church, my heart swells with pride as I look at my children: my sons, both fine men, better men than I could ever hope to be, both of whom call me "Dad" now, instead of "Peter." Jade, who looks stunning and much too grown-up in her floor-length gown. She twirls around in front of me. "Do I look pretty, Daddy?" I swallow the lump in my throat and assure her that she does. We're getting the old Jade back, a little each day.

And just before the ceremony is supposed to start, I take my place beside Cassie. She's radiant. "You're so beautiful, sweetie," I tell her.

The ceremony is beautiful, of course, and after a million pictures, we head over to the reception. I can't stop the tears as I watch Ian and Cassie share their first dance. It's astounding to think that just six months ago they weren't sure they had a future together at all; they went through so much heartache to get to this day, but it's obvious that it was all worth it.

Cassie has flatly refused to tell me what song she picked for the father/daughter dance, so I'm a little nervous as I step onto the dance floor and take her into my arms. The first strains of "Butterfly Kisses" start to play, and I stifle a groan. "You *want* me to bawl like a baby, don't you?" I whisper to her.

She shakes her head, a mischievous glint in her eyes. "This was our song when I was little, don't you remember? I always said I was going to play this at my wedding reception."

Do I remember? How could I forget? Every night when she was little, I'd tuck her in, and she'd give me butterfly kisses. *"Sleep well, Princess." It feels like just yesterday …*

Remembering the days of butterfly kisses, the days when I was her hero, I feel a stinging pain in my chest as I also remember the question she asked me that day in Dr. Rogers's office: *Did you really love me? Curse you, Peter, for making her doubt it.* "Cass, that day in Dr. Rogers's office when you …"

She puts a finger to my lips. "Daddy. I'm going to tell you something right now, and then we're just going to enjoy my wedding reception. I could not have asked for a better father." There are tears in her eyes, but she holds my gaze. "I couldn't have had a better father," she repeats.

Later that night, I'm asked to offer a toast. I look around the table at my family; in a room filled with our friends and relatives, it's only the six of us who truly understand the significance of this moment. It's several moments before I'm able to compose myself enough to speak, I feel overcome as I look at each of their faces and realize how far we've come over the past six years. Things aren't perfect, of course, but they're better than they've ever been. Against all odds, contrary to everything I deserve, I have my family back.

Finally I raise my glass and simply say: "To new beginnings."

The glasses clink together, and the photographer motions us all to lean in for a picture. There's a lot of laughing and shrieking from the girls as we all try to squeeze in. Everyone eventually maneuvers into place, and I glance around at my children, my heart swelling with pride at how much they've all grown and matured over the past several months.

"All right, everybody, big smiles," the photographer calls out, as if any of us could *stop* smiling.

Click.

Lightning Source UK Ltd.
Milton Keynes UK
UKOW041447120313

207523UK00002B/19/P